GRANNY BOO
Legacy of the Puma Man

A Novel by

Phil Whitley

To Martha

Phil Whitley

Published – December 2009
First Printing – January 2010
ISBN: 978-0-9819654-1-3

R. J. Buckley Publishing
Queen Creek, AZ

www.rjbuckleypublishing.com

DEDICATION

For their patience and understanding during the three years this work was researched, written, rewritten, edited and obsessed over, I dedicate this book to my wife, Reba Lynn, and my daughter, Destiny. Both are immortalized as characters in this story.

I love you both.

ACKNOWLEDGEMENTS

I would like to acknowledge the Native American and First Nation peoples everywhere. My intent in writing this book was to honor your wonderful cultural heritages and traditions that a paleface will only ever know from the outside. Any misrepresentation or offense should be considered completely unintentional and without malice, so please accept my apologies in advance as I continue to learn.

A special acknowledgement is also due to all my online message board friends who were there when the idea for *Keechie* and later, *Granny Boo,* was first formulated. You gave me the motivation to write when I did not feel like a writer and the courage to continue writing when that feeling seemed to be true.

Special thanks also to my Creek Indian friend, Richard Thornton, Creek historian and city planner, for his advice and assistance with the Muscogean language and customs.

And to E. Don Harpe, Mollie Moon, Sandra McClellan Carter and Catherine Wilkinson, who were among the first to read the raw manuscript looking for spelling and typographical errors (there were many), I offer my heartfelt appreciation.

My author/artist friend and fellow researcher of ancient history, Andy Lloyd, deserves all the praise for the beautiful painting you see on the cover. Andy has been painting for twenty years, both in acrylic and watercolor. His work has been exhibited many times in Gloucestershire, England and can be seen at http://cheltenham-art.com/andylloyd.htm. I owe you one, mate.

Principal Indian Characters and Their Name Meanings

Pu-Can (Passionflower): (Called "Granny Boo" by Keechie) born 1859, dies in 1949 at 90. (Stayed in GA) (Had Gift)

Panet -Semoli (Wild Dancer): Pu-Can's Gr Gr Grandmother, came to Georgia from the west, born 1767. (Had Gift)

Echo-Ochee (Little Deer): Pu-Can's Great Uncle and Hechee-Lana's brother, medicine man. (Had gift)

Hechee Lana (Yellow Eyes): Pu-Can's grandmother, born 1807. (Stayed in GA) (Had Gift)

Achena Nakla (Burning Cedar): Pu-Can's Mother, born 1827 (Time of Removal).

Apelka-Haya (Laugh Maker): Pu-Can's older brother.

Wekiwa (Spring of Water): Keechie's mother, born 1879, Keechie called her "Mam."

*Keechi*e (Kachina): born 1899, Granddaughter of Pu-Can. (Had Gift)

Cornsilk: Boo's great aunt, born 1800, went to Okla. with husband and pregnant.

Tysoyaha (Child of the Sun): Boo's husband of the Wind Clan, Mother was Yuchi.

Chatto-Nokose (Stone Bear): Tysoyaha's father, Mico of the Wind Clan.

Locha-Luste (Black Turtle): Brother to Chatto-Nokose, Medicine Man of the Wind Clan.

Owa-Hatke (White Water): Medicine Woman of the Wind Clan, sister of Locha-Luste and Chatto-Nokose.

CHAPTER 1

The dream came again during the night.

The man, who looked like a cat, was trying to tell her something, but she didn't understand.

Alex looked over at her parents, who were still sleeping. As she tried to recall the dream, she felt compelled to go into the deeper room of the cave where all the "Indian stuff" was stored. Keechie had shown her dad the relics of her people and told him about them. As Alex entered the room, she remembered the "Power Bundle" that had belonged to Granny Boo, Keechie's grandmother.

The old leather bag was hanging just inside the opening. She reached out and touched it as the light from her candle reflected on its surface. Taking it down from the peg, she carried it back to her blankets beside her parents. It felt natural to hold it against her chest as she tried to decide whether to open it or not. The cave had grown cold so she lay back and pulled her blankets up around her neck. Within minutes, she was again fast asleep, and the dream returned.

The cat man was standing before her; but this time he spoke. "*Do you accept your birthright, granddaughter of the Spirit Singer?*" *the entity asked her.* "*Power has assured that the bloodline of Pu-Can is unbroken to you. Ask your father to tell you of Pu-Can. Pu-Can of the Puma Clan.*"

When she awoke, Alex quickly returned Granny Boo's Power Bundle to the other room, just as her parents woke up. She walked quickly past them. "Good morning. I'm going to sit outside and watch the sunrise."

She felt sure that she remembered the cat man, but from *where* escaped her. As soon as she was alone outside, she recalled a dream from before they had come to this cave. She tried to remember. *Yes! It was after Dad had finished reading me his Keechie manuscript. Puma Man! That was what Dad had called him,* she thought as she turned, satisfied, and went back inside with her parents.

While her mother, Mary, was preparing breakfast, Alex asked, "Who is Pu-Can, Dad?"

"Pu-Can? I don't know. Wait, where did you hear that name?"

"I had another dream last night, and the cat man said to ask you about Pu-Can."

So the Puma Man returns, Brian thought as he touched his daughter on the shoulder. "Remember Granny Boo, Alex? Her real name was Pu-Can. Keechie told me that when she was young, she called her grandmother 'Boo-Can', instead of Pu-Can. They thought it was funny, because there is no 'B' sound in their language. It kinda stuck with the family, and everyone began calling her Boo. But Pu-Can is the Creek word for the passionflower vine. You know, the one with the pretty flowers and the green fruit that we call maypops."

"Well, what did Keechie tell you about Granny Boo, Dad? The cat man, Puma Man, said to ask you."

"Well, she did tell me some interesting stories about her, Alex. I wrote them down since I was studying the history of her people. They are mixed in with my other journals here somewhere. After dinner tonight, I'll get them out for you, if I can find the right box. Pu-Can was a very powerful Spirit Singer. Did the Puma Man say anything else?"

"Only something about her bloodline being unbroken down to me, and he asked if I accepted my birthright."

Brian frowned. "But Keechie's bloodline ended with her. However, she did predict that I would have a girl-child someday who would make a difference in the world. I always thought that she, in her own way, had adopted us into her family."

While Mary and Alex were busy inside the cave, Brian went outside and climbed the rocks above the entrance. He wanted to check the solar panels he had placed there to charge the bank of batteries inside the cave. He worried about the presence of the panels giving away their secret hiding place, but their benefits outweighed the risk. He had a shortwave radio that was their only contact with the outside world, plus several small battery-powered appliances that made life in the cave more bearable.

Gazing out over the valley, he thought back to the events that had brought him and his family to Keechie's cave nearly a year ago. Shortly after reading his old manuscript of Keechie to his then twelve-year-old daughter, Alexis, there was a series of terrorist attacks on America.

First, there were a few cases of an unknown disease, similar to Ebola, detected in several major cities across the nation. The authorities could only trace them to "persons unknown" traveling on major airlines. The passenger lists were large and the potentially exposed victims were too numerous to count.

Then the suicide bombers came to cities great and small all across the land. Always striking at large crowds, the intentionally infected terrorists only used very small explosive charges strapped to their bodies. The explosions themselves didn't cause much physical damage – usually only the bomber was killed outright, but everyone else in the crowd was sprayed with blood, body fluids and parts.

The spread of the mystery disease intensified. The Centers for Disease Control in Atlanta became as secure and closely guarded as the White House. A state of national emergency was declared and martial law enacted. Homeland Security, made up of people only minimally trained in airport security, went into action. They were guided mostly by panic and acted without adequate instruction or direction. Fortunately, a vast majority of these ill-trained professionals deserted the ranks in fear for their own lives.

Then, as the public panic reached its maximum, the power grids were sabotaged across the land. Communication systems failed. The Internet was no more. Radio and television, so secure with their "Emergency Broadcasting System," went off the air. Cities and rural areas alike were in the dark. Water purification plants shut down. No stores were open. No airlines were flying. No trucks were making deliveries. The remaining fuel could not be pumped from the storage tanks.

There was no public transportation, and the sick and dying went uncared for. Hospitals remained open until the fuel for their emergency generators ran out; then the medical staff, fearing for their own lives and those of their families, failed to report for duty. The patients who were able to leave did so. Many of them, too sick to leave, died in the dark—deserted by those entrusted with their care.

Mass panic ensued, and mobs ran through the streets, stealing anything they could find. Money was useless. Food, guns, ammunition, drugs and antibiotics became the new currency. The military began closing down all major routes into and out of the cities. They quarantined entire neighborhoods where the sickness seemed worst. Local governments enacted strict curfews, but due to the lack of personnel, they were not adequately enforced.

Brian had already prepared his emergency supplies. Ever since the Y2K scares, he had been stocking his "grab bags", and they had been maintained and added to ever since. Without the knowledge of his family or any other living soul, he had safely deposited the larger portions of these supplies in the very cave where they now lived.

He looked behind him toward the top of the mountain and the old Indian burial ground where he had buried Keechie with her ancestors. *Thank you, my old friend. Without the knowledge you passed on to me and the protection of Puma Man, we most likely would not have survived.*

He had met Keechie when he was sixteen while looking for arrowheads near his old home place at the foot of the mountain. She began teaching him her survival skills and inspired in him a love for the natural world and how everything was connected in what she called the "Wheel of Life." For many years both he and his parents thought of her as part of their family. Even so, she would never leave her mountain cave. It had been her own family's refuge since the time of "The Removal" and the bones of her people were still there.

Alex called out from below, breaking his reverie, "Dad, where are you?"

"Up here, Alex. I was checking on the solar cells."

"Well, c'mon down. Mom wants to work on the drying racks, and then you said we would check on the rabbit traps."

"I sure did, baby. I almost forgot. Maybe we can have rabbit for dinner tonight."

Mary had found more herbs in their small garden that needed drying and there were more tomatoes and onions that needed picking.

When the drying racks were set up, Brian and Alex headed out to check on the traps. Alex had her trusty hunting knife and her backpack, and Brian had his ever-present crossbow over his shoulder. The traps were all near the small spring where he had first met Keechie. The first one was empty, but the bait was gone. He placed a small piece of carrot on the trigger stick and reset the trap. The next two boxes each had a rabbit inside, which he quickly dispatched. While he was field-dressing them, Alex noticed his mouth moving.

"What are you saying, Dad?"

"Oh, I'm thanking the rabbits for giving us their meat. It's something Keechie taught me to do. She called all the animals brothers and sisters. She would thank the rabbit for its meat and fur, then promise to honor its spirit, always."

Brian knelt down at the spring to wash the blood from his hands. As he did, he remembered that he should tell Alex about the water there. Keechie had warned him about drinking it. "Alex, never drink the water here. It's okay to wash your hands, though."

"How do you know that?"

"Keechie told me," Brian said, and then he laughed.

"Well, what's so funny?"

"That was the first thing I ever heard her say. I was squatting right here, about to take a drink, when from right over there," he pointed across the spring, "came this voice that said, '*Dat wada give you da shits fer sho. You gots t' bile it furs*'. I nearly jumped out of my skin! I thought I was all alone and the woods were quiet. That was the day I first met her."

"How old were you then?" Alex asked.

"I was sixteen, and thought I knew all there was to know about the area. Boy, was I wrong! When we get back to the cave, I'll show you how to cure the hides. We can make pouches out of them if you want to."

On the trail back to the cave, Alex stopped and pointed out a small tree. "I think I know this one already. You told me about it before, and I think you can make tea from the roots. Right?"

Brian looked at the mitten-shaped leaves and smiled. "You'll get a gold star for that if you can tell me its name."

Alex thought for a moment, and then said, "Sassafras! It's what root beer is made from."

"You get two gold stars, baby. Remember where it is so we can find it again. Your mom may want to dry some of the root bark. Keechie called it a blood purifier and my grandmother used it for all sorts of things, but mainly she just liked to make tea from it."

"Dad, is it true that for every ailment, there is something in nature that will cure it?"

"Keechie believed that, and so did Granny Barnes. They both also warned me that there are things that can kill you, or make you very sick."

All the way back to the cave Alex kept asking about certain plants she saw along the way. Brian knew some of them, but others he admitted that he didn't know.

"I started a project when Keechie was teaching me about plants and herbs," he explained. "I made drawings of them and tried to identify them later but I never finished. I think I still have my old sketchbook. I'll look for it later and we'll see if we can identify some more of the plants Keechie showed me."

Mary was just coming from the garden when they walked up. She carried a basket of fresh vegetables in her hands, and over her shoulder was her crossbow pistol.

"Hey, you guys! I see that we're going to have fried rabbit after all. It'll be a good change from venison, and we can have a fresh garden salad to go with it."

Brian finished skinning the rabbits, being careful to keep the hides intact. "Keechie used deer sinew to stretch them, but I'll cheat and use thumbtacks. We'll need some salt to rub on them, but first we have to scrape off all the flesh. You can do that while I go get the salt, Alex."

Brian placed the hides fur-side down on an old board and tacked them all around, stretching them as he went. Then he watched as Alex scraped the flesh from them.

"Now we have to rub them down with salt and leave them out in the sun for a few days. After they're dry we can then chew them until they're good and soft," he said with a grin.

"Ewww! Chew them? That will have to be your job."

"Well, that's what Keechie did, but I think we can come up with a more modern way, baby, 'cause I'm not chewing them either."

By the time they were finished, Mary called them in, announcing that the rabbit was nearly done. "By the time y'all get cleaned up, supper will be ready."

After their evening meal, Brian and Alex went into the storeroom to look for the journal that he had written about Granny Boo.

"Ahhh, here it is," Brian said, as he pulled the old spiral notebook out of the box. "This is the one with the old stories that Keechie told me. She was a wonderful storyteller. She could make you feel like you were there. You could even smell the smells and see the scene she was describing. I tried to capture some of that in these stories."

The three of them sat near the fire as Brian began reading Keechie's memories of her Granny Boo's life.

"Boo's mother, Achena-Nakla, which means 'burning cedar', told this first one to Keechie when she was very young, but she recalled it vividly."

Hechee-Lana entered the cave and everyone scattered. The old woman not only had the yellow eyes of a cat as her name indicated, but she seemed to have its meaner disposition as well. She threw down the bundle of herbs she was carrying and went to Achena-Nakla.

"The child comes early, Daughter. She must be anxious to meet her grandmother. Let me feel your belly, girl. How fast are the pains coming?"

"Three hands of heartbeats, Mother. It will be soon, I hope. This child will be much smaller than Apelka-Haya. I swear he came out sideways—" Achena grunted as the next contraction hit her.

Hechee-Lana went about her duties as she had done for every child that had been born into the clan for the past twenty seasons. As she swept the room with the sweet smoke of cedar and sage, she chanted prayers to her spirit helper, Puma Man, who had been with the Clan since time began.

It was he who bestowed "The Gift" of Spirit Singing and Medicine Making to every other generation of girl-children in her family. Since her daughter had only two boys before this birthing, Hechee-Lana hoped that this would be the girl that Puma had foretold. She was getting old and wanted plenty of time to teach her successor the rituals, the medicinal plants and the duties of the Spirit Singer. It was an important position in the Clan, and not always the easiest path.

Her own grandmother, Wild Dancer, had been a young girl when the Clan came to this valley from the Land Where the Sun Sleeps. She was born during the journey, and was said to have been the most powerful Spirit Singer ever.

With the next contraction the baby was born.

"It is a girl-child!" Hechee-Lana announced, mostly to her daughter. She quickly tied the umbilical cord with deer sinew, and then deftly cut it. The baby was small, but otherwise seemed perfectly healthy. She washed the crying child, dried it off and placed it on her daughter's breast.

The naming of a child was usually the duty of the Clan's Hilis Haya – the Keeper of the People. He had been up on the Rock all day singing prayers for the dead. Echo-Ochee, which meant "Little Deer" was the older brother of Hechee-Lana. Like his sister, he carried the Gift of the Puma Clan, although grudgingly. It was not an easy path for anyone to take, but he had accepted it.

As he completed his rituals at the burial place of his father, the old chief Bull Killer, a familiar sensation of an approaching *Power* came over him. He looked toward the setting sun, shielding his eyes against the glare. In the glowing clouds of sunset the face of Puma Man appeared.

The voice of the entity spoke directly to his mind. *"The grandchild of your sister is born. Name her for the five-pointed flower that grows on the vine at your feet. Her souls are already known to me."*

Never before had Echo-Ochee heard the actual voice of the Puma Man, nor had he experienced a waking encounter with him. So shaken was he by the vision, he fell face down on the ground.

When he opened his eyes, he saw the Pu-Can vine growing amidst the rocks. The blossoms were open and displaying their full splendor of color and complexity. He quickly gathered one of the flowers, remembering to ask permission of the vine, and made his way to the cave as fast as his shaking old legs would permit.

Hechee-Lana went outside where the people waited and announced, "It is a healthy girl-child. If she is the one that Puma has foretold, she will be the next Spirit Singer, and a most powerful one. She comes from the line of my grandmother, Wild Dancer."

The people were all very familiar with the story of Paneta Semoli, the Wild Dancer. She had been born during their ancestors' migration to this place. They traveled all the way from the shores of the great saltwater where the sun sleeps, bringing with them the sacred corn of their people. Just as they crossed the Yazoo River, Wild Dancer's mother went into labor and she was born. They built their first village there.

Just as Hechee-Lana finished speaking, her brother came stumbling into the assembly. When he had caught his breath he pulled his sister aside and said, "The Puma Man told me. The girl is born, yes?"

"You move like your namesake, Little Deer. What has happened? And yes, Brother, she is born, but how did you know?"

"Puma Man. He came to me in the sunset … gave me her name." He was still clutching the passionflower blossom in his hand, and he held it out to his sister.

"Pu-Can? It is too early in the season for them to be blooming. Surely this is a sign of *Power*, Brother, and it is a good name. I will bring the child out so all can see her and hear the naming."

Hechee-Lana returned with the child and handed it to Echo-Ochee and then asked for the peoples' silence.

Echo-Ochee spoke. "It has been our tradition to wait for the full moon for our naming ceremony, but the Puma Man has given me this girl-child's name this day. He said to name her for the flower that was at my feet." He held the blossom up for all to see. "And so I name this child, the many-times granddaughter of Paneta-Semoli, Pu-Can. Pu-Can of the Kowakatchu Clan."

The people cheered and soon a huge fire was burning. The drumming and dancing lasted well into the night, for this was the child they had all been waiting for. Was she not of the direct line of their Spirit Singers? The Master of Breath had caused the Gift of Singing and Healing to only every other generation of women. With her grandmother Hechee-Lana to guide and instruct her in the shaman path, this would surely be the greatest of all their Singers.

CHAPTER 2

Alex was trying hard to not fall asleep while her dad read the story. "Dad, can we finish this tomorrow? I'm so sleepy."

"Sure, honey. I'm tired too. Tomorrow I will show you some more of Granny Boo's possessions and finish reading about that part of her life. I've got more—when she was a young woman, and when she got married and had Keechie's mom."

Mary and Brian went outside as soon as they prepared their sleeping mats after Alex had gone to sleep. They sat silently for a long while just listening to the night sounds, both realizing that the ceremony that Brian had read took place right where they were sitting.

Mary looked at Brian intently. "This Puma Man thing, is this something we should be worried about? It is more than just dreams, isn't it?"

Brian nodded. "Yes, honey. I've seen him myself many times since I met Keechie. He even told Keechie that my daughter would be the one to carry on the 'Gift', and that was even before I met you. He seems to be our protector, just as he was to Keechie and her ancestors."

"I know we have both experienced these things," Mary said. "I just worry about Alex not being ready for it. We must be ready to help her deal with it, if she needs us."

Brian nodded again. "The Puma Man sometimes does come in a dream. The only times I have seen him when I was awake was when Keechie was Spirit Singing, or performing a ritual. He seems to wait until he is called upon at those times."

He thought of the time nearly fifty years ago when Keechie had told him that he would have a daughter.

"You's gonna have a girl-child wit' de Gift, same as me an' Granny Boo. Puma done tol' me dat too. She gonna make a diff'ernce in dis worl'."

Brian put his arm around Mary's shoulders and they just sat there, watching as the clouds drifted across the full moon. He tightened his arm around her and said in a whisper, "I sit out here sometimes and wonder about the lives of Keechie and her family, you know? Just trying to imagine what it must have been like for them after the majority of their tribe was either killed or forced off this land and sent to the Indian Territory in Oklahoma."

"Me too. Was Keechie and her immediate family all that was left?" Mary asked.

"She told me that there were others who stayed, but their town—they called it a talofa—was burned and ploughed over. It was over that way on the bank of the river," Brian answered, pointing northward, "about a half-mile upstream. I've been there many times looking for potsherds and arrowheads. It's mostly grown over now with pine trees and kudzu. The town had about five hundred people in it. When their towns got any larger than that, they usually divided it up and some of the people would move away and form a new town. After the Removal, which it was then called, Keechie's great-grandparents came to this cave to hide. There wasn't much effort made to round up any stragglers, as long as they weren't causing the locals any trouble."

"But their normal way of life changed though, didn't it?"

Mary asked, thinking about their own recent change from their accustomed way of life.

"Well, there were a few small families scattered around within a day's walk, but they had to learn to operate on their own, instead of working as a co-op with the entire tribe. When they were in a town, each family had a small garden, but all of them worked in the communal fields. The crops were stored for all to use as needed and for trade with other towns. It was a good system until the white man came."

"It must have been terrible for them, since from what I've learned from your journals, they seemed so community-minded." Mary leaned her head on his shoulder.

"Yes, and you should have seen Keechie when we found her relatives and other people in Oklahoma. She had come to my college graduation with my parents. That was in College Station, Texas. That's when I took her to Indian Territory. From that day on she was torn between staying there with them and coming back here where her ancestors were buried. She really loved it here."

"I love it here too," Mary whispered, looking up at her husband of nearly thirty years with an expression of sincerity.

Brian smiled. "Me too, honey. Sometimes I think about us not ever leaving – not even if the world comes back to its senses. But Alex, she needs to be around people her own age. She needs an education, but then maybe the one she's getting here is more valuable."

"She's only twelve, Brian, so we can teach her for now. You're a country boy and you didn't turn out too bad," Mary teased.

"But a country boy who lived in a house with electricity and had schools to go to."

"Yep, but it's the things you learned from Keechie that make the difference for us now, right? Not the formal education."

Brian chuckled. "Okay, you win. And I'm getting chilly out here. Let's go back inside, okay?"

When they entered the cave they could hear Alex talking softly, as if she were chanting under her breath. Mary went to her and was about to ask what she was saying, when she realized that her daughter was sound asleep. She motioned to Brian to come closer. "What is she saying? Do you think she's alright?"

Brian knelt down beside Alex and listened for a moment in astonishment.

"It's the Song, Mary," he whispered. "It's the one Keechie called the 'Come to Me' song. They called it Spirit Singing. She seems all right. Maybe when she wakes up she'll remember the dream. Wait here. I want to read you something."

Brian went into the storeroom and came back with the manuscript that he had read to Alex just before they'd come to the cave. "Here it is," he said as he leafed through the first few pages. "This is what I dreamed right after meeting Keechie."

An old woman stood on the big rock at the top of the mountain. Her arms were outstretched toward the sky and she was singing. The words were not recognizable but I knew what they meant. Her voice, although soft, was heard by all living things. She was calling the animals to her valley. She was asking for them to give their lives for her tribe for food. She promised them honor and gratitude. She was asking the fish to fill the streams and rivers, the deer to provide clothing from their hides and their flesh for nourishment, and the beaver and mink for their hides for trade. The Song was irresistible, and I sensed the animals responding in great numbers. She called them Brothers and Sisters.

"When I told Keechie about my dream, she asked me, 'Was it like this?' and began singing the same song. She said it was the song that the Spirit Singers sang to call the game to the hunters, and that the words were what she called the 'Old Language'. Alex must be having the same dream. I think Puma Man is taking care of her education right now." Then he noticed that Alex had Granny Boo's Power Bundle clutched to her chest. "And when I had my dream, I was holding the medicine bag that Keechie had given me. She said it contained some of that same Power Bundle. 'Dat be pow'ful medicine', she used to say."

Alex shifted in her blankets and became quiet, apparently

drifting into a deeper sleep. She had a contented smile on her face, so they went to their own blankets for the night.

Alex was the first one up the next morning and was in the process of building up the fire when Brian and Mary awoke. "Hey, you two, I'm going to fix breakfast for us today. I've already been outside, checked on the solar cells, watched the sunrise, chased a rabbit out of the garden, and picked a ripe tomato, but I already ate it," she said with such cheerful enthusiasm that her parents laughed. "What? I'm just feeling good today, that's all."

"Oh, it's just good to see you in such a good mood, honey," Mary said, relieved that the dream of the night before had not had an adverse affect on her. "Need any help?"

"I want to do it myself, Mom. I do want some advice on herbs and spices that you use though, stuff that grows around here that we can use. Keechie told Dad about some of them, and his grandma knew some things too. I want to learn about the herbs, not just for cooking like the things you know; but how to make medicine from them too."

Mary looked at Brian with a questioning expression. He nodded in agreement. Puma Man had shown Alex the Healing Path of shamanism. It was something Alex was already attuned to, obvious from her love of animals and nature, which had already been apparent. But this, if one could foresee the future, was the path she was meant to take. The dream had only confirmed it.

And Alex couldn't have found a better person to ask about herbs. Mary, although she was accustomed to using herbs for cooking, had a wealth of knowledge to share. Her maternal grandmother from the Appalachian Mountains of north Georgia was said to be a full-blooded Cherokee Indian Medicine Woman. The family stories about her were many. The woman had lived to be ninety-three years old, and never once went to a doctor in her entire life. Mary had spent much of her young childhood in her presence. She had often said that Mary had the "Gift".

While Alex and Mary prepared breakfast, Brian went back

into the storeroom and located his box of journals and notebooks, which he carried into the main room. He was a meticulous organizer, so finding the journal he was looking for was easy. He had labeled it "Keechie's Herbs and Medicinal Plant."

Thumbing through it caused a wave of nostalgia to come over him. He remembered the trips he had taken with Keechie through the woods and swamps, where she had pointed out the different plants she knew.

Keechie would say things like, "Dis `un hyer, hit be fer coughing," pointing at a small plant, or "Fer dis `un, you gots t' bile de roots, den let `em sit fer a day."

Brian would try to identify the plant from memory. If he couldn't, he would make a sketch and look it up. He had several good books on herbs in his collection. His own Grandmother Barnes had taught him about many of the local plants and their uses, and all this together had proved invaluable over the years. When he was young, one of his friends had nearly died from tasting an unknown berry. It turned out to be poison sumac, locally known as "thunderwood". On the skin, it causes blisters much like poison ivy, but much worse. Internally, it caused his friend's tongue and throat to swell, nearly suffocating him. He had spent a week in the hospital. Sumac was usually found as a small bush, but Brian had seen it grow into a fairly large tree.

After they had eaten, he and Alex looked through the journal together.

"Some of these plants that I sketched haven't been identified yet," he said. "Why don't you make a project out of it? I'll dig out a good book on herbs and we'll try to figure out what they are. We might even be able to locate some of the plants themselves. Keechie didn't know their real names, so she just called them whatever her people called them. Their names were usually whatever the plant was used for, like 'Headache Plant', or 'Fever Plant', Actually, that's not such a bad system." He smiled at his daughter.

When he found *The Field Guide to Herbs* and gave it to her, Alex was immediately into the project. She spent most of the morning reading and comparing her dad's sketches with the illustrations in the book.

"Hey, Dad, for some of these we need to see the actual plant, you know? Could we look around today and see if we can find any of them? Please?"

"I guess so. We need to check on the corn anyway. There's a small creek near there. It should be a good place to start. Want to go with us, Mary?"

"Sure. Maybe some of the snow peas are ready. I'll get a basket," Mary said, eager to get out of the cave for a while.

The three of them walked single file to the patch of Osochi corn. Brian had begun calling it that when Keechie told him that her tribe was Osochi, and it was they who had first brought their corn into the southeast from "out west." He had researched their migration, and the best he could determine, they had came originally from the northwestern coast of Mexico in the early sixteenth century. By the mid 1500s they had reached what is now Alabama and Georgia.

Keechie had amazed her people in the Oklahoma Indian Territory when they discovered that she had preserved the original strain of corn all those years. Brian intended to carry on that tradition in honor of Keechie and her ancestors.

The corn was nearly five feet high, and some ears were beginning to appear. What was especially pleasing was that the snow peas that Mary had planted beside each stalk when it was only a foot tall had done well, too. The vines were climbing the cornstalks and were full of peas ready for picking. There were many more blossoms promising an even greater harvest, but the deer had also found the succulent vines. There were tracks throughout the field, and Brian knew where he would be hunting in the coming fall.

To the west, Pine Mountain loomed. Between them and the mountain was the creek, bordered by a low, swampy area. It was there that they began looking for the plants that Alex wanted to investigate.

She immediately found one that Brian had sketched.

"Hey, Dad! Look at this. Keechie was right. Your notes said that she used this one for coughs and dying flesh. Gangrene is what she meant, right?"

Brian took the field guide and compared it to the plant. It was, without a doubt, marshmallow (althea officinalis). Brian studied his notes and the text of the book that said: *MEDICINAL: Marshmallow aids in the expectoration of difficult mucous and phlegm. It helps to relax and soothe the bronchial tubes, making it valuable for all lung ailments. It is an anti-irritant and anti-inflammatory for joints and the digestive system. It is often used externally with cayenne to treat blood poisoning, burns, and gangrene. GROWING: Marshmallow needs marshes and swamps to grow. It is a perennial, growing to 4 feet tall.*

The photo in the book and the plant Alex had found were the same. The identification was even further conclusive by the swampy land they were now in, which, according to the book, was the correct place for it to grow. The medicinal uses described in the book and those simple words of Keechie, as taught to her by Granny Boo, were also in perfect agreement.

Alex made some additional notes in the journal and then exclaimed, "Oops! Dad, I just wrote in your old journal. Is it okay?"

"Sure, honey. You're completing a project that I started many years ago. I always did want to finish it, but never seemed to find the time. Now, with our situation as it is, we may need these plants."

He had stored at least a year's worth of medicinal supplies; but in reality, that was only an estimate.

Puma Man is leading her to the Healing Path. This may be the meaning of Keechie's words that foretold that my daughter-to-be would 'make a diff'ernce in dis worl', Brian thought, feeling proud of his daughter. The very air seemed to crackle with *Power*. The presence of unseen forces made the whole scene appear surreal.

Mary had felt the *Power* too, and she placed her arms around both their shoulders and gave them a loving hug.

"It's getting late, so why don't we start back?" she said,

trying to sound cheerful. She looked at the darkening sky and shivered as she made a silent plea … *Puma Man, Great Spirit, God, whatever it is that is at work here, please protect our family.*

As they gathered their belongings, a large white owl swooped down and landed on a tree branch just a few yards from them. Unblinking, it watched them as they began their trip back to the cave.

"Remember Brother Owl there, guys? In one of the later stories I have of Granny Boo's people, he plays an important role," Brian told them.

When they passed the cornfield, Mary picked up the basket of snow peas she had gathered earlier, feeling a closeness to the way of life that had been forced upon them. *Keechie would be very proud of us right now.*

After a meal of venison stew, fresh snow peas and boiled potatoes, Brian read to them again from his notebook on the life of Granny Boo, as told to him by Keechie …

CHAPTER 3

When Pu-Can was three summers old, white men discovered her father while he fished at the river. They told him of the war among the white men, North against South, and took him away with them. A young boy was with him, who had escaped to tell the story. He did not know which side took Pu-Can's father, only that they promised him great riches if he went with them as a guide. He was never seen again.

Young Pu-Can was never far away from her grandmother, Hechee-Lana. The old medicine woman knew that this child was the one they were expecting, and she intended to teach her the ways of the spirit world as early as the child could accept them.

Power has a way of making its presence known and Pu-Can was already showing interest in the supernatural world. She would frequently have conversations when there was apparently no one there.

Her mother was worried that there was something wrong with her and would scold her and try to get her interested in other things. Pu-Can would wait until her mother left her alone, and would then continue her conversation with her unseen companions. Of course, Pu-Can's grandmother encouraged her and asked questions about the special visitors.

Hechee-Lana and Pu-Can both communicated with the animals of the forest, but Pu-Can's Gift was exceeding her grandmother's in the ability to hear and see the spiritual entities. Hers was the unbiased world of a child, and Hechee-Lana wanted to nurture that part of the Gift so that it would remain into adulthood.

Kowakatcu, the Puma Man, was a gatekeeper to the unseen realms, and had been her Clan's totem since there had been people. Pu-Can had described the "Cat Man" to her, so she knew that her granddaughter's visions were real. He was one of the more powerful of the guides and had caused the death of more than one person through fear alone.

One of his tactics in teaching the shaman path was to suddenly and unexpectedly leap at the initiate and swallow him whole. Those who showed no fear he took to the heights of a spiritual journey. Those who cowered were not suited for the shamanistic life, and never received the opportunity again.

Hechee-Lana was twenty summers old when she fasted for several days, took the black purging drink, and sang and danced for many hours before Puma Man confronted her. Now here was young Pu-Can already talking to him, and was no more than eight summers old. Surely she was to be the Spirit Singer that her Clan had been expecting since the time of her own grandmother, Paneta-Semoli, the Wild Dancer.

"That old woman could even scare the Puma Man himself," Hechee-Lana muttered under her breath as she remembered her own experiences when she was a young girl. Her grandmother would put on the ancient mask and leopard skins, then dance around the fire. She would dance and dance, then suddenly spring toward the children with a feline shriek. Children scattered in all directions, screaming in fear, but not Hechee-Lana. She stood her ground—her heart nearly jumping out of her chest—but never, ever showing fear.

Her grandmother would laugh and allow Hechee-Lana to join in the dance, and sometimes, when no one else was around, would let her put on the old mask. This was a very special honor, because the mask, like all ritual items, was sacred and reserved for only the Spirit Singers and Medicine Men.

When Pu-Can was in her twentieth summer, her older brother, Apelka-Haya, came running into the clearing in front of the cave.

"White men come!" he shouted. "They have already killed two of ours near the river, now they are coming this way." He gasped for breath and drank deeply from the water gourd that Pu-Can offered. "I warned the ones who were in the cornfield. There is not much time!"

Since the Removal the cave had become the hiding place for the few remaining from the Clan and it had seemed to become invisible to outsiders.

"How many of the whites did you see, Apelka?" Hechee-Lana asked. "Who did they kill?"

"There were four of them, Grandmother, and they shot old Turtle and his son while they were fishing. They never even saw them from across the river. I was in the trees behind them, repairing my cast net. They had a boat and crossed while I watched. There was nothing I could do but run to warn the rest." Apelka bowed his head in shame.

"You did the right thing, Grandson. Here come the others. Help us to move everything inside the cave that could give us away," the old Medicine Woman said.

She began giving orders to everyone within the sound of her voice. Soon all the people were gathered inside the cave, its entrance concealed with fresh branches so that it looked as natural as the rest of the scenery.

Apelka-Haya and two of the younger men climbed the rocks above the cave to stand watch. They had only their bows and arrows against the white man's guns, but with their knowledge of the terrain and their expertise, it could be enough. It would have to be enough.

The most important thing was, if they killed a white man, more were sure to come. Sooner or later, they would find the rest of the Clan and kill them all.

It was only a hand of time before the people in the cave heard the pre-arranged signal that warned of approaching danger. A pebble was thrown from the rocks above, rattling as it bounced down the boulders, landing in front of the cave. The women silenced the children and everyone waited, helpless except for going into the deeper recesses of the cave.

The Puma Man had protected them in the past in times just like this.

Blind their eyes again, Kowakatcu, Protect us as you have protected our people since time began. We honor you, Hechee-Lana prayed silently.

Only two of the white men came into the clearing in front of the cave, as far as Apelka could see. He was straight above the cave entrance—less than a bowshot away. He nocked an arrow, but remained hidden from sight behind the brush and rock above their heads.

The two men were obviously drunk, and were still passing a flask between them.

"Where they's one Injun, they's always mo'. I saw that 'un run this-a-way, but he be long gone by now," one of them said.

"You right, Elmer, but I sho wanna get me one. I ain't never kilt me an Injun befo'," the other answered.

"Hey, look at this!" The man picked up the water gourd from which Apelka had recently sipped.

Somehow, it was overlooked when the people hurriedly cleared the area.

"Hit's still got water in it. They's close, man. I can smell 'em!"

The men began looking closely at the ground in front of the cave.

"Looky hyer, Slim, here's some tracks a'goin' right up to

those rocks—and this branch hyer's been cut!" he said as he pulled it away from the opening.

"Looks like we got us a cave hyer," Slim said, backing away as he brought his rifle up to bear on the entrance.

Apelka, seeing the man bring his rifle up to his shoulder, wasted no time. He drew his bow and released the arrow. The man died where he stood. The arrow, coming from above him, entered his throat at a downward angle, penetrated his lungs and severed his spinal cord. He fell backward without a sound.

Elmer saw his companion fall and brought his rifle up and turned wildly, looking for the one who had loosed the arrow. Then he saw Apelka standing on the rock above him.

"Gotcha, you bastid," he said as he brought his weapon up and aimed.

Two arrows almost simultaneously struck him in the chest.

Apelka waved to his two companions on the opposite side of the cliff wall. He motioned for them to be silent and remain where they were. He climbed down to the clearing and went into the cave.

"Is everyone safe in here?" he asked Pu-Can, who was guarding the entrance with a spear that was longer than her height. Apelka recognized the spear as the ceremonial one that had belonged to their ancestor, old Bull Killer, but said nothing.

"Yes, my brother, we are safe, but you said there were more of the white men. These two," she said, indicating the two dead men with contempt "need to be hidden until we can decide what to do with them."

Apelka-Haya thought for a minute and said, "We will hide them for now, but the others will be looking for them. Now they must all die, or we will be hunted down like animals."

He saw Pu-Can's eyes widen as she looked over his shoulder. Just as he turned to see what she was looking at, she charged past him, bringing the spear down until it was pointed straight ahead of her.

One of the two remaining men had wandered into the clearing. When he saw his companions lying dead on the ground he brought his rifle up and took aim at Apelka's back just as Pu-Can ran him through with the ancient spear. His rifle discharged into the ground and he fell forward onto the shaft of the spear that was protruding from his belly.

Looking up at his companions, Apelka gave a signal for them to remain vigilant for the fourth man. They signed back in understanding.

Turning to Pu-Can he said, "Thank you, Sister. You saved my life. Now send some of the men out here. We must hide these bodies until we find the other man. There were only four of them. He must not escape."

Pu-Can had never killed a man before. She had never even thought about what it meant to kill another human being. She stood transfixed by what had just occurred—a look of horror etched on her face.

Then she pulled the spear violently from the man and raised it up to the sky. Blood ran down the shaft and onto her hands as she called upon Kowakatcu the Puma Man for strength and guidance.

Just as Pu-Can turned to enter the cave to get more men to help hide the bodies, her grandmother came out of the cave with two men.

Hechee-Lana ordered them to hide the bodies, and then turned to Pu-Can. "You did what was necessary, child. No one likes to kill. Sometimes it is necessary. You saved your brother's life."

Pu-Can looked at her grandmother, then at the blood on her hands and nodded. "I am alright, Grandmother. What must we do now?"

Hechee-Lana opened her mouth to reply when a shot rang out from the edge of the clearing. The bullet struck her in her chest below her left shoulder, and she sank slowly to the ground.

Pu-Can crouched to the ground as she turned around, just in time to see the fourth man struck by an arrow. His rifle dropped from his hands, and as he clutched at the shaft protruding from his chest, a second arrow struck him. He fell dead to the ground.

"Grandmother!" Pu-Can cried as she knelt beside the old

woman. She looked at the wound closely. It was bubbling with every breath the old Medicine Woman took. Pu-Can placed her hand over the wound and leaned close to hear what Hechee-Lana was trying to say.

"Puma … Kowakatcu," the old woman whispered, pointing up at the sky. "He comes … he will show you what to do …" With a last breath, still pointing at the sky, she said, "Wild Dancer … Grandmother … wait … I come …" and then she died in Pu-Can's arms.

Two of the women came out of the cave and silently took Hechee-Lana inside.

Pu-Can stood up, then in a wild dash toward the man who had killed her grandmother, she fell upon him with only her fists. She grabbed the arrows that were in his body—twisting and pulling them. "Die, vermin! May your souls wander the earth and never find peace!"

"He is already dead, my sister-warrior. But you can ask Puma Man to eat his souls so that he will never find peace in the other world," her brother said, spitting on the dead man.

The others came slowly out of the cave and stood transfixed in shock over the day's events. No one spoke as they tried to understand what had happened to their peaceful life.

Echo-Ochee came out of the cave last. He had donned the robes and ornaments of his position as Keeper of the People. He first examined the bodies of the four white men, shaking his gourd rattle and chanting under his breath.

He turned to his people, pointed at the dead men and said, "Carry this meat to the river. If their boat is still there, turn it over and let it drift downstream. Weigh their bodies with stone and let the turtles and fish have them.

"No trace of them will ever be found, and their people will think they drowned. Now! This must be done quickly! Bring old Turtle and his son back here. We will honor our dead in the way of our ancestors." He shook his rattle violently once more at the white men and walked away.

Apelka-Haya and the two warriors who had defended their people put the dead men onto two hastily built travois. Three more of the men joined them, and began the journey to the river. Several of the women walked behind them with pine branches, sweeping the drag marks away. There would be no trail left to follow if anyone tried to discover the fate of the white men.

Just as the sun was setting, they reached the river. The boat was still resting on the sandy beach and old Turtle and his son lay not far away. They were both scalped and their bodies mutilated. They found the scalps in the boat and recovered them.

"What kind of men do these things?" one of them asked.

"None with honor, Brother," Apelka said with contempt. "We are not people to them. We would not treat an animal this way." They removed the white men's clothing, then tied large rocks to the bodies and put them into the boat. Two of the men paddled it to the middle of the river where it was the deepest and tipped the boat over. As they swam back to shore, the overturned boat drifted slowly downstream and was soon out of sight.

They made camp on the river for the night, just far enough into the forest that their fire would not be seen from the opposite shore. Apelka sent sentries up and downstream to watch for danger.

The women cleaned the bodies of old Turtle and his son and wrapped them in blankets, ready for transport to their home the next day.

Apelka caught enough fish with his cast net for the group. Someone had brought a pot of sofkee to which the fish were added. There was enough for all to satisfy their hunger. At dawn, one of the sentries ran into the encampment and told Apelka that there was another boat on the river. They quickly extinguished their fire and two of the older warriors made their way cautiously to a place where they could see the river. They watched as two men paddled against the current, searching the banks on both sides.

"They are not fishing. They are looking for the other white men," one of them whispered.

"Let us hope they find the boat. They will think that the four men were drunk and drowned when their boat overturned."

The men allowed their boat to drift downstream and the observers watched until it disappeared around a bend. Owl, the younger of the two sentries, followed along the bank, staying out of sight. The other one returned to their camp to report what they had seen.

The bodies of Turtle and his son were already on the travois and they were about to begin the journey back to the cave.

"We must now be more vigilant than ever, my brothers. The whites are increasing in numbers. They are hunting and fishing where we hunt and fish," Apelka-Haya said solemnly. "In that regard we are fortunate our numbers are small and our needs are few."

Old Echo-Ochee met them when they were halfway back to the cave. "What news, Apelka?" he asked, gasping for breath.

"We sank the four men in the river as you instructed, Grandfather, and overturned their boat. There were some men searching for them, I think. They were not fishing. Owl is following them as they drift downstream to see if they find the boat," Apelka told him. "We hope that the boat did not go far and they will find it and think the men were drowned."

Echo-Ochee looked toward the two bodies on the travois.

"How did they die?" the old man asked softly.

"They were shot with rifles, Grandfather. But then …" Apelka hesitated before completing his sentence. "Then they were scalped and mutilated with knives," he said, looking down, not wanting to see the reaction on his grandfather's face.

Echo-Ochee slumped forward and almost fell. Just as Apelka was about to grab him to keep him from falling, he heard a deep growling snarl like a wolf about to attack. The sound was coming from his grandfather.

The old man stood up straight, and the snarling increased in volume until it sounded like a leopard's shriek. Apelka drew back in shock at the expression on his grandfather's face, and the sound that was coming from him.

Birds, startled by the sound, took to the sky in flocks as Echo-Ochee raised his arms to the sky and began singing in the Old Tongue. The sky darkened and thunder reverberated between the two mountains as the old shaman continued the Song. Steadily increasing the tempo and volume, his voice soon blended with the thunder until it became one with it.

A huge, black thundercloud gathered above them as the swirling clouds spun faster and faster, climbing higher and higher into the sky. Lightning flashed with such intensity that it temporarily blinded them.

Apelka and the others knew that they were witnessing great Power and they became silent, each mouthing prayers to the spirits of their ancestors.

The great thundercloud drifted toward the river and continued to produce violent lightning as it went. Then ice began falling from the sky. Ice the size of bird eggs fell upon them as they rushed for the cover of trees. Soon the ground was covered with a thick layer and then the storm passed as suddenly as it had started.

"Did you see him, Apelka? Did you see the Puma Man?" his grandfather asked in a tone of reverence.

"No, Grandfather, I did not see him. But you did?"

"He was in the great cloud that passed over us. He smiled at me, and it was a terrible, yet beautiful smile. He has eaten the souls of the four men who killed our people. I do not envy their fate," his grandfather said. "Now we must bury our dead and honor them as our tradition requires."

Apelka took the old man's shoulders in his hands and looked directly into his eyes. "The children of my children will know of this day, Grandfather, I swear to you. Surely, Echo-Ochee is the most powerful Keeper who has ever lived. You called down the wrath of Kowakatcu upon our enemies."

Just then Owl appeared out of the forest. He had cut cross-country from the river, hoping to meet them on their way back. Between gasps for air he said to them, "I followed the two white men … as they searched downstream, Grandfather. They found the overturned boat … just as the great storm struck … but I think they are both dead." He paused for air, and with his voice shaking with emotion he continued, "Just as they were pulling the overturned boat to shore … lightning struck them. There was a huge flash and then … then they were gone … even the boats. Then the rocks of ice fell from the sky. Kowakatcu has destroyed our enemies."

CHAPTER 4

Brian closed the journal and told his wife and daughter, "They had very strict traditions about burying their dead back then. Because of their small numbers, some of it had changed, but they usually waited four days before the actual burial, and they never left the bodies alone during those four days. Then they buried them in swampy, wet ground for as long as it took for the flesh to decompose. The bones were then dug up and sewn into deer hides, or placed in large clay pots and re-buried at the burial ground—just like I did with Keechie."

Alex nodded and said, "I remember that story. And you showed us the burial ground up at the Rock. Are all these people there?"

Brian nodded. "I think so. Keechie never mentioned any other place where they buried their dead.

"Now, if y'all are as sleepy as I am, we better get some sleep. Tomorrow night I'll read you the story of how Granny Boo, Pu-Can, took over the duties of her uncle, Echo-Ochee, after he died. It happened soon after what I read tonight."

Brian went outside and sat for a while reflecting on the story he had just read. It had reminded him of the man he had killed in almost the same way that Apelka had killed the first man from above the cave. *I wonder how many have died right here in front of this cave. Keechie told me that the Puma Man protected it. I hope he still does.*

With that thought, he looked up at the star-filled sky and silently repeated his plea. Just at that moment a shooting star flashed across the sky and he took it as a sign that his plea was heard.

When Brian brought his family to this place nearly a year ago from Atlanta, the entire nation was in confusion, and many people abandoned the cities and metropolitan areas. The competition for food and necessities was too great for a dense population.

Then there was the danger of disease with so many people clustered so closely together. Even most of the people living in the small community in the valley nearby had left. Further south the death rates and food competition were lower, and many had gone there.

When they begin returning, if they haven't already, our danger of discovery will increase. Hunters will be looking for game, and there will be people fishing on the river. I really should check out the area—and soon.

Mary came out just as he finished the thought and said to her, "I'm thinking about making a trip into town tomorrow."

"Town? What are you sitting out here dreaming up, Yoholo?" she asked, teasing him about the name given to him by the Creek Indian mikko, or chief, when he had taken Keechie to Oklahoma. His Creek name, Yoholo, meant "Loud Speaker" and was a result of the tribal council's reading of his college thesis on the Muskogee/Creek history.

"We need to find out just how many people have returned to the valley," he explained. "There will be more hunters, and more people fishing the river, and, well, we just need to know what's going on in the world. Not to mention, we need to know if the truck will still run. Its battery will probably need recharging, and I need to see if there's any gasoline to be had so we can fill the tank."

Mary thought for a moment, and then said, "We all will go. I don't want to sit here worried about you."

"Okay, so are you ready for an adventure?" He put his arm around her and waited for her answer.

"What will we need to take besides food? What if there are still bandits and thieves?"

Brian smiled. "We will be careful, and we'll have our weapons, of course," he said. "This could be good for Alex too. She hasn't seen any other people since we came here … except for that one man—" He stopped himself too late for it to get by her. The only other person Alex had seen besides the two of them since coming to the cave, he had killed. The man had been holding Alex with a knife to her throat and Brian had shot him with a crossbow dart. It was not a pleasant memory.

"I'll start getting things ready," Mary said. "I'll be ready by the time you check the truck tomorrow morning', she added, trying to get past the memory of that awful day.

They woke early. Alexis was excited to have a chance to see where her dad had grown up. She was excited just to be able to go somewhere else. When Brian headed out to check on the truck, she insisted on going with him.

"I haven't been up on the Rock in a long time, Dad. And I want to see the burial ground again. Plus I can look for herbs on the way, and—"

Brian chuckled. "Okay, okay, baby girl. I get the message. Tell your mom you're going with me. I could use the company," he said, smiling at her.

She was practically jumping up and down with excitement.

They took the old path up to the base of the mountain, past the burial ground of Keechie and her people, and climbed the rock-lined trail to the top, where they had hidden the truck.

It was such a huge outcrop of granite and from the top of it, one could see the entire valley below. Brian had discovered it when he was just a boy, and had immediately felt the specialness of the place. It was his "Place of Power" and now, knowing how Keechie's ancestors had used the place, he knew that the ancients had probably felt the power too.

He had pulled the truck into the brush and scrub oaks at the end of the old sawmill road that ended near the outcropping.

They pulled away the camouflage of limbs and brush, and then Brian unlocked the door and climbed inside. The engine was slow in turning over at first, but it finally caught, and seemed to be running just as well as it had when he had parked it a year earlier.

They let it run while Brian found his small air compressor and inflated two of the tires that were just a little low. While the battery was charging, the two of them removed some of the larger limbs that had fallen across the old road.

A car passed on the main road, but neither they nor the truck could be seen from the road, but they listened until the sound of its engine was out of hearing range.

"Let's go back and get your mom and the rest of the stuff we're taking with us," he said to Alex, thinking mostly about the weapons, as well as the food for the day. He switched off the ignition, locked the doors on the truck and they began the hike back to the cave.

Mary had everything ready when they arrived: food in two large backpacks, and a third that contained a first aid kit, their two Colt .380s, extra ammunition, a couple of hunting knives and extra bolts for Brian's crossbow that was hanging over her shoulder.

"Can either of you think of anything else?" Brian asked.

"It's not like we're going to be gone for a week."

Brian gave Mary a hug and answered, "Right, and it looks like you thought of everything. I remembered to get some cash, just in case there's a store open. Remember those? They were where we used to buy the things we needed," he joked, but not without a bit of sarcasm.

It was almost noon by the time they reached the Rock and loaded the truck for their venture into what once was civilization. Brian carefully backed the truck to a place where he could turn it around. When they neared the main road, he switched off the ignition and listened for other vehicles before pulling out. He didn't want anyone to see them as they pulled out of the old weed-covered sawmill road.

The road they were now on was what was locally known as "The Scenic Highway". It ran along the crest of Pine Mountain, offering views of the valley below on either side. It was part of the Franklin D. Roosevelt State Park and ran northward almost to Warm Springs, Georgia, home of Roosevelt's "Little White House."

It had been Roosevelt's idea to form the little community of Pine Mountain Valley where Brian was born. His grandfather had joined the W.P.A. workforce in the early 1930s, and helped build the houses in the community, even the one in which Brian had been born.

His grandfather and his dad had each bought a house and sixteen acres of land in the young community. Brian still owned his family's house and land, but the house had been rented out for years. It was vacant now and he hoped it was still boarded up. That was where he wanted to visit first.

At the end of the Scenic Highway, he made a left U-turn onto the road that went down the mountainside to the valley below. His old home was just past the bridge that crossed the creek that he had followed so many times in his youth. It was on one of those excursions, up this same creek, where he had found Keechie, the old half-breed Indian woman living alone in the cave that they now occupied.

He was still reminiscing about Keechie when he nearly passed his old home. The yard was so overgrown with weeds and brush that he almost didn't recognize it. The most familiar landmark was the huge old oak tree that stood beside the house. He had spent many hours high up in its branches, pretending that he was in the crow's nest of a pirate ship, or that he was Tarzan of the Apes.

Waves of nostalgia washed over him as they sat in the driveway. There were bittersweet memories of family, childhood, and a more innocent time before terrorism and weapons of mass destruction. He remembered the "duck and cover" period of the Cold War when everyone feared the Russians and the atomic bomb.

They got out of the truck and checked the house, which seemed to be in fairly good condition. There was no evidence of vandalism or unwelcome occupation, other than mice. The barn that stood behind the house was still there, and he made a mental note to check it out thoroughly later. He and his family had stored many possessions there, locked it up and made it clear that it was not part of the rental agreement.

Satisfied that the house was in order, they continued on through Brian's old neighborhood. Only a few of the houses nearby had cars in the driveways, but no people were evident. The windows were all heavily curtained on these few, but there were still some signs of occupation, although less obvious. A few small gardens looked maintained and they saw a couple of cows behind one of the homes.

Next they drove to Hamilton, the nearest town that was five miles away, where his dad's old country store had been. Here they found people—not a lot of them, but people, nonetheless. There were a few older black men gathered in front of his dad's old store, which appeared to be open, but there was no sign of electricity in use.

The men were sitting on the concrete steps, a scene that was very familiar to Brian from the days when he worked at the store as a young boy. It was a meeting place to swap stories of fishing and hunting, success or failure of crops, and in general all the recent gossip. The men paused and watched as Brian and his family drove slowly past, suspicion apparent in their stares.

Brian wanted to stop and talk, but thought better of it, and continued on through the town. Neither of the two red lights was in operation, and the only gas station was closed and boarded up. He drove as far as his old high school on the outskirts, then turned around and headed back into town.

"I'm going to check out the store and try to get a feel for what's been going on lately," he told Mary and Alex. "If it seems alright, the two of you can get out and come in. Just let me make sure first, okay?"

He parked in front of the store, but away from the men gathered there, and got out, locking the driver's door behind him. He saw Mary reach into the backpack, trying to be discrete, but he knew she was getting her Colt ready. He gave her a quick smile and walked toward the store entrance.

One of the men standing at the steps next door approached him slowly just as he reached the door.

"Dey's spicious o' strangers in dere, mista" he said softly to Brian. "You folks from 'roun' hyer?"

"I was born here, friend. But I haven't been around for a long time. My daddy used to own this store."

"You be Mista Brine's son?" the man asked, his eyes suddenly lighting up.

"Yep. Did you know him?" Brian asked, immediately feeling a hint of recognition.

"Sho did. My mama an' daddy usta brang us kids hyer on Saddys to get groceries. Yo daddy used t' give me canny an' stuff. He were a good man, yo daddy. I 'member you, too. I even worked hyer fer a while, same as you. Me an' you usta deliver groceries on a bicycle! You be mista little Brine, ain'tcha? We usta go fishin' togedder n' stuff!"

"Maurice! Is it really you?" Brian asked him excitedly. "You look just like your daddy. I went to your mama's funeral the year before I went off to school."

They grabbed each other in a bear hug, laughing at their unexpected reunion. The other men walked over at this sign of recognition, wanting to know just who this stranger could be that caused this sudden outburst of emotion.

Maurice told them who Brian was and introduced them. None of the others had been around when Brian was young, but since Maurice knew him, that made him all right in their eyes.

Brian asked Maurice about the store, trying to get an idea of how they did business.

"Are the owners from around here and do they want money or trade?"

"Money be da best, but mos' folks 'roun' hyer ain't got much o' dat leff. Dey trades mos'ly. Dey don't be from 'roun' hyer neither. I thank dey came up from Columbus. Dey's 'bout as po as de rest o' us, truf be tol'."

Brian and Maurice walked in together, and Maurice introduced him to the man behind the counter.

"Mista Epstein, dis be my ol' frien', Brine. His daddy usta own dis sto back in de ol' days," he said. "Mista Brine work hyer when he wuz a youngun, fo' he went off t' school. He knowed my folks."

"Pleased to meet you, Brian. What brings you back to these parts?" the man asked with a poorly hidden hint of suspicion. "And what can I do for you today?"

"Just checking out the old homeplace, Mister Epstein, and thinking about maybe moving my family back here. Trying to get an idea about what's available. Mind if I look around?"

"No, not at all. Look around. There isn't much to see, but it's all for sale." Mister Epstein laughed at his own humor.

"Let me get my family then. They're waiting in the truck. I'll be right back." Brian went outside and waved to Mary, motioning for them to join him. Then the three of them went inside and Brian introduced Mary and Alex first to Maurice, then to the storeowner.

Mr. Epstein was looking past them, probably trying to see what was in the back of the truck that possibly could be used for trade.

Brian had noticed that the old manual gas pump was still outside on the curb and asked about it.

"Gasoline ran out almost a year ago. That's like gold around here these days. A gallon of gas will get you ten pounds of flour or a ham," Mr. Epstein told him with a wink.

"What's that come to in money, Mister Epstein?" Brian asked, trying to get an idea of values again.

"Flour is a dollar a pound, so ten dollars a gallon for gasoline, I reckon," Mr. Epstein said without flinching. "I've heard rumors that gasoline is being produced in small quantities, but it costs more to produce and transport than it's worth. There's been talk of alternative fuels, but no one knows what or even when that will be."

Mary and Alex checked out the available goods while Brian talked. They were both bent over one of the counters looking at something closely. Brian went over to see what had caught their interest.

Expecting it to be some foodstuff that they didn't have, or something that they really didn't need, he laughed aloud when he saw what had got their attention. It was a stack of magazines with titles like *Ladies Home Journal* and *Better Homes and Gardens*. They all had a good laugh at the irony of it all. Then Brian saw some of his favorites from times past. There were several issues of *Mother Earth News* and *Organic Gardening* with dates from almost two years ago. He already had all of them.

The meat and produce sections were nearly bare because of the lack of electricity to keep things cold, but there were salted meats and some produce, apparently taken in trade from local gardens.

They realized that they were actually better supplied at their cave than the meager offerings that were available here. Obviously the local people had reverted to subsistence farming and were providing for themselves, much the same as they were.

They still had staples such as flour, cornmeal, and dried beans stored at the cave, but the flour was getting low. Brian thought it wise to at least buy something, so he located the flour. He picked up two ten-pound bags and placed them on the counter.

"Does someone around here have a mill?" he asked, noticing that the bags had no label.

Mister Epstein nodded. "Yep. Old man Calloway still runs

GRANNY BOO ~ Legacy of the Puma Man

his mill down on the Mulberry Creek, just like always. Problem is there aren't many people growing wheat around here, so he has it brought in. The mill is one thing that continued to operate, since it's water powered. Will there be anything else I can get for you today?"

"No, I think this will be it, but we'll be back," Brian said, reaching for his wallet.

"Will that be cash?" Mister Epstein asked. "It'll be twenty dollars, unless you have trade, of course."

Brian pulled out a twenty and handed it to the man who looked at it carefully before putting it into his own wallet. From the corner of his eye, Brian had noticed two white men entering the store just as he had reached for his wallet. His internal alarm bells went off, but he tried to appear as if he had not noticed them.

They were picking up items and replacing them, not really appearing interested in them, and then looking away when Brian tried to make eye contact.

Maurice walked out the door with Brian and his family and said, "I seen dem two befo'. Don' nobody 'roun' hyer know who dey is. Dey showed up 'bout a week ago. Dey don' evva buy nuthin', but dey always snoopin' 'roun'." He took Brian's hand and said, "Hit sho good t' see you 'gin, Brine. Y'all be keerful now, you heah?"

Brian thanked him. "Sure is good to find someone I know from around here, Maurice, and I appreciate the warning. Strange times, my old friend. We'll see you again soon."

As they got in the truck, Alex said, "Those men are getting into that little car, Dad."

"I see them, honey. Don't worry. We're strangers to most of these people and they're probably just checking us out because we're new," he said, not really believing it himself.

He watched in the rearview mirror as the car pulled out behind them, just as they went through the intersection with no red light. The hairs on the back of his neck were alerting him to danger, and as he began the ascent to the mountain, he saw that the car was remaining just far enough back to not appear conspicuous. During the entire day's outing, they had seen only one other car, and now there was one following him. When they got to the top of the mountain where he should have taken the right fork to enter the Scenic Highway, he continued driving straight ahead.

"Wasn't that the road you should have taken?" Mary asked.

"Yep, but I'm not going to lead those two right to where we live," Brian explained. "I think they're trying to find that out. At any rate, I'm being cautious. I'm going to pull in just up the road and turn around. Let's see if they follow."

He remembered that there was a picnic area just ahead that had a turn-around drive. It was one of the scenic view areas, and it was just past a sharp curve that would allow him time to turn in before the car behind them could see them make the turn.

He pulled into the drive and stopped, facing back the way they had come. Seconds later, the car went past and braked, then continued on as if they hadn't seen them. Brian waited. If the men were following them, they couldn't wait long before giving themselves away.

Just when he figured that they had waited long enough and was about to pull out, the car returned, slowed slightly, then continued on, back toward Hamilton, the way they had come.

"Now I'm on to you," Brian said under his breath. "But what do we do now?"

He thought for a minute, and then pulled out in the opposite direction, toward Chipley.

The men in the other car would have to turn around again if they wanted to follow them.

Better to have them follow us to where there are other people, Brian thought.

Chipley was only about two miles down the mountain, and there was another road which connected to the other end of the Scenic Highway—just outside the city limits. It would be more proof that the men were following them if they saw their car again and not that much out of the way if they were not. Chipley was just a little more occupied than Hamilton, but still had no evidence of electricity in use. Several people were congregated outside the "Feed and Seed" hardware store, and they all watched as Brian pulled into the parking lot.

They sat there for a few minutes until Brian said, "Well, we're attracting more attention just sitting here. Let's go in. Wait. One of us should stay here and watch for the car."

"You and Alexis go in. I'll stay here," Mary volunteered.

"Thanks, baby. We can look for some late season seeds while we're in there. Can't ever have too many seeds." Brian said as he kissed Mary on the cheek. "We won't be long, just long enough to see if those guys are still following or not. We'll keep an eye on you. Lock the doors, okay?"

Brian and Alex went inside, and Mary pulled the Colt from beneath the seat, never taking her eyes off the main road in front of her.

Less than five minutes passed before she saw it. The car drove slowly past on the main road and parked across the street. The men remained inside, not looking in her direction, but she knew that they had seen the truck. *They think either that they are very good at this, or they assume that no one is clever enough to spot them*, she thought. Either way, Mary had seen her husband kill a man for threatening his family, and she knew that she was fully capable of doing the same. She racked a shell into the chamber of the .380 and waited.

Brian and Alex returned shortly and nodded to her.

"I saw the car, honey," he said. "Don't look toward them. I have a plan." He handed her a paper bag of seed through the window and got in behind the wheel. He backed out of the parking spot and headed north on the main road toward Atlanta—where they really had no desire to go. It was in the opposite direction from where they needed to go to return to the cave. The car soon followed.

"It's either the truck they want, or they saw the cash in my wallet," he said. "And they're not getting either, if I can help it. Their car has an out-of-state tag—Louisiana, I think, so I may have the advantage by knowing the back roads. I know of at least three different ways to get back to where we want to go."

When they rounded a curve and could no longer see the car behind them, Brian quickly turned into a dirt road off to the right, but not so fast as to cause dust to rise. He sped up and made another curve, then pulled over far enough to turn around. He waited a moment, and then drove back toward the main road just in time to see the car disappearing around another curve.

"I think we've lost them. By the time they realize we're not in front of them, we'll be gone."

He turned back toward Chipley, and the road back to the Rock, driving faster than the law had allowed in much different times. He suddenly laughed out loud.

"What's so funny, Brian? We have a serious problem here, you know?" Mary asked.

"It's just that when I was young and foolish, you couldn't get away with anything in Chipley. The cops watched for us boys in our cars back then, and would chase us down for sneezing at a red light. Where are they now? I would really like to see a cop right now."

Brian made a quick left turn just before they got back to the center of town.

"Just in case they ask anyone if they saw us," he explained. "I know a road that leads up to the mountain. It's a dirt road, but it used to be pretty well maintained."

The road was in poor condition, with deep washouts. Just after navigating around one of the worst ones, he came to an abrupt stop. In front of them was a huge fallen tree lying across the road. He got out of the truck and looked at it. There was no way around it. They had to go back.

"We've got to go back through town now. There's no other way from here."

Just as they came to the main road, the car with the two men drove past. He saw the driver look directly at them with a surprised expression on his face. Brian pulled out behind them, back toward town.

"If we're going to have a confrontation, I think it's best that we have it where there are people."

The car pulled into a parking place in front of the Feed and Seed store, where they had just been. Brian drove on past, then thought, *What the hell. I can't have them searching for us forever. Let's see what they have to say.* He pulled in and stopped, two parking spaces away from them.

"Alex, be ready to duck down, okay? Mary, cover me, but don't let them see the gun."

He got out of the truck and walked around in front of it, then headed directly toward the car, which immediately started up and backed away rapidly, heading south, back toward Hamilton. Brian ran toward the car, waving at them as if he wanted to ask them a question, but they sped away. To his horror, he had gotten close enough to see a third person in the back seat, and Brian had the distinct impression that the person he saw had been bound with a rope. It was too quick to get a good look, but it appeared to be a black man, wearing a faded denim shirt—just like the one Maurice was wearing earlier. He ran back to the truck and quickly started the ignition, backed out and followed the car as it sped away.

"I think they have Maurice tied up in the backseat," Brian explained. "This is not a good thing. We can't call for help, and there's no one to help, anyway. What should we do? We can't let Maurice get hurt because of us. Why do you suppose they took him?" he asked, mostly thinking out loud.

"They wanted to know who we were, and they saw you greet and hug Maurice. Does he know where your old home place is?" Mary asked.

"Yep. He used to come over and go hunting and fishing with me. His mother worked for us at one time, so we practically grew up together. But he doesn't know about the cave," Brian added with relief.

The car was still in front of them, but gaining distance between them quickly.

"If they release him, they give themselves away. Maurice

will know what they wanted. Maybe I was wrong. What I saw could have been—no! I know what I saw, and whoever is in that backseat, Maurice or not, is in terrible danger."

He accelerated as fast as the sharply curving road would allow. They were now heading down the mountain.

"There's only one road they could turn into between here and Hamilton. We need to see if they turn in there, or go on into town."

As he made the last downhill curve and hit the straightaway, he saw the dust rising from the side road that he remembered, and the car was not visible on the road ahead.

"This is the road to Mr. Williams' pond. It doesn't go anywhere but down to the pond and a couple of fields," Brian said as he turned into the road and stopped.

"The pond is just over that rise," he said, pointing ahead. "I can get there and see them without them seeing me, if that's where they've gone.

"Mary, turn the truck around and pull back out toward the main road. Go just a short way and park. We don't want them to see us if they come back out too soon."

He reached into the back and grabbed his crossbow and darts. Mary handed him the other Colt .380, which he slid into his back pocket. "Now hurry. Don't let them surprise us. I love y'all," he said as he quickly walked toward the overgrown field, then to the hill and the pond below.

When he neared the hill overlooking the pond, he began "Injun Walking" as Keechie had taught him. Through the brush he could see the car parked at the pond's edge. The men were not in it. Moving closer, and making sure that he was not silhouetted against the sky, he saw them. They seemed to be having an argument, waving their hands and speaking loudly, although he couldn't understand their words.

He moved in closer, now almost on his belly.

"We gotta kill him now, Jack. He knows too much. What's another one to you?"

"I never wanted to kill anyone, Preston—not unless they were trying to kill me. I told you that!"

"I'll do it myself then," Preston said with obvious anger. "Go get the guy out of the backseat, then sit in the car. You can get rid of the body. Do something right. You couldn't even follow that truck without losing it."

Brian had heard enough. Whoever they had tied up was about to die, and he thought it was because of him. He crept up a little closer while the men were arguing and prepared his crossbow.

The man called Jack opened the rear door and pulled the bound man out onto the ground, dragging him around to the front of the car. The man appeared to be unconscious, since he was not struggling against the ropes. Jack turned and got into the front passenger seat, slamming the door behind him.

Preston pulled a revolver out of his back pocket and walked over to the man. He rolled him over and leaned down, placing the revolver against the man's head.

The crossbow bolt struck him in the chest and protruded slightly from his back. He dropped the gun as he straightened up and looked down at the bolt. He dropped to his knees, and then fell across the bound man.

Brian quickly cocked the crossbow and slid another dart in place. Jack got out of the car and walked around to the front.

"What the hell you doing now? Did you chicken out, big man?"

Then he saw the dart sticking out of Preston's back. He looked around wildly as he grabbed the revolver that had fallen from his companion's hand. He kept looking for the source, and at the same time realized how vulnerable he was standing there. He crouched down, holding the gun out in front of him with both hands. That's when he saw Brian with the crossbow leveled at him. Instead of dropping the gun, he pulled the trigger in fear, firing a wild shot over Brian's head. It was the last sound he ever heard, for at that moment Brian released his dart, which struck the man in the throat. He fell across Preston and died on the spot.

Brian's heart was racing and adrenaline was surging through his body as he went quickly to the bound, unconscious man. He dragged the two men off him, and saw that it was indeed Maurice, and that he was still alive.

He didn't even try to untie the rope around his friend's arms and legs. He pulled out his knife and cut it.

Maurice, in his confusion and pain, began thrashing around wildly as he regained consciousness.

"It's okay, Maurice. It's Brian. You're okay now. Can you sit up?"

"Whar you come from, Brine? I didn't tell 'em—" he stopped when he saw the two men lying on the ground beside him. He scrambled away from them in horror.

"They're not going to hurt you again. They're dead. I killed them," Brian said with resignation. "What did they do to you?"

"Dey made me get in dey car when y'all leff de sto. Dey wanted to know who you wuz, whar you wuz stayin', an' stuff lak dat. I din' tell 'em nuthin. Ohhhh," he said, grabbing his head.

"It can wait. Let me check your head. Is that the only place they hurt you?" Brian asked as he pulled Maurice's hands away from his head.

There was a nasty gash just above his left ear, but it wasn't bleeding badly. It needed cleaning, and possibly even stitching, but as he pressed around the wound, his skull seemed to be unbroken.

As his mind became clearer, Maurice tried to stand, and with Brian's help, was able to stagger over to the car, away from the dead men. Brian opened the back door and had him lie down on the seat.

"I've got to go get my family now. Will you be okay for a few minutes?" Brian asked.

"Sho, I be all right – juss as long as dose two don' get up," Maurice said. "You be comin' back directly, right?" he asked, looking at Brian intently.

"They aren't getting up, my friend, and yes, I will be back in just a minute with the truck." Brian assured him. He didn't want to leave him, but he knew Maurice wasn't able to walk without help yet.

Brian ran back through the field to the dirt road where he had left Mary and Alex. The truck wasn't there, but as he made his way to the main road he saw it slowly driving past the access road. He waved with both arms over his head and Mary saw him. She backed up and turned in. He got behind the wheel and tried to fill them in as he drove around to the lake. He parked well behind the car so they couldn't see the two dead men.

"The two of you wait here while I get Maurice. He's hurt pretty badly, and needs someone to look after him," Brian said, hoping that would distract them enough to keep them away from the dead men.

He felt no pride in killing the men, but had done what was necessary. Now he had to decide what to do about them and their car. They were preparing to commit murder, and they had probably killed before; but in the course of one afternoon, he had gone from trying to figure out why they were following them, to what to do with their bodies. The first question hadn't even been answered yet. *So much for a nice outing for my family,* he thought sadly.

He helped Maurice over to the truck, and Mary brought out the first aid kit they had brought along with them. As she and Alex got him settled on a blanket in the bed of the truck and began cleaning the wound, Brian went over to the two men.

First, he unscrewed the razor-sharp hunting points from the shafts, and then pulled the darts from their bodies. He went through their pockets slowly and methodically, removing everything that was there, but neither of them was carrying any identification. There were no driver's licenses, no photos or letters—nothing that told who they were. Both men were wearing wallets with chains that attached to their belts.

The man called Preston was carrying a bankroll. There was probably over a thousand dollars in his wallet. The other man— Jack—was carrying less, but still there were many bills in there. There was some small change in Preston's front pockets and probably twenty rounds of hollow-point ammunition for the 38-

caliber revolver. Both men had large hunting knives in belt sheaths, which he removed.

Then he began looking around the lake. There was a small johnboat overturned and pulled halfway out of the water near him, and he went and turned it over. It appeared to be seaworthy enough for his purposes. Beneath the boat were two cement blocks, which had probably been used as anchors. Those would be useful as well.

He dragged the bodies one at a time to the boat and placed them inside. Using the same rope that they had used to bind Maurice, he tied the men together and attached the cement blocks to them. Realizing that there was no paddle, he removed his shoes, socks and shirt, and slid the boat into the water. He waded out, pushing the boat in front of him until he could no longer reach the bottom, then he swam. When he guessed that he was at the deepest point, he overturned the boat, dumping the bodies into the murky water. Then he pushed the boat back to shore and turned it over, leaving it just as he had found it.

He went over to the truck and checked on Maurice. "Are the doctors treating you well?" he asked his childhood friend.

"I thank I'se gonna live, Brine. At leas' I ain't so dizzy now," Maurice said with a forced smile. "I ken hep ya now, I believe."

"I've got everything handled so far. But we have to decide what to do with the car. We can't leave it here, because it would lead anyone who was looking for them right to the pond. Not that I think anyone's going to be looking for them."

He thought for a moment, then added, "We also need to search the car for anything that would identify them, or for that matter, anything that we can use."

The two of them went over the car thoroughly. On the floorboard there were a couple of flashlights, spare batteries, and a greasy, canvas toolkit. Beneath the seat, Brian found a sawed-off pump-action shotgun. It was loaded, so he pumped the action until it was empty. There were two boxes of 12-gauge shells in the glove compartment, along with several maps. He put the shells from the shotgun into one of the boxes and handed Mary the maps.

"See if they made any marks on these, honey. We may get an idea of what they've been up to."

Among them were maps of Georgia, Alabama, Mississippi, Louisiana and Texas. Mary unfolded the map of Alabama and studied it briefly. "Yep, there are notations all along I-20. Looks like some sort of code or something." Then in her wry sense of humor added, "Maybe it's where they buried the bodies."

"Looky hyer, Brine. Dis oughtta say sompin' 'bout whut dey up to." Maurice said. From beneath the seat, he pulled three license plates, all from different states–a good indication that the car was more than likely stolen.

"That clinches it for me, my friend. What honest person needs more than one tag for their car?"

But the one thing that Brian was the most pleased to find was the citizens' band radio that was inexpertly mounted beneath the dashboard. It had been left on, and it crackled when he turned the ignition switch. This could mean only one of two things—the men were in contact with someone, or there was radio traffic to hear. No one left one of these annoying things on unless there was a reason.

He made a mental note of the channel it was on, then removed it and stashed it in the truck. Now they could have two-way communication from the cave to the truck. Brian had one in the cave, attached to his bank of solar batteries, but there had been no radio traffic to listen to since they had moved in.

The trunk of the car was more productive. Along with the expected spare tire, jack and tool kit, was what Maurice called "trade goods." There were two cases of liquor in half-pint bottles, at least twenty pounds of vacuum-sealed Columbian coffee, and a slightly smaller amount of loose tobacco. With these three items, a person could trade for anything he wanted. They were more valuable than gold in times like these. They removed everything but the spare tire and the jack and put it all in the back of the truck, covering the lot with a tarp.

The gas gauge on the car displayed almost three-quarters of a tank. Brian asked Maurice about the old junkyard outside of Hamilton.

"Yep, hit's still dere. Ain't nobody a'runnin' it no mo' though. Ain't nothin' worth anythang leff. Evvathang's done been took dat be worth takin'," Maurice answered, then realizing what Brian was thinking, said, "We get dis car ova dere, hit ain't gonna be noticed fer a long spell. You perdy good at dis stuff, Brine."

"It's not something that I'm proud of, Maurice. But in these times, you got to do what you got to do." Brian replied, actually feeling prouder than he cared to admit.

"Now, if someone will hand me that gas can and piece of hosepipe."

They siphoned almost all of the gas from the car, leaving just enough to make the trip to the junkyard, which was only about two miles away. Brian poured nearly ten gallons into the truck tank, filling it, and still had a full five-gallon jerry can left over.

Mary followed in the truck with Maurice and Alex. Brian drove the car to the old abandoned junkyard. He pulled the car around to the back of the lot, and then rammed it into the pile of old wrecks. They smashed all the windows and lights, making it look more like it belonged there. Then they removed the battery and put it in the truck with the rest of the booty. It could be used as a spare or an addition to the bank in the back of the cave.

"Is there anyone waiting for you at home?" Brian asked his friend.

Maurice shook his head. "Nope. I stays 'lone, Brine. Evvabody's gone but me. I don' even lak t' stay at the ol' house no mo. De walls start closin' in on me. I goes dere t' sleep an' take keer o' my li'l garden I gots dere, but dat's 'bout it."

Brian looked over at Mary with a questioning look, and she nodded in agreement.

He looked at his old friend and asked, "Want to come stay with us a while? It's because of us you were hurt today, and you need help with that scalp wound."

Maurice looked at the three of them, glancing at each one by one to see their reaction.

"I ain't had no real frien' fer so long… what you all want wid an ol' black man hangin' 'roun'?" he asked with his eyes tearing up.

"Oh, are you black? I didn't notice," Brian teased. "I guess that must change everything, right? It didn't matter when we were kids, so I guess it doesn't matter now, my friend. What do you say?"

"Well, dey sho ain't nobody gone t' miss me. Dose guys at de sto saw dem men take me 'way and dey din' do nothin'."

After a long pause, he finally said, "I reckon I kin stay wit' y'all fer a spell. Least 'til my head gets well," he said, his voice breaking with emotion. "But I needs t' get m' clothes an' stuff. Mebbe pick whut's ready in da garden. Ain't much else t' worry 'bout."

It was crowded in the truck with the three adults in the front seat, and Alex sitting in the drop-down seat behind them. Brian remembered that Maurice's house was on the outskirts of Hamilton. He had been old enough to drive when Maurice's mother had worked for them, and he had driven her home many times.

Maurice went inside, got the few items he wanted, and the four of them went out back to his little garden. They picked a few tomatoes, some squash and snap beans. The corn wasn't ready yet, so they left it.

Within an hour, they were on their way back to the top of the mountain and the cave they called home.

Maurice had a huge surprise in store for him!

CHAPTER 5

As they drove past the road that went to the valley, Maurice asked, "Ain't you goin' to yo ol' house, Brine?"

"Nope, we have another place now. One I don't think you know about. Did you ever meet my friend, Keechie, back when we were in high school? She was an old Indian woman."

Brian remembered that in those days of segregation of the races, Maurice had attended a different school altogether, but he could have heard about her. As they had grown older, they hadn't spent as much time together as they had in their youth, and Maurice was a few years older than him.

"I heerd sompin' about you an' a Injun woman, but I nevva did see her, though."

"Well, my friend, when you see where we now live you will understand what she has to do with all this."

When Brian turned onto the Scenic Highway and entered Franklin D. Roosevelt State Park, Maurice said, "Dey don' be no houses up hyer. You goin' all de way t' Warm Springs?"

"Nope. We're almost there now, except for a little hike," Brian told him. "Feel up to a little bit of walking?"

The old sawmill road was so overgrown that Brian almost missed it himself. As he pulled the truck into the weed-filled road, he stopped. Mary and Alex both already knew why; it was so they could get out and brush the weeds back up where the tires had bent them over.

Maurice watched in admiration. "Guess you cain't be too keerful dese days." He got out to help them as Brian drove slowly down the trail to the Rock.

They took everything out of the truck and piled it near the Rock. Brian left the CB radio in the truck to be installed later, but removed everything else they had taken from the men's car. It was getting too late to try to get everything to the cave right away, so they moved the pile down to the base of the Rock, covering it with a tarp for retrieval the next day. The two men concealed the truck.

Brian asked Maurice with a smile, "Are you ready to see our home?"

"I cain't 'magine where you done hid a house 'roun' hyer, an' you been right 'spishus 'bout it. I thank y'all mus' live in a hole in da groun'!" Everyone but Maurice began laughing so hard that they couldn't speak. Maurice looked at them with astonishment. "Oh, no! Did I done guess yo secret? You be a'livin' in a cave?"

"You'll see, my friend. You'll see," Brian said, wiping the tears from his eyes.

The four of them made their way down the mountain with Alex showing Maurice how to avoid leaving tracks where the earth was exposed. "We call it 'Injun Walking'," she told him with an air of professionalism.

When they got to the clearing in front of the cave, they all stepped aside and looked at Maurice to see if he could find the cave.

"Well, here we are, Maurice. Welcome to our home. Go on in and make yourself comfortable!" Brian said.

Maurice looked around, and finally discovered the concealed opening. Once you knew where to look, it wasn't all that difficult to find behind the laurel bushes Brian had planted. Mary entered first and lit a lamp. Maurice followed and was immediately awestruck.

They had made it look very homey inside—not what anyone would expect a cave to look like. As Maurice walked around in open-mouthed wonder, Mary lit more lamps and added to the fire. She had left a pot of stew simmering over the coals before they left, and it would soon be their dinner. She and Alex began mixing the ingredients to make cornbread to go along with the stew while Brian began filling Maurice in on the history of the cave.

Maurice held his hand up to interrupt and with an intent stare, asked, "Befo' you gets too fer in dis story, Brine, I gots t' ask you sompin', 'cause I thank you saved my life t'day. Dose men not a'goin' t' let me go today, wuz dey?"

Only then did Brian realize that he had not told Maurice about the events that had occurred while he was unconscious. He had tried to not think about what he had done until he could be alone and think it through, but now it was time to tell.

Brian returned the stare that Maurice was giving him and said in almost one breath, "The men argued about killing you. The driver told the other guy to 'just sit in the car if he couldn't do it'. He pulled that 38—the one over there with the stuff from the car—and put it to the back of your head. Even then, I didn't shoot him until I saw the hammer going back. I shot him dead with my crossbow. Then the other man ran over from the car and picked up the gun. When he saw me, he fired at me once and missed. I had already reloaded the crossbow, so I shot him before he could take another shot. I killed him too. That one, at least, was in self-defense." Brian let out a deep breath and said, "No. I didn't save your life today. I saved mine."

"Saved dis ol' black ass fer as I concerned," Maurice said, fighting back tears.

"What if I had let him shoot you? How could I live the rest of my life with that memory? Carrying that guilt would have ruined my life. So you see? I saved my own life today," Brian repeated. Then, to lighten the moment, added, "Not to mention the fact that I didn't want those two out there somewhere, looking for my bony white ass!"

Maurice took Brian's hand between both of his. "Brine, you wuz a good friend when we wuz young'uns. You mo dan a frien' now. You fambly. I ain't had one o' dose in a long time." During their conversation they had moved outside.

Alex appeared at the opening and said, "Soup's on!" She took Maurice's hand and led him back inside. "I need to change your bandage tonight, too," she said nonchalantly, as if it was something she did every day.

They sat cross-legged on blankets in front of the fire to eat. "Do y'all mind if I say the blessing?" Alex asked.

In the past, Brian had always been the one to offer a prayer of thanks, although infrequently. He had adopted Keechie's tradition of thanking an animal for giving its life after he had killed it. Slightly surprised at Alex's request he answered, "Sure, honey, that would be nice."

Alex closed her eyes and bowed her head. "Lord, Puma Man, Great Spirit, whoever is listening, we thank you for the food that we are about to eat. We also thank you for protecting us today and we especially thank you for our new friend, Maurice. Amen."

Brian and Mary looked at each other, then at Alex, then at Maurice. The reference to Puma Man surprised them, but they understood the prayer, and agreed with it. But they wondered what Maurice was thinking.

Maurice saw the exchanged looks and asked, "Who dis Puma Man? If he hepped save my life t'day, I be a'thankin' him too!" He had just taken a big bite of the steaming cornbread but his full mouth muffled his words. "An' dis be de bes' conebread I et since my mama died."

"I've had your mama's cornbread, and you're right," Brian said. "She used to put whole kernel corn in it, and sometimes chopped-up onions. He paused a moment, then added in a soft voice, "I sure did love your mama."

"Hehe, don' I know it! You wuz the only white person come

t' her funeral. Don' thank I din' notice!" Maurice said as he cleaned his bowl.

Mary refilled Maurice's bowl and passed it back to him, then said to Brian, "Go ahead and tell him about the Puma Man. Turning to Maurice, she said, "He's still new to me too, so I wouldn't mind hearing it again myself."

"It would be better to let you read my journal about Keechie, Maurice," Brian said. "It's all in there. Besides, to tell the whole story would take the rest of the night and part of tomorrow. But for a quick answer, Puma Man is a spirit being, kinda like a guardian angel. He adopted me after I met Keechie. He was her spirit helper and her Clan's protector for many generations. For some reason, our involvement seems to have a lot to do with Alex. The Puma Man told Keechie that I would have a girl-child one day, and that she was the one who was going to make a difference in this world. Those were her exact words, and that was over thirty years before Alex was born. It seems he is still watching over this cave and us. When you read the story you'll get a better idea of him."

After dinner Alex and Mary washed all their bowls and put the stew back over the coals.

Alex added some water and replaced the lid. "Shouldn't we add a few more potatoes and carrots, Mom? They'll cook real slow and be ready by tomorrow."

"Good idea, honey. I'll help you peel and cut them up. Let's let the men talk man-stuff a while. Men like to do that, you know," Mary said with an exaggerated wink.

Maurice and Brian both thanked the cooks for the meal, and went outside into the cool night air.

"How long y'all been hyer?" Maurice asked, looking up at the night sky.

"Almost a year now," Brian admitted. "We left Atlanta right after the world went crazy. The mobs had just started making trouble. I had kept this cave a secret ever since Keechie died. I've been storing stuff here for years, just in case something like this ever happened. But you know, in my heart I never really thought that it would," he murmured, feeling a sense of relief to have another man to talk to.

"How was it down here? You know … at first … when the terrorists attacked?" He had often wondered how soon it had been after the major cities had collapsed under mob rule that the effects were felt in the rural areas.

Maurice thought for a moment. "Well, at firs', when the radios and TV's wuz still a'workin', we heerd all 'bout whut wuz a'goin' on in da big cities. People started firs' by gettin' evvathang dey could get they hands on. Stockin' up, you know? Den da sickness started. Den evvabody wuz 'fraid o' evvabody else. Den da 'lectricity quit workin'. Dat wuz when it got real bad. People wuz a'skeered. De law got as bad or wors' dan evvabody else. Dey wuz a'skeered too. Dey even kilt some folks dey caught a'stealin' food. Den dey started stealin' it deyselves. Dat's when mos' folks wid any sense kep' 'way from evvabody else. Mos' o' us black folks went back out inta da country. We din' go inta town fer nuthin'!"

"It was the same in the city," Brian confessed. "Except that there were more people living closer together. They couldn't get away from each other. The sickness spread like wildfire. We got out just in time, and we were fortunate to have this cave to come to that no one in the whole world knew about but me. Keechie saved our lives, Maurice. When you read the story you will understand better." He paused, and then said, "And you will also learn that Keechie was half black. Her Pap, as she called him, was a black man. Her mother was a full-blooded Indian. And people back then hated Indians worse than black folks, if you can believe that."

Maurice laughed, but then grew solemn. "'Member de only time I evva got mad at you, Brine? I mean really mad?"

Brian nodded, equally solemn. "I've told that story a thousand times. Yep, I sure do remember. It was right after Mr. Delton said the word "nigger" in front of you. It hurt your feelings so bad, and I felt so ashamed of my race, that I followed you into the store's warehouse and tried to make you feel better. You were crying, and I said, 'I know how you feel', and you went berserk. You told me in no uncertain terms that no, I didn't know how you felt, and I could never know unless my skin was black. Then you told me what it was like. I never forgot that. It became one of my most treasured memories."

"Mine too," Maurice said. "'Cause I knowed dat day dat you wuz differnt from mos' white folks. Yo white friends even teased you 'cause you had a black frien'. I knowed 'bout it. I got a li'l bit o' teasin' myself from my black friends. Dey called me "honky boy" an' stuff lak dat. Whut yo friends call you?" he asked with a laugh. "Don' tell me, I already know. Nigga lover, right?"

They both laughed at the ease in which they could talk about it, and even say the demeaning words.

Maurice said in a hushed voice, "Whut I 'member de mos' 'bout dat day is when I tol' you whut it wuz lak to be a li'l black boy, you cried. I nevva fergot dat, 'cause you 'uz da firs' white person I evva knowed dat liked me fer who I was, not in spite o' whut I wuz. An' let me tell you, I ain't seed many more lak dat in my whole life. I liked yo' daddy, but I knew dat he saw my black skin firs'. He din' lak it when you spent mo time wit' me dan you did wit' de white boys. But you did it anyway. I thank it 'cause o' you dat I din' grow up hatin' all white folks. I knowed dere wuz at leas' some dat din' thank I wuz 'juss a nigga'."

"That word still bothers me, Maurice," Brian said. "We taught Alex that that was the dirtiest thing you could call a person, black or white."

Maurice smiled at him, and they just sat there not saying a word, but each feeling so close, and so amazed at finding each other again after all the years, and at the circumstances that had brought them back together. They both knew that it was more than chance, and it was obvious to them that there was a higher power at work.

Brian broke the silence. "This is how the Puma Man works, if you want to call him that. It could be God, the Great Spirit, or something that we just don't understand, but it's more than just coincidence that today happened like it did."

The men walked into the cave just as Alex was coming out. She had everything prepared to clean and re-bandage Maurice's head, and had prepared a place for him near the fire. He sat down and let her begin.

She asked him to lie back and then she washed the wound clean, using small towels that were soaking in warm water, changing them frequently. "I boiled them first to sterilize them," she told him.

She used one of her dad's razors to shave the hair from around the wound, and then cleaned it again. There was a small boiler on the grill that she removed and placed on the floor beside him. She dipped one of the towels in the liquid, waited a moment for it to cool a little, then pressed it against the wound and held it there. "This has some herbs and stuff in it that will help it to heal. I'll do this twice a day until it starts to get better."

From their well-stocked medicinal supplies, Mary handed her some steri-strips that would hold the wound together almost as good as stitches.

"Thanks, Mom. I was hoping I wouldn't have to sew it up, but I was ready, just in case." She pointed to the tray on which she had placed her preparations. There was a curved suture needle lying there. "The thread is in the water. I boiled it, too."

Maurice propped himself up on his elbows. "You gots gentle hands, Alex. My mama had hands like dat. An' she knew 'bout healin' an' herbs, too. She told me 'bout some a' dem, an' I usta hep her pick 'em. Most times it wuz de only medicine we had. She say hit wuz better dan de sto-bought stuff anyhow."

Alex nodded. "Mom and I have been studying about them too. We have a book with pictures in it, and some things that Dad drew pictures of when Keechie showed them to him. I wish I had known her."

"Yo daddy done tol' me some 'bout her. I wish I had knowed her too. He's gonna let me read his story 'bout her. He say if I wants to know de whole story I needs to read it," Maurice said, turning his head toward Brian.

Brian smirked at him. "I get the hint. I'll go get the

manuscript right now. Are you sure you feel up to reading?"

"Too much done happen today fer me t' sleep. I feels right glad to be alive an' hyer wit' y'all. Hate to waste all dat good feelin' by sleepin'," Maurice grinned. "I loves t' read, an' I gots two books dat I had since I wuz a young'un, an' I done mos' read all de words off the pages. Bet yo daddy know one a' dem, afta the talk we had tonight 'bout us, when we wuz kids."

Brian heard the last part of the conversation when he returned with the manuscript in his hand. He thought about what they'd talked about outside, recalling the part about being teased because of their different races.

"Now, let's see. What book do I recall that had to do with a white kid and a black kid being friends?" He looked at Alex for the answer. "I think I know, because it's one of my favorites, too. I know you've read it, honey."

Alex shrugged. "I don't know any book like that. I can't— wait a minute—Huckleberry Finn! Is that right? Maurice, is that it?"

"Dat be da one, chile. Dat book 'minded me so much 'bout yo daddy ... I usta preten' lak it was me n' him out dere on dat raff, floatin' down de Mississippi. Ol' Nigga Jim—dat wuz me. Yo daddy wuz Huck, case you wonderin'."

Alex was shocked by his use of that "N" word, but then Maurice burst out laughing. Soon all four of them were gasping for air, trying to stop.

"I remember now!" Alex exclaimed. "Dad has told us over and over about this black friend that he had when he worked at his dad's store. You're the one that got so mad at him when he tried to cheer you up or something. Someone had just called you that word and you, it was you, wasn't it?" Not waiting for an answer, she continued, "And your mama's name was ... Jessie Mae, and your brother worked at the service station. Am I right?"

Maurice was astonished. All those years that they had been apart, and Brian had been telling that story to Alex. What really astonished him was that he too had been telling the same story to his friends since then, too. Even after all his family and friends had gone, he recalled it to himself, savoring the memory.

"Me an' yo daddy sho done shared us some times, all right. He be real special t' me, an' now you special t' me too, an' yo mama, too. Now, whut y'all thank de otha' book was? Brine, since you knowed my mama, dat oughtta give it away."

Brian didn't hesitate. "The Bible, if I know your mama. She could quote a passage and then name the chapter and verse it came from. She knew it as well as my granddaddy, and some called him a preacher."

Maurice laughed at the memory Brian had stirred.

"My mama knew just the right verse to throw at you too, fer any situation. 'An' you cain't argue wit' de Bible', she say. 'You want God to whup you, boy? God whup you an' you 'member it fer a long time!'"

He took both Mary's and Alex's hands and said, "Now I gots to read this book hyer and fine out 'bout dis Puma Man. I thank maybe you right 'bout how he got sompin' t' do wid us findin' each other again." He looked at Mary and asked, "Now, where you wants me t' sleep? I don' wanna get in de way 'roun' hyer. Sho don' wanna wear out my welcome right off de bat!"

"I've made you a place right over there," Mary said, indicating a place near the fire. "But you can sleep anywhere you can find an empty spot if you get too hot, or too cold. That's the way we do it. At night, the whole floor is the bed. Drinking water's over there in the bucket with the gourd sticking out, and the 'restroom' is out there," she said, pointing at the entrance with a smile. "Now good night, our new friend. Sleep well. Brian's got plans for us all tomorrow!"

Maurice took a lamp over to his blankets and snuggled in and began reading Brian's manuscript. Soon he was engrossed in the story of Keechie, the woman who had made all this possible for Brian and his family.

An' now me, he thought. *Thank you, Lawd, for leadin' me here, an' I promise I gonna perteck my new fambly lak day is my own blood.*

Brian got up during the night and turned Maurice's lamp off. His friend had gone to sleep reading, but he noticed that he had finished it, since it was opened to the last page. He knew that Maurice's head must hurt badly, and he had just had a really bad day, even if he had been unconscious for part of it.

He quietly stepped outside to watch the sunrise. He loved this time of day, when everything was still, and the magic feeling of the night was still hanging on. He looked up at the dark mountain where the Rock loomed, and where his old friend Keechie was buried alongside all her ancestors.

In the deepest part of his mind he again heard the drums, and recalled Keechie's words from so long ago: *Didja hyer da drums, Brine? As long as dey's someone dat kin hyer da drums, de people will never die.*

"I hear them, Keechie. I can hear the drums, my friend," he said aloud to the sky.

CHAPTER 6

Oak Mountain, straight across the valley from the cave, hid the rising sun which caused the sky to light up and change colors long before the sun itself became visible. It made dawn last much longer than it would have otherwise.

Brian heard someone moving around in the cave, so he went back inside.

Mary was stirring the coals and adding fresh wood to them. Alex was with Maurice, checking on his bandaged head.

"How's that hard head, Alex? Did your patient survive the night?" Brian's eyes displayed admiration for his daughter. *She's really getting serious about this healing stuff lately. And she seems to be good at it too. She has never done the things that she did last night with Maurice's head. Granny Boo and the Puma Man must be busy with her.*

Alex smiled. "He'll live, Dad, as long as he does what I tell him. You men think you're so tough sometimes, so somebody's got to take care of you."

Mary called for them to get ready for breakfast. "It'll be ready in a few minutes, you guys. Grits and fried venison. I tried to make it taste like ham."

In a few minutes they were eating. Mary looked sheepishly at Brian and said, "Notice anything different about the coffee?"

He took a sip and smiled at her. "You sneaked some of that coffee from the car, didn't you? This isn't that instant stuff we've been drinking."

Maurice was digging into the fried venison. "Man, dat stew las' night, and den dis hyer deer steak be da firs' meat I had in a long spell! Right afta the `lectristy went off, people had a few chickens an' pigs. Dey wuz soon either stole or et up. Den sometimes we kilt a deer or a rabbit. Den dey got hard t' fin' too. I ain't even seed a deer track in my garden since I planted it, an' de rabbits eats the stuff in da garden, an' not even look at my traps I set fer `em."

"Why didn't you shoot the rabbits?" Alex asked with a mouth full of grits.

"Daddy's ol' shotgun got stole while I wuz out a' workin'," he explained. "Din' have nuttin to shoot `em with."

"Mary has a crossbow pistol, and has already killed a rabbit with it. Too bad you didn't have one of those," Brian said.

"I probly couldn't a hit one wit' it iffen I had one. But I sho would lak t' learn," Maurice said as he pushed his empty plate away from him. "Mary, dat wuz de bes' meal I done had in `mos' two y'ars. I'se full as a tick!"

Mary thanked him for the compliment, then pointed to the rack of slowly smoking sausages hanging above the fireplace. "Just wait'll you try some of that," she said. "Alex did the spices and seasoning in the sausage. You can't even tell it's deer."

Maurice smacked his lips as if he could already taste it. "An' I bet you kin take dat flour y'all bought yesterday and make some big ol' cathead biscuits. I'se gettin' hongry `gin jus' thankin' `bout `em."

Brian had already gone outside to get things ready for the trip up the mountain to retrieve the stuff they had left there the night before. He had two poles and a couple of blankets from which to fashion a travois. He handed Maurice and Mary each a full canteen of water for their belts.

Alex was wearing a backpack and had *The Field Guide to Herbs* in her hand and Brian chuckled when he saw the sheath knife she was wearing on her hip, because it was almost bigger than she was.

"Everybody ready?" Brian asked, already starting up the nearly invisible trail.

They walked single-file up the trail, skirting the clearings and stepping on rocks when they were available. Alex continued Maurice's education on "Injun Walking," and he was getting pretty good at it, having been a country boy all his life.

Brian was hoping that they could carry everything in one trip, and when they began loading the travois, he saw that it was going to be possible. Even though they might have to hand-carry a few items, seeing it in the daylight it didn't appear to be as huge a pile as he remembered.

Just as they started the trek back to the cave, they all froze in their tracks. A car or truck was passing on the main road above them. They all let out a breath when the sound of its engine died away in the distance.

"We don't hear that many cars up here, but when we do, it's 'Full Alert', you know?" Brian said to Maurice.

"I sho do know, Brine. I got t' da point whar I din' trus' nobody but myseff, an' sometime I din' trus' me neither!" Maurice replied, and everyone laughed.

On the return trip, Brian stopped on the perimeter of a small clearing and pointed out a set of deer tracks.

"Those weren't here when we came by a while ago. I always look here, because this is one of their trails. Pretty big one, by the size of these tracks. I don't want to take any doe this time of year, because they might still have fawns with them. Besides, we're pretty well stocked up anyway."

"Ain't you worried 'bout somebody hearin' yo' gunshots?" Maurice asked.

"Nope, because I always use this," he answered, indicating the crossbow slung over his shoulder. For a moment, he just stood there, staring out into space with a sad expression. "At least I've killed more deer with it than I have men … so far."

"But I bet you ain't nevva kilt neither one 'lest you had to," Maurice told him. "I ain't 'shamed of nuttin' I evva done, my frien', but den dere's some thangs I ain't very proud of, either. Will you teach me how t' use dat thang?" he asked, pointing to the crossbow.

"I sure will. All three of us are getting pretty good with it. I've got another one back at the cave. I'd feel a lot better if you carried it anytime you go out. At thirty or forty yards, they're as accurate as a rifle. Further away gets a little trickier. And they're quiet. I've taken two deer from the same herd before, and the rest didn't even look up."

Mary noticed that Brian's dark mood seemed to leave him as quickly as it had hit him, but she knew her husband. She knew he still had nightmares about the first man he had killed here. She thought back to when the mean drunk held a knife to Alex's throat. *I was so proud of him afterwards. He never hesitated when he saw we were in danger, and then he took care of everything afterwards, despite the fact that he had just killed a man for the first time in his life—just like he took care of everything yesterday.*

They took a break after they hauled everything to the cave. Alex had found a new plant she was trying to identify, and Maurice was looking over her shoulder. They were comparing the leaves she had picked with the pictures in the book.

Mary began storing away some of the items in the storeroom, and Brian was working on a fish net he had begun a few days earlier. He was trying to make a cast net like the one that Granny Boo had described to Keechie. That reminded him about the stories he had been reading to Alex, about Granny Boo and her Clan. Keechie had told him everything that she could remember from her grandmother's stories of "the old times" here at the cave. That was when Alex had become so intensely interested in herbs and the healing arts.

"Hey, Maurice, did you finish reading about Keechie last night?" Brian asked.

"Sho did, Brine. An' I lak de way you wrote the soun' o' her voice. I kep' thankin' dat she soun' a lot lak me! Hehe!"

"Yeah, I told Dad that I wish I could hear Keechie's voice for real," Alex chimed in. "Now I know what she sounded like. This is just too cool!" She laughed at her own choice of words and added, "I guess Keechie wouldn't have said, 'too cool', would she?"

Brian chuckled. "Well, you're welcome to join us when I read these old stories about Keechie and her ancestors," he told Maurice. "You are now almost caught up with everything these two know about Keechie. These stories are about her ancestors who lived in this valley, and sometimes, right here in this very cave, almost two hundred years ago."

When they finished their evening meal, they all gathered in front of the old fireplace, ready to hear more stories. The fire was just a bed of glowing embers, and the kerosene lamp cast a yellow glow over the four of them as Brian began reading.

Sitting in the very place where the stories took place made them almost magical, and Alex said in an almost whisper, "Granny Boo may have even told Keechie these very stories in front of this fireplace."

CHAPTER 7

Pu-Can was waiting anxiously for her people to return from the river. Too many bad things had happened today. She was afraid that they had discovered more of the white people, and could be in trouble. *My uncle should have sent more warriors with them, but that would have left too few here to guard the women and children. We know too little about the ways of these white people, except that they do not want us here. What a strange god they worship!*

The older women were preparing the body of Hechee-Lana for burial. In four days, they would place her into the ground alongside Turtle and his son, Taske. Young Taske, Woodpecker, was to have become a man during the Green Corn Festival this very summer.

There were far too few people remaining for the tribe to be called a talofa, or town, and many of those living nearby were related. Nearly all of the population was going to gather with other nearby villages at the nearest italwa, which was two days' journey upriver. The largest italwa was on the Chattahoochee River, but it was too far away for Pu-Can's small clan. In the past they had made the journey to the larger italwa, Chatta-Hochee, named for the river whose name meant 'Red River'. Their river was much smaller, no more than a large creek. It ran into the Chatta-Hochee, and was a three-day walk to the south. Occasionally some of the men would follow their river downstream, then they would paddle against the current up the Chatta-Hochee, but it was not an easy journey.

Many marriages were arranged at these festivals, and it was hoped that some of the young unmarried girls would meet prospective husbands there. The men in a matriarchal society always came to live with the women's clan, which brought in new blood. This year they would be sending almost three times the number of girls than young men to the festival. The talofa would increase in number with the addition of these new husbands, and many children would follow.

Pu-Can thought of the stories she had heard of her people in the happier times, before the white men had become so numerous. Their talofa, which was then located on the river near the spot where Turtle and Woodpecker were killed, had been destroyed at the time of the Removal.

The soldiers had driven most of their people to the Oklahoma Indian Territory, but more than the white men realized had escaped capture. They had remained hidden for several years and eventually had built rectangular wooden houses, raised livestock, and tried to adopt a lifestyle more like that of the white men.

The Muskogee people had never felt prejudiced toward other races or cultures, and consequently, very few families were not of mixed blood. Freed and escaped slaves were taken in and treated as equals. They had married into the clans, raised families, adopted the traditions and religion, and learned the languages. They had adopted the Indian way of life more completely in just a few years than a century of enslavement by the white man had changed them.

From the small hill where she was standing, Pu-Can saw movement at the edge of the forest. Squinting her eyes against the glare of the setting sun, she saw that it was her people returning from the river. She breathed a prayer of gratitude to Kowakatcu the Puma Man, and rushed to meet them.

Echo-Ochee was the last to emerge from the forest and appeared to Pu-Can to have suddenly aged. He was walking bent over as if he was carrying a heavy weight on his back. His gait was unsteady, and when she spoke to him, his response came between gasps for air.

"Are you all right, Grandfather?" she asked him.

"I am just tired, Pu-Can … and my heart is heavy. Turtle was my friend … and my sister—" His voice broke with emotion. "I saw Kowakatcu today. It was after the storm … when the ice fell. He … he has eaten the souls of the white men … but I saw something else—"

"What did you see, Grandfather? Have we offended him in some way?" Pu-Can asked with dread in her heart.

"No … we have not offended him … my child. He protects us still. There were two other white men on the river today. They were searching for the ones we killed. He sent lightning down on them … during the storm. Owl was watching … as the lightning struck the boat they were in. When the thunder ended they were gone." He paused to catch his breath, then, in a low voice, said to her, "Then I saw you standing on a hill. You were alone … wearing the old leopard mask. You were both Spirit Singer … and Medicine Woman."

"Why was I alone, Grandfather? Why were you not wearing the mask of power?"

"He calls to me, Pu-Can. I will soon … be returning to my ancestors. Old Cat Eyes won't have to wait long … for her brother," he said with such finality that Pu-Can did not respond.

She took his arm and walked beside him to the clearing in front of the cave. The people were gathered around the bodies of Turtle and Woodpecker, and there was a building of tension in the atmosphere that could be felt.

Three of their people had been murdered the day before.

None of them were carrying weapons. All three were killed simply because they were Indian; their lives stamped out like vermin, as if they were no more important than the woven mats the young boys used for bow and arrow practice.

Echo-Ochee felt the tension and anger as he approached the circle of people. He raised his arms for attention and said, "The spirits of my sister, the Spirit Singer, and those of my friends … Turtle and his son … have no need to cry out for revenge this night. Kowakatcu, our protector, ate the murderers' souls. He told me this himself yesterday … as the storm passed. There were two others on the river looking for them … he destroyed them with a lightning bolt. He did this … so that we would not lose more of our people in a hopeless attempt to avenge our dead. For every one of our dead … the whites lost two of theirs. Now … let us honor our dead according to our traditions and continue to thrive … as a people. Our responsibility is to our children … who will carry on after us."

He paused, looking around the gathering at the effect his words were having. When he knew they were listening, he spoke in a loud voice, "Do we teach them the hopelessness of revenge … or do we teach them of the power of the Master of Breath … as he turns the Wheel of Life?"

At that moment, Pu-Can came out of the cave wearing the ancient leopard robe and mask of her ancestors. She was beating a small drum and singing in their ancient tongue. It was a song of *Power*; a song that told of a people who survived in the face of impossible odds. It was a song of a people who traveled across a great land with enemies on every side, yet still arrived at this place where they now stood grieving their dead. She danced slowly around the circle of people, chanting softly to each one as she passed. When she completed the circle, she raised the drum above her head and continued to beat out the slow rhythm.

"Do you hear my drum, my people?" Pu-Can asked.

"Yes!" the people shouted.

"But do you hear the spirit drums that beat with mine?"

"Yes!"

"Then the people will never die! My grandmother, Hechee-Lana," she pointed to the wrapped body beside her, "told me this many times during my training, as she tells us now. As long as there is someone who can hear the drums, the people will never die."

Maurice was thrilled by the story. "My mama say dat her grandma wuz an Injun woman. I never thought 'bout her bein' from 'round hyer though. Mebbe I'se related to Keechie. Hehe."

Brian had reached the end of the notebook and was searching through the box for the next one. "There's a good chance of that," he agreed. "Since the population was so small, they frequently had no other choice but to marry cousins. That's why they went to the festivals and tribal meetings—to arrange marriages outside their immediate area. The Green Corn Festival was one of their biggest gatherings, and the people would travel great distances to get there. It was a time of thanksgiving, trading, catching up on the events of the past year of the other clans, and it marked the beginning of their new year. It was usually in July, and celebrated the corn harvest."

He realized that he sounded like he was lecturing in a classroom and handed the notebook to Maurice. "Here's the first of the Granny Boo notebooks. I already read it to Alex and Mary just the other night. It ought to catch you up with them. Now where is the next one?" He continued to shuffle through the stack of journals. "Ah, here it is," he said, holding up a spiral-bound journal. "I labeled it *'Granny Boo's First Green Corn Festival'*. Are you all ready for another piece of the story?"

"I am," Alex answered gleefully.

Maurice and Mary both agreed, so Brian opened the journal and began reading.

Old Echo-Ochee was able to conduct all three burial ceremonies with Pu-Can's help. It seemed as if his spirit had left his body. He was having difficulty remembering even routine things, and he kept talking to the Puma Man as if he was right there in the physical world beside him. Only he could see the entity hovering above them as he looked out over the peoples' heads. "Not yet, Kowakatcu, I have unfinished business here," he said at one point.

The people turned and looked in the direction in which he was speaking, but there was no one there. They looked at each other knowingly. Their Keeper would soon be joining his sister, Hechee-Lana, and he had no male apprentice to take his place. They all knew that Pu-Can was not only a gifted Spirit Singer like her grandmother, but she also had the skills of a Medicine Woman. Everyone had assumed that she would one day take the roles of both Hechee-Lana and her great uncle, Echo-Ochee—but now? She was only twenty summers old, but there was no one else to consider; and after all, she was directly descended from the Wild Dancer, the most powerful Spirit Singer in her Clan's memory.

With the burials complete, Pu-Can accompanied her uncle to his dwelling. He lived alone and she was concerned about him. "Let me prepare you a meal, Grandfather. I will make some special tea as well. It will help you rest and regain your strength."

"I am not hungry, Pu-Can, but I would appreciate the tea. My souls are restless, and I mostly appreciate the company. There are things that I must tell you," he said, accepting the offer of her arm as he half-stumbled up to his cabin. The interior was a mess. He had never taken a wife, insisting that the life of a shaman was too difficult for the spouse. "A wife would eventually grow tired of me, and would probably kill me in my sleep," he had said many times.

Pu-Can finally located the herbs that she needed for his tea, and put them in a pot of water to simmer over the coals of his fire. Then she began cleaning up the clutter.

Echo-Ochee settled himself onto his sleeping furs, watching as she moved about the small room. "Granddaughter, you know that I must soon join my ancestors, do you not?"

"We all will join our ancestors soon enough, Grandfather. Do not speak of such things. You are just tired and grieving for your sister and the others," she replied as she checked on the tea.

"No, I know the time is drawing near. The Puma Man has told me this himself, and I am ready, except for the burden it places on you. Only once before has a woman had such a burden, and that was your grandmother's grandmother, Paneta-Semoli—the Wild Dancer. I knew her when I was a child, and the stories I heard—," he looked at the ceiling as he reminisced, temporarily forgetting that he had a point to make. "And so," he said as he came back to the present, "it is up to you to carry on the Gift. You are so young, my child, but you carry the power of Kowakatcu. Even from the time of your childhood, you have been seeing and talking to him." He drifted off again with his memories as Pu-Can poured him a bowl of the steaming tea.

"Here, Grandfather. Take your tea. It's hot, so do not burn yourself," she said as she handed him the bowl, and then took one for herself. She sat down across the coals from him.

"You are going to the Green Corn Festival, are you not?" he asked.

"Yes, I was planning on attending this year, but now that Grandmother is gone, I wonder if I should. I do not want to leave you alone with all the duties."

"I think it is important for our people that you attend, Pu-Can. We are too few, and the alliances made during these festivals could help us to grow strong again. It is not only the people here that need a powerful Spirit Singer, the whole Muskogee nation needs you. With most of our nation either living on a reservation or dead, the few remaining need someone who can keep them connected to the spirit world of our ancestors." The old man hardly paused for a breath.

"But I fear that the old ways have already gone, Grandfather. The italwas have all been burned, and the white man now grows crops where they once stood. There are only remnants of the people left, just like us, here. More and more, we are taking on the ways of the whites to survive. Some are even accepting their religion, thinking that their god must be more powerful." Pu-Can looked into her grandfather's eyes and realized that she had only saddened him further. "Yes, Grandfather, I will attend the Green Corn Festival. Perhaps it is not too late for the people. The drums will play loud, and the people will hear."

They sat silently for a while, lost in their own thoughts. Echo-Ochee was nodding off to sleep as he sat cross-legged on his furs. Pu-Can helped him lie down and banked his fire. She covered him with his blanket, and then left quietly, heading for the cave and her own blankets. Her mother was still awake as she entered the cave.

Achena-Nakla was living up to her name, Burning Cedar, by waving a smoking cedar branch around the room. It was said to purify the air and drive away unfriendly spirits. "The ghosts are busy tonight," Pu-Can's mother said. Achena-Nakla had never experienced the Gift directly as her mother and daughter had, but she had learned the herbs and their uses. Being the daughter of the powerful Medicine Woman and Spirit Singer, she knew and believed in the spirit world.

Pu-Can told her about Echo-Ochee's condition. "He says that he will soon join his ancestors, Mother. Puma Man told him so. I don't think there is anything we can do for him."

"My uncle is old, Pu-Can. My mother's death took the last of his spirit away. She was his only sister, and they shared the Gift. It is unusual for a man to have as much power as he does." She threw the smoking cedar into the fire, and turned to face Pu-Can. "Did he not call down the Puma Man to destroy our enemies?"

"He wants me to go to the Green Corn Festival, Mother. I told him I would go."

"Yes, you must go. You have a duty to the people to go, even if you don't want to. You will soon take over the roles of both your grandmother as Spirit Singer, and his of Hilis Haya, the Medicine Maker." She placed her hands on Pu-Can's shoulders. "You are young, my daughter, but I see in you the strength of our people."

Pu-Can looked around the cave and thought of all her family who had lived in it, in this hole in the mountain. She remembered her grandmother's stories of the first of their ancestors who had come there. They had all been of the Kowakatcu Clan—the Osochi

Creeks. They had come from the west, seeking 'the land where the sun was born each day'. Some of the other clans had continued on to the eastern ocean the white people called the Atlantic, but her people stayed on or near the Chatta-Hochee and Flint Rivers.

"Tell me again the story of the Removal, Mother, and I will prepare us some tea. The ghosts that you feel also like the stories and they will be appeased," Pu-Can said as she put a pot of fresh water over the coals.

Achena-Nakla smiled at her daughter and spread blankets in front of the fireplace for them to sit upon as she began. "I was born the year that the soldiers came to take us away. My grandmother was the wife of Bull Killer, whose spear you so recently held. She brought all her family to this cave when the soldiers came. Grandfather Bull Killer went to the top of the great rock where our people are buried, refusing to leave the bones of his people. He fell dead right there on the rock, dressed in all his ceremonial robes. My mother's sister, Corn Silk, was at the spring when they came, and did not get here in time. They took her away even though she was pregnant. She was older than your grandmother by seven summers. She was a very powerful Spirit Singer, even more so than Hechee-Lana. Your grandmother never completely got over losing her."

Pu-Can checked the pot of tea, and poured them both a bowl. She handed one to her mother, and sat down beside her again. "The others, the ones who did not get to this cave in time, were they all taken away?"

"Most of them were taken, yes, and some were killed as they tried to escape, but the soldiers were not very thorough. Some were able to hide in the forest, watching as their houses were burned to the ground. We later heard from others up and down the river that the same had happened to them. The soldiers gathered up all they could readily find, then burned the italwas and the homes. We heard from some that escaped that many died along the way. They had been driven like cattle, without enough food or water. The children and the old ones suffered the most."

Achena-Nakla sipped her tea and stared into the coals of the fire. "Then there were some who could have come to this cave, but refused. They believed that nothing except animals and witches lived in the ground. They were afraid, and because our clan, the Kowakatcu, had the power of Puma Man and were already using the cave, only confirmed their fear. To them, a Medicine Woman is just a step away from a witch, anyway."

She looked at her daughter and laughed. "My little witch, Pu-Can, of the Kowakatcu, you will be feared only by the man who chooses you for his wife. He will not stand a chance. Now let us sleep and dream of better times. You were right about the ghosts. They are silent now. The Puma Man watches over us still."

CHAPTER 8

"And that is a good place to stop for the night," Brian said with a yawn. "You all look like you're about to fall asleep, and I can barely hold my eyes open to read."

Alex, with a tone of reverence in her voice said, "Can you imagine? Granny Boo's mother sat right here in front of this very fireplace and told her those stories—the same stories that she told Keechie, probably right here, too. Now Dad is telling us the same stories in front of the same fireplace. There is something magic about this place. Can't you just feel it?"

Maurice was the first to answer. "I knows I feels it, Alex. Dis be a spechul place, fer sho. Hit makes me feel safer dan I felt in a long time."

"Not only did Granny Boo and Keechie hear these stories right here in front of this fireplace, but both of them were born right here, too," Brian said as he put away the journal. "This cave has protected many people over the years—including us."

Brian went out at dawn to check on his rabbit traps. When he returned, Mary was preparing breakfast and Alex was cleaning Maurice's head wound.

"We have dinner," he announced. "Rabbit and dumplings sounds pretty good to me. How about you, Maurice? I got two this time. A `coon tore up one of the box traps. It'll need replacing."

"Ohhh, I ain't had no rabbit and dumplings since Mama died. Dat soun' real good t'me!" Maurice exclaimed. "An' Alex say my head healin' up real good. She sho be a good docta. I coulda died widout her hep."

Alex beamed at him. "Just try to keep it clean. I want to leave the bandage off for a while."

"You be de docta, Alex. I do whut you say," Maurice said.

"You two have time to clean those rabbits before breakfast," Mary said to Brian. "I'll have to start cooking them as soon as they're dressed. Otherwise they'll spoil. What are the plans for the day?"

"I thought I would show Maurice the corn, and begin his crossbow lessons. Anyone else want to go?" Brian answered. "We can begin hunting deer in a couple of months."

"If you'll wait until I get the rabbits simmering, we'll all go," Mary replied. "Alex and I want to gather some fresh herbs, and see how many plants we can identify." Mary had always possessed a special knack for herbs. Her grandmother, a Cherokee Indian woman, had come from the Appalachian Mountains of North Georgia, and had passed on her knowledge of plants to her.

Mary had learned a great deal from her, but the rest just seemed to be a natural gift of "knowing." She could taste a new food and know what herbs and spices were in it, even in minute quantities. Often she would not know its name, but when she found it in the wild, would recognize it at once. Now she and Alex could put a name to it with the help of *The Field Guide to Herbs,* along with Brian's notebook of Keechie's teachings.

Maurice already knew how to dress a rabbit. "We larned t'

skin rabbits an' squirrels `fo we could talk, I thank. Sometime dat be all we ate fer a spell. Dat an' poke sallat," he said with a smile. "Mama say de Lawd put evvathang we need on dis earth. Hit juss be up t' us to find it."

"And that kind of knowledge is priceless in times like these, my friend. There are many who would starve if left on their own, without a store to run to," Brian said, just as Mary called them in to breakfast.

"Venison bacon again and powdered eggs. I mixed them in with the grits," Mary said. "But the coffee is the real thing."

By mid-morning they were on the way to the cornfield. Brian took them first to the spring where he had found Keechie so long ago—mainly to show Maurice, but also felt it would be a good place for Mary and Alex to find herbs. The corn was still not quite ready, but there were many more sweet peas to be picked. Mary and Alex began picking them while Brian and Maurice went to the edge of the field for crossbow practice. On their way across the field, Brian stopped to examine some fresh tracks beside some broken-over cornstalks.

"Something likes corn as much as we do, it appears," he said. "I hope whatever it is leaves some for us when it's ready. It isn't deer. Whatever it is I can't tell from these tracks. They're not clear enough—"

Screams from Mary and Alex stopped him dead in his tracks.

Brian had his crossbow off his shoulder and readied by the time he saw them running toward him. He motioned at them to turn aside, hoping they would go opposite directions until he could see what or who they were running from.

Mary darted to his left, Alex veered to his right; and charging right behind them was a huge, feral boar. It paused in confusion, and then it followed on Alex's heels. The corn hid them, but Brian knew the hog was much too close to her, and would overtake her quickly.

Without a moment's hesitation, Maurice ran diagonally across the field to intercept them. "Brine! Stay dere!" he hollered.

Brian could just see the top of Maurice's head as his friend gave a loud yell directed at the boar, then turned back toward Brian.

"He right behind me!" Maurice said as he emerged from the corn. He motioned to his right, indicating that was the way he was going to turn.

Brian raised the crossbow and prepared himself, just in time for Maurice to make a quick, diving turn to his right, allowing Brian to get off one quick shot. The bolt struck it high in the shoulder, but it only seemed to infuriate the beast as it continued straight ahead, directly toward him. It was nearly upon him and there was no time to reload his crossbow. As a last resort he reached for his sheath knife and braced himself.

A shot rang out and the boar staggered, then tumbled into Brian, knocking him over. He scrambled away from the beast and looked in the direction from where the shot had come.

There stood Mary, still in firing position with a smoking Colt, ready to fire again. She slowly lowered the weapon and let the hammer down.

All Brian could manage was, "Thanks, baby," as he got to his feet.

"Is it dead?" Mary asked, eyeing it warily.

Maurice kicked the boar from the side, checking for signs of life, and then slit its throat. "Needs t' bleed it good," he said. "Look at dese tusks. Dey must be four or five inches long. I ain't never seen one o' dese, but my daddy tol' me 'bout'em. He say dey be de mos' dangerous animals in dese woods!"

Alex ran to Maurice and gave him a huge hug. "You saved my life, Maurice! When you came out of that corn screaming, it scared me almost as much as it did that pig! Then I fell and it took off after you."

"Now he's thinking more about how to best butcher a hog than he is about how close it came to running him down," Brian grinned. But he was still shaking, thinking about how close they had all come to disaster.

Mary looked at the three of them and held her arms out for a group hug. "That's the first moving target I ever tried to hit, you know, and I couldn't have fired again, it was on you. I was hoping it would follow me instead of Alex. Well, at least we have real pork for a change," she said with obviously false bravado.

"We'll call you 'One-Shot Mary' from now on," Brian said. "You hit it right in the head. A knife is no match for an animal like that and that was all I had."

"Then I probably shouldn't tell you that I was aiming for its heart," Mary said sheepishly.

"Let's get this big ol' pig to a tree so we can do dis thang right," Maurice said, trying to hide his shaking hands. "We sho had us a close call dere, but now we got us some real poke. Be a shame to let it go to waste."

They dragged the huge boar to a tree near the edge of the field, and with a large vine taking the place of a rope, hoisted it up, head down. Brian and Maurice quickly field-dressed it.

"Back home, we would have a big ol' drum o' boilin' water. Den we dip it in, den scrape de hair offen it. How us gonna do dat out hyer?"

"No choice but to quarter it here and take it back to the cave," Brian said. "This thing must weigh over two hundred pounds."

Brian and Maurice each took one of the heavier hindquarters and Mary and Alex took the front quarters and they all headed for the cave. Once there, they built a hot fire outside and put on a large pot of water to boil. Since it was summer, there was no choice of preservation, except to use the curing salt Brian had stashed away. Once the water was boiling, they poured it slowly over the hide and scraped away the bristly hair.

It took the remainder of the day to prepare the meat for storage. Most of the fat was rendered and canned for lard. Brian cleaned the small intestines for use as sausage casing; and everything—except for the hams, shoulder roasts, and pork chops—was cut into small pieces and ran once through the old food grinder.

Then Alex and Mary added their special seasoning. For the

second grinding, they placed the special stuffing attachment on the grinder. That finished, they hung the long links of sausage on a rack over the fireplace for smoking.

Dinner that night, instead of the rabbit and dumplings, would be fresh pork liver with white gravy, biscuits, and freshly picked sweet peas from the cornfield.

"The rabbit stew will be even better tomorrow because this liver needs eating right away," Mary said.

"Lordy, I juss cain't believe dat hyer I is, living in a cave, an' eatin' better'n I ate in mo years dan I care t' `member!" Maurice said. "Y'all sho knows how t' git by."

"You're now a part of us, my friend," Brian said. "You brought some pretty impressive talents of your own, not to mention saving Alex's life today. I think Keechie would be very proud of us if she were here tonight. Actually, it feels like she never left." He smiled at Alex and added, "But she would have fought you over who was going to turn the handle of the grinder, baby. She loved to do that part."

The fire repeatedly flared up, lighting the cave brightly before dying back down as the sausage links dripped fat into it. Every drip flamed and sizzled, filling the cave with a wonderful aroma.

After dinner, the four of them sat quietly around the fireplace, each lost in their own thoughts of the day's events.

Mary broke the long silence. "I think we should go back tomorrow and finish what we started today. Alex and I still need to collect herbs and learn what's available. I'm not going to allow a pig to scare me into hiding out here, afraid to go outside. How about y'all?"

"Well, we be eatin' de pig, ain't we?" Maurice said with a grin. "Besides, I still gots t' larn how t' shoot dat crossbow. Dat be my vote."

Alex nodded. "Fine with me, Mom, but tonight I want to hear some more of Granny Boo's story. How about it, Dad?"

Brian was sitting, watching the flames and feeling very

proud of his family.

"Sure, honey. I'll get the notebook. I think that's a great idea."

CHAPTER 9

The Green Corn Festival was less than a week away, and everyone going was making final preparations. From the entire valley region the tribe was only sending twelve girls of marriageable age, four unmarried young men, and twenty adults.

Most of the party planned to make the two-day journey upriver on foot, since there were not enough canoes to carry them and their supplies. Four of the elders would be carried in two canoes, each paddled by two of the stronger warriors. There were wagers placed on which would arrive first, the canoes or the walkers.

On the day of departure, Pu-Can visited Echo-Ochee, hoping that he would decide to go after all. He had not missed a Green Corn Festival since she could remember. "Grandfather," she called at his doorway. "It is Pu-Can. May I enter?"

The old man opened the door and let her inside. He was dressed in his ceremonial robes and seemed to have been expecting her. "I wish I was going with you today, Granddaughter, but I will remain here. The ones left behind may need me, and I have to conduct special ceremonies to protect those of you who are going."

Pu-Can knew that he was simply physically unable to make the journey, and was just making excuses, but she respected him for trying to make her feel at ease for leaving him. "I will carry your greetings to all of your old friends, Grandfather. They will hear the stories of the great Echo-Ochee, Keeper of the Osochi People and the Kowakatcu Clan. They will hear of his visions of the Puma Man on the day the white men's souls were eaten, and how he called down the lightning and the ice-rocks from the sky."

Echo-Ochee stood a bit taller with pride and smiled at her. "Do not tell them how afraid I was that day, Pu-Can. I nearly died of fright when that terrible storm came upon us."

"I will not tell, Grandfather. Your secret is safe with me." Pu-Can returned the smile. "They will know only that the Puma Man, your totem and your friend, heeds your call."

"I will walk with you to the river and make prayers for a safe journey. I will watch the people as they leave, and I have a special request to ask of you." He opened the chest that was sitting beside his sleeping furs and took out an old leather pouch. "This contains a portion of the oldest Power Bundle in our tribe, from the days of our first ancestors who came to this place. It has great power. I want you to give it to the old Hilis Haya, Locha-Luste. He is of the Wind Clan, but he is also of the bloodline of our Wild Dancer. If he is no longer there, give it to the one who holds the Medicine Bundle of the Kowakatcu Clan. It is to be added to it. When all the portions are together again, our people will be united and prosper once again."

"I will do as you say, Grandfather." Pu-Can placed the pouch strap around her neck. She felt its power surge through her as it touched her skin next to her own pouch that her grandmother had given her the day she became a woman.

The two of them went first to the cave to fetch Pu-Can's personal supplies for the journey, and then walked with several others to the river. They had quite a load of supplies to carry; there were trading goods, changes of clothing, and one travois containing nothing but the very best of this year's corn crop, vital to the success of a Green Corn Festival. They would taste none of the new corn until the final ceremony in which the corn was blessed. Then everyone would share it, ending the two-day fast.

In a special bag was a large quantity of the pollen from the new corn. It was the corn of the Osochi people—the original strain that was brought to this land by Pu-Can's great-great grandmother, Paneta-Semoli, the Wild Dancer, and the most powerful Spirit Singer of the Kowakatcu Clan.

The canoes were ready and waiting at the river when the departing villagers arrived. The corn and the supplies were loaded into the canoes first, then the four elders climbed in.

Echo-Ochee, in all his finest robes, chanted a special blessing for the travelers' safety, and the journey began. There were only a few open trails that the ones who were walking could follow, but the young warriors knew the best route to follow. Two of the fastest runners went ahead, checking for danger. They would also prepare a camp for the entourage to spend the night.

At sunset, they arrived at the halfway point. They were tired but excited, for tomorrow evening they would again gather with many others of their nation. There would be old friends, as well as relatives, among them.

The camp was alive with the telling of stories from previous Festivals for the benefit of the young ones who had never attended one. The ones who were hoping to find husbands and wives were teased relentlessly, but all in good-natured fun.

Pu-Can sat at her fire with her brother, Apelka-Haya, who had spent the day paddling one of the canoes. "How was the journey upriver, Brother?"

"We had little difficulty. Windmaker put his breath to our backs all day and the current was slow. We were here two hands of time before you," he teased.

"Yes, but you did not have the bramble-vines and fallen trees to slow you down as we did," Pu-Can said, showing him her scratched legs and arms. "And we had many more people to keep together." She poured him a bowl of tea from her fire and passed it to him, then leaned back against her large backpack, stretching her feet out toward the fire. "Will we make the Stomp Dance Grounds before sundown tomorrow, Apelka?"

"If we make as good time as we did today, we will be there well before the sun has gone, Sister. That is, we in the canoes will. We have shoals that we must carry the canoes around, but the rest will be easy," he said, looking past her to the large pack she was leaning against. "Did you bring all your possessions, Pu-Can? Are you planning on staying with the Hitchiti?"

Pu-Can smiled at his joke. The Hitchiti were the most numerous of the Creeks who remained in the area after the Removal. They adopted many of the white man's ways very early, including their religion. They were not driven west as many of the tribes had been. They did not live collectively in italwas, and so the white men did not consider them as great a threat as the others. "The Hitchitis have no need of a Spirit Singer, Laugh-Maker," she teased back. "And this is not all that I bring. There is another pack that contains the ceremonial relics of our ancestors. I have Grandmother Wild Dancer's mask and drum, along with her leopard robe and, most important of all, I have brought her fire-starter. Hechee-Lana told me that it was used to start our very first fire in this land. I guard it with my life."

"Then I will guard it with mine also, my Spirit Singing sister." Apelka-Haya looked at her with admiration. "The runners from other tribes that I have spoken to said that your fame has spread throughout the Nation. When our grandmother was killed by the white man, you became the youngest Spirit Singer since Wild Dancer," he said with pride. "I furthered your legend by telling them how you killed her murderer with Bull Killer's spear, and saved my life, all within a few heartbeats after she had fallen."

He stared into the fire for a long moment. "You know Echo-Ochee has not long to live. He told me that I would become Mikko when he dies, but I am tastanagi—a warrior. I know nothing of being a chief."

"He told me the same just before we left, my brother. He says the Puma Man calls him."

"Kowakatcu has placed us both in positions usually held by those who have had many more years to gain the wisdom required. Are we prepared for this?"

Pu-Can started to tease him, but saw the seriousness in his eyes. Her brother was not one to say that much at once, and he was usually trying to make people laugh, as his name, Laugh-Maker, indicated. "Just think about the ones who taught us, Apelka. Our grandparents were the most powerful of the Spirit Singers and Medicine Makers, all the way back to the beginning of time. Kowakatcu himself is our Spirit Guide. The Puma Man placed us in this time and this place. Look to him for guidance. You are a good man, my brother. You will do well."

"Thank you, Pu-Can. Now I must go relieve one of the sentries." He finished the tea in his bowl and handed it back to her. "And that tea was as good as Hechee-Lana made. You did learn something from her after all." He rose from her fire and took one of her hands in both of his. "Sleep well, Sister, for we travel early tomorrow." Then he disappeared into the forest toward the river.

Pu-Can sat there a while, just gazing at the stars and listening to the night sounds. Looking around their small camp, she saw that everyone else had settled down to sleep and their fires were now beds of glowing coals. She added a few small sticks to her fire, covered herself with her blanket, and was soon asleep.

Just before sunrise, with barely enough light to see, the camp was already a bustle of activity. The smell of sofkee awakened Pu-Can. She stretched her body, then walked to the edge of the forest to relieve her bladder.

She was about to build up her fire when one of the other women came to her and said, "We have enough sofkee for everyone at our fire, Pu-Can. Bring your bowl. It will save time and trouble, and will allow us to get started earlier."

Pu-Can thanked her and covered the coals with sand. She

picked up her bowls and went to the central fire where the others had gathered. The older woman took her bowl and filled it with sofkee, then filled the other bowl with water. She sat on her blanket to eat. The spoon she was using had been carved for her by Echo-Ochee, which made her think of him. *He would have loved to come with us on this trip. He hasn't missed a Green Corn Festival since he became the Keeper of the People.*

Apelka-Haya and another of the sentries appeared from the forest and joined Pu-Can. "Do you have bowls for us, Sister? We could smell the sofkee all the way to our outpost."

"I am finished with mine, Brother. You can use them." She used the water from one to rinse the other and handed them to him. "Are the canoes ready? We will be traveling soon, I hope."

"They are ready. I just need to get the elders into them and we will be off," Apelka said. "And thank you for the bowls. I will return them before I leave."

When everyone had eaten and gathered their belongings for the journey, Pu-Can looked carefully over the campsite. There was no evidence of anyone ever having been there. It was the way of her people, and it had served them well for many generations.

By the time the sun had risen completely, they were on their way again. A light rain fell on them at midday, but it was a welcome relief from the heat. Even the mosquitoes and biting flies left them alone for a while.

By mid-afternoon, they encountered a sentry from the big encampment who told them they were within two hands of time from their destination. There was much excitement as they realized they were almost there.

Earlier in the day, they had begun moving steadily away from the river. Pu-Can asked the man, "How close is the river from the main camp?"

"It is on a hill overlooking the river, Sister. Many are coming by canoe, and many are already there," the man told her as he looked at her appreciatively.

"My name is Tysoyaha, of the Wind Clan. May I ask yours?"

"I am Pu-Can, of the Osochi tribe. My Clan is Kowakatcu. Your name is strange to me. What language is it?" she asked, realizing how beautiful he was.

He laughed easily. "I am sorry. It means 'Child of the Sun' in my mother's tongue. She was of the Yuchi tribe. She and a few of her people did not go west with the others and remained here with my father's people, the Hota, or Wind Clan. He is Mikko Hese' – the Great Sun. I have heard many stories about you, Spirit Singer of the Puma Clan. It is said that you killed a white man with a spear."

"I would rather not be remembered by that reputation, Child of the Sun. I am not proud of killing," she said, secretly pleased that he had heard of her.

Tysoyaha accompanied them the rest of the way to the Stomp Ground, staying beside Pu-Can the whole way. The women were already giggling behind her back at her good fortune in finding such a prize before they even arrived at the Festival.

As soon as they reached the Stomp Ground, Pu-Can went immediately down to the river. There were many canoes at the landing, but no sign of her brother. Making her way to a group of young men standing there, she asked, "Has anyone seen Apelka-Haya of the Kowakatcu Clan? There were two canoes—"

"No, we have not seen him, Sister, but I will gladly take his place," one of the men said, elbowing one of his companions. They all laughed, but stopped as soon as they saw who was standing behind her.

Tysoyaha waved them away and gave them a stern look. "I will find him, Pu-Can. I apologize for those rude ones. It will not happen again."

"Apelka-Haya is my brother," Pu-Can explained. "He has four of our elders in the canoes. He said there were shoals that they would have to go around. I will wait here for him. It shouldn't be very long."

"The shoals are not far downstream, Pu-Can. I will go. They may need help, and I have a canoe here."

"Thank you, Tysoyaha. I will go with you. I can paddle a

canoe, and two paddles make it easier than one."

Tysoyaha slid one of the canoes into the water and held it while Pu-Can stepped in. She sat in the bow as he jumped into the stern, giving the craft a push as he did. They quickly entered the current and headed downstream. Tysoyaha guided the canoe expertly into the center of the river, but there was little paddling necessary as the current swept them away.

Around the second bend in the river were the shoals. Tysoyaha steered the canoe over to the western side and pulled it up onto a sandbank.

"If he knows the river, this will be the side he would choose. Over there," he said, pointing to the opposite bank "is almost impassable on foot. The rocks go all the way to the river's edge, and the cliff is too steep to climb."

"He knows the river," Pu-Can said. "Should we wait for them here, or should we try to find him?"

"There is a good trail around the shoals. Let us walk a little ways downstream and see if we see them."

The noise of the water gushing over the rocks drowned all other sounds. Calling out to her brother was useless. As they reached the bottom of the shoals, they smelled smoke.

Tysoyaha went to the bank of the river, and then called to her. He pointed out into midstream, where a single canoe lay capsized and pinned between two rocks. On the opposite shore was the other canoe, safely pulled up onto a sandbank. There was no one around that they could see.

Pu-Can was in the water immediately, already up to her waist and fighting the current before he could stop her. Tysoyaha quickly followed her. Together, slipping and sliding over the rocks, then wading through the shallower water, they made it to the beached canoe.

"Fortunately, this was the one that held the corn. I was afraid they had lost it. But where are they?" Pu-Can looked around. Tysoyaha looked at the sand closely. "Several people walked here, and they went that way," he said, pointing upriver. "They made several trips in both directions."

Then they smelled the smoke again. As they began following the tracks, Apelka appeared from the heavy brush in front of them, as startled to see them as they were to see him.

"Apelka!" Pu-Can cried, running to embrace him. "Are the others safe?"

"They are safe, Sister. Wet and bruised, but they are all right. We salvaged everything but the canoe so far. We built a fire for the two elders who got dumped into the river. I was coming back to see if I could get the canoe."

"I will help you, brother of Pu-Can," Tysoyaha said, extending his hand. "I am Tysoyaha, of the Wind Clan."

Apelka took the offered hand and replied, "I am Apelka-Haya of the Kowakatcu, and I accept your generous offer. I hope that the canoe is undamaged. We have four elders with us."

The two men waded out to the capsized canoe and began righting it, fighting the current that kept it pinned between the boulders. When they had it freed and afloat, they realized they had no paddles for it, so they pulled it to the shore, wading through the swift water. Once on shore, they examined the canoe, and found it was undamaged.

While waiting for them, Pu-Can saw one of the paddles caught in an eddy a little further downstream and went to get it. When the two men pulled the canoe onto the sand, she placed the paddle inside.

"One paddle is better than none," she said.

While the men were turning the canoe back over to empty the remaining water, Pu-Can went on ahead to the makeshift camp where the elders were drying themselves and their clothing.

Everyone was in good spirits in spite of their mishap. The two men and two women were laughing, each blaming the other for capsizing the canoe. Apelka and the other men had retrieved all the supplies that were in the canoe, but everything was wet. The elders decided that they would rather proceed now than wait for their clothes to dry.

Pu-Can checked their various scrapes and bruises, and agreed that they were not serious. They transported everyone, including the supplies, to the opposite shore. Dividing as much as they could carry among them, they took everything but the canoes to the top of the shoals, where Tysoyaha's canoe was waiting. Four of the young men went back for the canoes. Once they had them in the water, they reloaded everything. It would be easier now since Tysoyaha and Pu-Can put the corn into their canoe. Now that they were going against the current, Pu-Can was able to show off her paddling skills. It was a much slower trip going upriver, but they were back at the Stomp Dance Grounds just before sundown, as Apelka had predicted.

The same man who had been rude to Pu-Can was waiting at the landing when she and Tysoyaha beached their canoe. He came up to her, and looking at the ground, said, "Forgive me for my behavior today, Spirit Singer. I acted like a child. May I help you in some way?"

"It is already forgotten; but you may help us get these bags of corn up the hill and taken to where it is being stored. I thank you." Pu-Can smiled.

He glanced shamefaced at Tysoyaha, who smiled at him as well and passed him one of the large bags of corn. Apelka and the other men helped the elders from the canoes, and then began unloading the supplies.

From above, they could hear the drums and rattles of a beginning dance. The main ceremony of the Green Corn Festival was still two days away, but there would be many dances, games and special events for four days.

As the party of Osochi Creeks approached the main courtyard, with Pu-Can and Tysoyaha in the lead, a very tall, dignified man came toward them. He was dressed in fine cloth robes, and wore a red turban on his head.

Tysoyaha went up to him and took his hand, leading him back to Pu-Can. "This is my father, Chatto-Nokose, of the Wind Clan. Father, this is Pu-Can, Spirit Singer of the Kowakatcu."

Pu-Can smiled. "Greetings, Mikko Hese'. I am honored to be here."

"Welcome, young Spirit Singer. I knew your grandmother, Hechee-Lana. I was saddened to hear of her death, and we will miss seeing her brother, Echo-Ochee, this year. Was he well when you left him?"

"Yes, my uncle is doing quite well, but he could not make the trip this year. He is feeling his years."

"Ah, as do we all, daughter. They said your group had some trouble on the way. Is there anything we can do to help? Is everyone safe?"

"Yes, they are safe, Mikko. Your son has helped us already. Some of our elders got wet and bruised at the shoals, but they are all right, in spite of the bruises."

"When you are settled in and rested, Pu-Can, I would like for you to join me at my tent for the evening fire. We have plans to make for the Festival that involve you."

CHAPTER 10

At the eastern edge of the paskova, the large circular clearing where the dances and games would be held, towered a large earthen mound. Sitting atop the mound was the temple of the Great Sun, constructed of poles and covered by a thatched roof. It was rebuilt each year, since on the final night of the Festival it would be burned, and then covered over with earth. Because of this, the mound grew a bit larger every year.

Pu-Can and her group had settled in and changed into better clothing when a messenger appeared. He told Pu-Can that the Mikko requested her presence. He waited for her to get her pack and then led her up to the mound.

She looked up at the impressive structure, feeling some reluctance. *What could he want with me?* Taking a long, deep breath, she climbed the stone-lined steps to the top.

The Great Sun, Chatto-Nokose, greeted her and led her inside where two others were waiting. He introduced them to her as his brother and sister. The oldest of the trio was Owa-Hatke, the renowned Medicine Woman of the Wind Clan.

Owa-Hatke said, "We have known your grandmother Hechee-Lana since she was a young girl like you, Pu-Can. I even met you once when you were a child. Your grandmother and I knew you were to be Spirit Singer many years ago, now here you are. I welcome you."

"Thank you. Grandmother Hechee-Lana was excited to be attending the Festival this year. I feel her souls are here with us."

Next to be introduced was Locha-Luste, the tribe's Shaman, and the older brother of the chief.

"I welcome you, young Spirit Singer of the Osochi."

"Greetings, Locha-Luste. My great uncle Echo-Ochee speaks highly of you, and asked me to convey his apologies for not attending this year."

"Echo-Ochee and I go back many years, Spirit Singer. We have traveled the Spirit Path together many times. I was hoping to do that once more with him. We were going to begin gathering the Nation's Power Bundle this year," he said, looking at her questioningly.

"Then you are the one I am to deliver this to," Pu-Can said with relief. "I was afraid I would give it to the wrong person." She took the small bag that her uncle had given her from around her neck and handed it to him. The bag seemed to grow warm as their hands touched.

"Ah, he did not forget." Locha-Luste took the bag with reverence and held it upraised. He went to a large bag near the central fire and took out another bag, slightly larger than the one Pu-Can had given him. 'We must do the ritual for combining these, but that can wait until tomorrow. Will you help us with the blessing, Pu-Can?"

"I would be honored, Locha-Luste, but I do not know the ritual."

"Your presence and power are all that is required, Spirit Singer, and that I felt when you entered the room. Kowakatcu walks with you," the Hilis Haya answered.

Chatto-Nokose had been standing silently as the three were talking. Now he said, "Your grandmother will be missed, Pu-Can, but she prepared you well for assuming the duties of Spirit Singer. No one expected the burden would pass to you this soon, but I am sure you will honor your Clan and your Nation. You have Wild Dancer's fire drill, do you not?"

"Yes, Mikko. I have it and the leopard robe and mask. Should I bring them to you?"

Locha-Luste looked at the two elders with him, and they both nodded their approval. "You are Paneta-Semoli's direct descendant by blood, young Spirit Singer. I offer to you the duty of starting the New Fire at the main ceremony in two days. Are you prepared, and do you accept?"

Pu-Can was speechless for a moment, and then answered with humility, "Yes, I accept the honor of beginning the New Fire, Mikko Hese, and I hope to bring no shame upon my ancestors."

"Good! That is settled. Now I want to hear from your lips the story of the white men who attacked your people and killed Hechee-Lana. Did you really kill the man with old Bull Killer's spear?" the chief asked with a kindly smile.

It was late evening when Pu-Can climbed back down the mound and walked alone to her fire. She had told the story of the four white men and of her people's actions afterward. She had remembered her promise to Echo-Ochee, and told them how he had called down the wrath of the Puma Man, who had destroyed the white men with fire from the sky. The Mikko seemed pleased and asked many questions during her telling of the story.

The next day would be Busk, the first official day of the Festival. The people would begin fasting and drinking the Black Drink that would purge their bodies. No one was allowed to take part in the Green Corn Dance who had not fasted and partaken of the Black Drink.

Pu-Can allowed herself a drink of water, and then went to her blankets. She had much to think about. As she lay there, looking at the stars, someone approached the fire.

"Pu-Can?" whispered a voice.

She sat up. "Yes? Who calls?"

"It is Tysoyaha. I was hoping to speak with you before you were asleep. Will you walk with me?"

"Yes," Pu-Can replied. Suddenly she was very much awake. "Let me get my moccasins. I could not sleep, anyway."

They walked down to the river and sat on a large boulder near the canoe landing. Tysoyaha waved at the sentry standing nearby, who waved back.

"My father can appear very intimidating sometimes. Did he tell you what he wanted?"

"Yes, he wants me to be Firestarter at the Festival. I brought the fire drill with me that was passed down from my many-times-grandmother, Wild Dancer, but I thought it was for one of the elders. It is a special honor, not usually given to one so young."

"As soon as we heard the news of your grandmother's death, their plans were set in motion. Your fame has reached far, Spirit Singer." He took her hand as if to make a point, but then held it, allowing their joined hands to lie between them.

Pu-Can almost withdrew her hand, but then realized that it felt nice and not at all threatening, so she allowed it to remain in his. She pointed to a group of stars. "See those two brightest ones? Grandmother said that those are the eyes of Kowakatcu, the Puma Man. And those over there," she pointed again, "are the seven sisters who fell in love with the same man."

He laughed. "And I know the one that shows me which direction north lies, and I recognize the moon when I see it. The Child of the Sun does not know the night sky so well." He seemed to be about to say something else, but became silent. He turned to wave again at the sentry.

"I asked him to watch us," he explained. "That way, your honor will be unquestioned. I do not want any rumors spreading about the two of us being alone. These Festivals are the only thing some people have to talk about until the next one. That sentry is the grandson of Owa-Hatke, the Medicine Woman you met tonight. There will be no rumors."

Pu-Can smiled appreciatively. "Thank you. I have much to learn about being around so many people. My people are nearly all related and very few in number. We do not live in an italwa, but are spread out in the valley between the two mountains. There are only two hands of people that I see daily."

A pebble clicked down the hill and Tysoyaha looked around at the sentry. He was being relieved and was giving notice that he would be leaving. Tysoyaha stood and helped Pu-Can down from the rock.

"We had best return now. I will walk with you to your fire. Will you dance with me at the Stomp Dance, or do you have other plans?"

The question caught her off-guard, but she replied that she would be honored to dance with him.

He placed his hands on her shoulders in a near hug, then took her hand again and walked her back to the top of the hill.

At her fire, he said, "Sleep well, Spirit Singer. I will see you tomorrow."

"Thank you for asking me, Tysoyaha. I think I can sleep now, if I do not dream of fire drills that do not work," Pu-Can replied, smiling at him.

Pu-Can woke early the next morning. She found her pack with her herbs and began selecting the ones she would use to make the Black Drink for her people. Satisfied that she had all her ingredients, she built the fire and put on a pot of water to boil.

Several children playing nearby gathered and watched as she prepared the herbs. One very pretty little girl came up to her and said something. Pu-Can, thinking that it was just a child's gibberish, just smiled at her and continued working. The girl repeated what she had said. Pu-Can knew that many of the Muskogee tribes spoke slightly different dialects, but they could always manage to communicate, using words that they had in common. This was different. There were no words that she recognized.

"I am sorry, but I do not know your language," Pu-Can said. Then she saw Tysoyaha, who was approaching as the little girl came over.

He laughed at Pu-Can's attempt to understand the girl and said, "She asked if you are a witch. She is Yuchi, the same as my mother. The Muskogee and Yuchi languages are completely different."

"Tell her I am not a witch, please. Some of my own people already think that of me anyway, because of where I live." She smiled at the girl as Tysoyaha relayed her message. "And tell me more of the Yuchi, and this strange language."

"I know very little of it myself, only that there are no common words between the tribes. No one even knows where the Yuchi came from. They later formed an alliance with the Muskogee because of their small numbers, and the white man calls them Creek like the rest of us, but even their legends and customs are different. I would like to know more about them too, since I am half Yuchi myself."

He sat down at her fire and watched as she prepared the Black Drink. From another bag she took a pinch of corn pollen and cast it in the four directions as she softly chanted a song in the Old Language.

"Would you sing that again?" he asked when the song had ended. "Some of it sounded very much like my mother's prayer-chant."

"We call it the Old Language," Pu-Can said, and repeated some of the lines.

"Yes! That seems the same as I remember, but the words are not Yuchi either. My mother also called it the Old Language. So perhaps there is yet a common bond from when the two people were one," he said, "but all that is buried by time."

Now the entire camp was awake, with many fires, and the aroma of Black Drink permeated the grounds. It seemed everyone had their own recipes for the special drink, but the end result was always the same—within minutes of drinking, it caused vomiting. The cleansing would begin.

Brian stopped reading and looked up at the others. Mary, Alex and Maurice were listening intently, waiting for more, but he could tell that they were getting sleepy.

"What do you say we continue this tomorrow night? Once again I'm about to fall asleep reading."

They all agreed, and almost reluctantly began preparing their blankets for the night.

"I was hoping we could have a Green Corn Festival of our own," Alex said, "but do we have to do that last part? You know, the Black Drink thing?"

They all laughed. "I think we'll be lucky if we can even do the fasting part," Brian answered. "I think that would be enough. Keechie gave me the Black Drink in Oklahoma at our first Stomp Dance. I don't want to ever taste that stuff again!"

An intense thunderstorm awakened them the following morning. Frequent lightning illuminated the cave, and the very earth trembled with the earsplitting booms of thunder. It was a perfect day for inside activities.

Maurice had not seen the storage room or the spring-fed pool in the further recesses of the cave, so they all gave him a tour. Brian pointed out the passageway that he had traveled through to find the remains of Keechie's father and brother. He admitted that he had always wanted to go back and investigate further, even to the tiny opening that had caved in on first Keechie's younger brother, Stikini, then again on their father, George Washington.

Maurice was horrified at the thought and said so. "I nevva did lak t' get myseff closed in. Spechully whar I cain't see, er tarn 'roun'. Please don' ask me t' go in dar, Brine."

"It's much too dangerous, my friend. As much as I would like to, I doubt if I'll ever go back. It's just my curiosity, and I did see wall paintings, so I know the Indians had gone into the deeper areas, but that was even before Keechie's ancestors, I believe. The legends of her people indicate that there had been people here before they arrived. No one knows who they were, or even when they got here. Now, is anyone ready for more of Granny Boo's story? The rain looks like it has set in for the day, anyway."

The first day of Busk was filled with excitement. The popular Ribbon Dance, led by four specially selected women, was to be the highlight of the evening, and preparations were being made for that event.

Just past noon, one of the more favored events began. Stickball was a tradition that all the different tribes shared. Even their old enemy, the Cherokee, played this ancient game, and it was frequently used to settle disputes instead of making war.

For this reason, it was called the "Little Brother of War." Two teams were selected to defend goals at opposite ends of the paskova. A small deerhide ball was maneuvered across the field using sticks with nets attached to one end. The ball was caught and tossed using only this stick. The main rule was that the ball was never touched with the hands. Other than that, it was a rough-and-tumble event – one which frequently resulted in severe injury, broken bones being the least of these. Much wagering took place among the spectators, who occasionally got into fights with each other. The teams were named either Red or White, identified by strips of colored cloth tied around the arms and legs of the participants.

Pu-Can and her group were there, cheering for the White team that Tysoyaha played on. He was the favorite among most of the spectators, not because he was the son of the Mikko Hese', but because he was so very talented at the sport. He was all over the field, blocking, catching and scoring with long, accurate throws; but it was his sportsmanship that was his most appealing virtue. He would stop to help a fallen opponent to his feet even at the expense of a goal, and the crowd would cheer him loudly.

The White team won by a small margin, and the opposing

Red team was thrown into the river in a good-natured victory celebration.

The paskova was again swept clean, and then blessed by Locha-Luste. He was dressed in full ceremonial attire, complete with a fearsome mask. On his ankles were turtle shell rattles, which accompanied the drum that he used to set the tempo of the dance of purification around the paskova.

Then, just as the sun was setting, the Ribbon Dance began.

After the purification ritual, the male singers encircled the paskova. With only gourd rattles, they set up a slow, sizzling tempo. Next they began chanting in rhythm. After a short while, the four chosen women entered the paskova from the four corners, each wearing long, multi-colored ribbons. Owa-Hatke, the Spirit Singer and Medicine Woman of the Wind Clan, led the dance. After one complete circuit, the rest of the women joined them. Several turtle shell rattles that were tied to their ankles added to the rhythm the men had begun. They stomp-danced single-file in a counter-clockwise direction around the paskova. Each woman carried a long stick, painted red at the tip, which she waved in time with the chanting of the men's voices. They made four rounds of the field and then rested; then they made four more rounds until sixteen rounds were completed.

At the conclusion of the Ribbon Dance, the tempo increased, and drums were added to the hypnotic music. Now everyone who wanted could participate in the dancing and foot-stomping celebration. Only a few of the spectators remained sitting. The nearly full moon was high in the sky when the dancing ended and the people returned to their fires.

Just as Pu-Can returned to her fire, Tysoyaha approached her. "Locha-Luste wants you to meet with him, Pu-Can. He said you knew the reason. I will escort you to his chikee."

The Power Bundles, she remembered. "I will only need my pack, Tysoyaha. Did he say I was to bring anything with me?"

"No, just your presence is all he told me. He did say that it would not take long."

The old shaman's chikee was a small oval structure, made from saplings covered with animal skins, much like a sweat lodge. She had to stoop to enter the enclosure where Locha-Luste waited. There was barely room for him to stand as he rose to greet her. He asked her to sit across from him at the small central fire, into which he began sprinkling tobacco and other herbs. The aroma filled the room. She saw a large Power Bundle lying next to him, along with the one she had brought beside it.

"Do you have pollen, Pu-Can?" he asked, knowing that a true Medicine Woman always had a small pouch of pollen and special herbs with her.

"Yes, Grandfather," she said as she removed her pouch from her waist. She took a small pinch of the golden pollen and sprinkled it on the fire, asking for the protection and blessing of Puma Man.

He began shaking a small gourd rattle and softly chanting in the Old Tongue.

Pu-Can realized that she knew this old incantation, so she added her voice to his. At first he looked surprised, then pleased, as he continued the chant. Suddenly Pu-Can realized that the room had filled with the presence of many spirits. At that instant, she and the old shaman were standing on a mountaintop, overlooking a fertile valley filled with large, shaggy-haired animals, grazing in uncountable numbers. The sky overhead was beautiful, with red and magenta clouds rolling past. Drums were throbbing like the combined heartbeats of every living thing, all in perfect unison.

The old shaman held a Power Bundle up to the sky and shouted, "Kowakatcu! Kowakatcu!"

The Puma Man, in his human form, was instantly standing there, his feline face smiling at them. He took The Power Bundle from the shaman and opened his mouth wider and wider, until his mouth was all Pu-Can could see. Then he swallowed the Bundle and faded away into the clouds.

The drumming stopped and Pu-Can found herself once again seated at the fire across from Locha-Luste, who was holding the large Power Bundle in his hands, but he was trembling with emotion. Or was it fear?

"Pu-Can, I saw you—we were—the Puma Man—," he stammered.

"You saw him too? We were both there, with the Power Bundle." She had never shared a dreamtime with anyone, but it had seemed so real to her.

"Yes. I saw him, and you were there with me. In my whole life, I have only felt the presence of the Puma Man. I have never seen him until this night. It was your vision, Spirit Woman. Never have I felt such power, nor had such a vision." He lowered the Power Bundle and held it with great reverence. "Just as you began singing with me, I added your bag to it. Then I was standing on a mountain with you. It was so beautiful … all those animals … and the sky … then Kowakatcu was there in his man form—"

"And he ate the Power Bundle," Pu-Can added. "I think he was pleased with your offering, Locha-Luste, great shaman of the Wind Clan. The Puma Man does not show himself to many, especially those of a different spirit guide. Surely your intentions were good and worthy."

"My many-times grandmother was of the Puma Clan, Spirit Singer. My sister had the Gift, as did our grandmother. She was taken during the Removal," he said. "Perhaps we share a common ancestor? Echo-Ochee and I tried many times to trace our roots back to one of the Old Ones, but we never could determine for certain."

"Hechee-Lana spoke often of her many-times grandmother, Wild Dancer, Grandfather. Is that name familiar to you?" Pu-Can asked.

Locha-Luste nodded. "Echo-Ochee told me of her, and she is mentioned in the story of the first people to come to this land. I will tell it to you before you leave if you wish. I received only a small part of the Gift, being a male. But my sister, if she were only here, she would know more than I about Wild Dancer. My sister is a very powerful Singer, and she remembers all the old stories. I was trained only in the medicine crafts. Our tradition required that those secrets were only for the women of the Gift. But what we shared tonight was the most power-filled event of my life."

He stood and helped her to her feet. He was still shaking, but it was from emotion. "I will walk you to your fire, Spirit Singer."

Tysoyaha was waiting outside the chikee when the two came out, but Locha-Luste waved him away.

"I will escort Pu-Can to her fire, young warrior, but you may walk with us if you wish," the old shaman added with a smile directed at Pu-Can. Suddenly he seemed to be many years younger and walked with his head held high, as if he had regained his youth. Once at her fire, he bid her goodnight.

"I must think about what happened tonight, Spirit Singer. I would like to speak more of this, if you would honor me with more of your time?"

"It is I who would be honored, Grandfather Locha-Luste," she said to him with great respect.

He clasped her hand in his, then turned and walked away toward his chikee.

Tysoyaha watched him go. "My uncle seems different tonight. Did something happen? He seems happier than I have seen him in years."

"Yes, a very special thing has happened," Pu-Can told him. "But I would rather that he tell you about it. Some things are best not discussed too soon. All is well, though. The spirit world is close to us tonight. I, too, feel the need to be alone with my thoughts. But tomorrow we dance. I hold you to your promise."

"I understand, Spirit Singer. I will leave you with your thoughts and bid you goodnight. Sleep well, my Pu-Can," he said, and left her fire before she could answer.

My Pu-Can. When did I become his Pu-Can? she asked herself. "Right after I first saw him on the journey here," she answered aloud, then smiled.

The dawn promised a beautiful day for the Green Corn Festival. There was an air of excitement around the camp. Even though there was no smell of food being prepared, there were fires being lit at every campsite. The children were already running around and playing loudly. Tonight they would have the biggest feast of the entire year, making the fast of the Busk all the more worthwhile.

Pu-Can pulled the old fire drill and bow from her pack and inspected the rawhide bowstring. The wood was very old, but still strong. The bowstring was still supple and did not need replacing. She did not want any surprises tonight when she brought the New Fire to life.

Gathering some of the tinder from her pouch, she began drawing the bow back and forth, spinning the fire drill in the cradle. Soon there was a wisp of smoke from the tinder. She quickly doused it. The New Fire was for tonight, and it would be a bad omen to start it too early. She was satisfied that it would work for her again. She carefully put it away and took out her special deer hide dress that she planned to wear. A few beads needed to be re-attached, and some of the colored quills required some attention, so she set about the task.

Another stickball game was under way, but this one was for the girls and women. Not nearly as rowdy and dangerous as the men's game, it was still just as entertaining and exciting for the spectators. The people would gamble on anything, even which leaf would fall next from a tree, and the games were no exception.

Just as she finished with her dress repair, Tysoyaha joined her and they walked to the paskova to watch the game together.

In mid-afternoon, after the women's game ended, Locha-Luste, dressed in his finest ceremonial robes and wearing his most fearsome-looking mask, walked to the center of the paskova. Two of his priest-initiates were with him, blowing on conch shell horns to get everyone's attention.

When they all had gathered, he made his announcement: "My people, people of all the Clans gathered here for this beginning of the New Year, we give thanks to the Master of Breath for our bountiful harvest. All the wrongs that were committed in the past year are forgiven. We will form new alliances among those gathered here. We pay tribute to the ones who are not with us, and invite their souls to watch over us and be pleased with our celebration of the Green Corn."

Drums began beating as Locha-Luste and his assistants went around the paskova with the ritual purification. In front of him were the sweepers, cleaning the dance grounds. No spot was missed, and even the houses and tents were cleaned and purified. They kindled a fire at one end of the paskova and the people brought out their old clothing, broken vessels, and tools, and cast them into the fire. After this was completed, all the fires in the encampment were extinguished.

Then four young men who had earned the privilege during the past year brought out four huge logs and placed them in the center of the paskova. Locha-Luste carefully oriented them to the four directions.

Just at sundown, when there was barely enough light to see, Chatto-Nokose and Locha-Luste stood at the logs and raised their hands for everyone's attention.

Locha-Luste announced, "It is customary for a male priest to begin the New Fire. The Spirits have spoken to me, and they have instructed me to break that tradition this year. They have sent us a very special Firestarter, one I am sure you have all heard of by now. She brings with her the very fire drill and bow that her great grandmother, the Wild Dancer, brought to this land. We welcome Pu-Can, Spirit Singer of the Kowakatcu Clan, granddaughter of the great Hechee-Lana, and we ask her to begin the New Fire."

The people cheered loudly as Pu-Can walked slowly to the center of the paskova and the waiting logs. Her heart was pounding so hard that she felt that everyone could see her chest heaving with her heartbeats as she knelt before the logs.

The people became silent as they watched her begin the age-old ritual. A single drum began a slow tempo as Pu-Can drew the bow faster and faster. It seemed as if time stood still, and she was beginning to worry, when the first wisp of smoke appeared in the cradle. She continued for a few more strokes until she saw a spark appear. She stopped and quickly added tinder, blowing gently on it. A flicker of flame appeared and she added yet more tinder, still blowing softly. Finally, a flame appeared that was large enough for her to add a few small twigs. She transferred the burning sticks to the center of the logs and carefully placed more wood around them.

As the flame grew higher, the people again cheered loudly and began stomping the ground in time with the drum. The men who had brought out the logs came with pine torches, which they ignited from the New Fire, and carried them to all the fire pits and houses around the grounds. Once all the fires were re-kindled with the New Fire, the Stomp Dance, the Green Corn Dance of the Muskogee, began.

All the participants formed a circle around the paskova. The women wore turtle shell rattles around their ankles. They began the ritual stomp-dance around the circle in a counter-clockwise direction, alternating man-woman-man until everyone was included. When the first line became too long, a second line formed within the first.

Tysoyaha had made sure he was next to Pu-Can when the dance began, so he could be her partner. He placed his hands on her waist as they made their way around and around the circle.

It seemed as if the very earth was shaking with the rhythm of the drums beaten by the men around the paskova, and the rattles of the dancers added their sizzle to the throbbing beat. When everyone became exhausted and began dropping out of the line to rest, the dance ended. The new corn, which had yet to be tasted, was brought out in steaming baskets. It had been roasting throughout the Stomp Dance, and was now ready.

One of the women handed Chatto-Nokose the first ear and he held it up to the sky. A priest threw an arc of yellow pollen into the air as the people watched in anticipation.

Chatto-Nokose slowly raised the ear of corn to his lips and bit into it. "It is good!" he shouted, and the people cheered and rushed to the waiting baskets for their own.

A huge amount of various foods was prepared for the

breaking of the fast, but the corn was the highlight of the celebration. From the youngest children to the oldest among them, everyone was feasting on roasted corn, fried corn cakes, sofkee, hominy, and the special Chud-da Ha-ga, blue bread made by adding the hulls from purple-hulled peas.

Afterwards, there were storytellers at several different fires, telling the many colorful and oft-repeated legends of the Muskogee Nation. No one ever tired of hearing them, especially the children, because the storytellers would act out the different characters from the stories—most of them being the animals from the forests that every child knew.

It was nearly dawn when Pu-Can and Tysoyaha walked hand-in-hand down to the river; and it was there, sitting on that same boulder, that Tysoyaha asked Pu-Can to be his wife.

CHAPTER 11

"Wow!" Alex exclaimed. "I was hoping they would get married! They do, don't they?"

"They sure do, honey, but they had all kinds of problems. Remember he told her that he was to become the chief - the Mikko - of his tribe when his father died, and the man always went to live with the woman's Clan. You'll just have to wait for the rest of the story, okay?"

Maurice went to the doorway and looked out. "We still got us some daylight leff, an' hit's quit rainin'. Can I finely get me a crossbow lesson?"

"Good idea, Maurice. I'll get the bows and meet you outside." Brian was glad to have an excuse to get out of the cave for a while.

Mary had a crossbow pistol that she was quite good with, so she and Alex joined the men for some target practice. She had already killed a rabbit with it. It had been eating her vegetables in the small "kitchen" garden near the cave, so she had felt justified, and the meat was not wasted.

Maurice turned out to be a fair marksman with the crossbow. He, like most boys in the south, had grown up with firearms. The crossbow, with the exception of loading and cocking, was aimed and fired much like a rifle at close range.

"Can we really have our own Green Corn Festival?" Alex asked her father. "It would be fun, plus it seems like the right thing to do, you know, out of respect for Keechie and her Indian corn we're raising."

Brian nodded. "We were going to let it be a surprise, but your mom and I have already discussed it. We also think it would be fun and it is the right thing to do. The corn will be ready in just about a week, I think, and the moon will be full about the same time. If we do it right, we should do it on a full moon, but we can't eat any of it until we have our Busk, or Stomp Dance. Everybody okay with that?"

They all agreed and began making plans right away. They would have parts to play. Alex wanted to be the Firestarter, like Pu-Can. Mary would be the Medicine Woman and leader of the Ribbon Dance, while Maurice would act as the chief priest—the Hilis Haya, and do the purification ritual. Brian would be the Mikko and double as the drummer and master of ceremonies.

Darkness was falling, so Mary and Alex set out immediately planning and making their costumes. They fashioned ankle rattles out of old cans. Maurice and Brian started reminiscing about the fishing trips they had made together when they were kids, and decided that tomorrow they would do some fishing on the river. Brian took Maurice into the storeroom to see what he had in the way of tackle. He was well stocked as it turned out, and he had completed the cast net like the one that Keechie described to him. But, since Brian was reluctant to leave Mary and Alex alone at the cave while they were fishing, they decided to have an all-day family outing and picnic at the river.

Shortly after their evening meal of barbecued pork ribs and fresh vegetables, they went to bed, planning on an early start the next morning.

Mary woke with a start in the middle of the night.

"Brian, are you awake?" she asked in a whisper.

"I am now, honey. What's wrong?" He was still half asleep.

"I thought I heard drums. Is Alex up?" She looked over at Alex's blankets. "No, she's there, and Maurice is asleep. I know I heard drums beating!"

"Probably just a dream. You know, from the stories I've been reading and all."

"You're probably right, but it seemed like it was the drums that woke me." She lay there listening intently to the night sounds, but she heard no more drums. Soon she was back to sleep.

But now Brian was awake, lying there, remembering Keechie's words. *Didja hyer da drums, Brine? As long as dey's someone dat kin hyer da drums, de people will nevva die.*

He went back to sleep with a smile on his face.

While Brian and Maurice got the fishing tackle ready, Mary and Alex prepared a picnic basket with enough food for the day. They had jerky, cold cuts of pork and a large loaf of homemade bread. They threw in a frying pan, some cornmeal, and a chunk of salted fatback to use for grease in case they decided to have a fish fry on the river.

As the sun was just appearing over the opposite mountain, they were off. Brian took the lead with his ever-present crossbow swinging from his shoulder. Maurice brought up the rear with the fishing poles and his own crossbow. Mary smiled at the sight, patting the bulge in her light jacket where her Colt .380 rested.

They all carried backpacks with various supplies in them. When you live on your own devices, survival depends on having what you need, when you need it. They had learned some things the hard way; but mostly they had learned from Keechie and the ways of her people.

The river, swollen from the rain, had a strong, fast-moving current. There was a light fog hanging over it, but not enough that they could not see the five deer on the opposite shore, cautiously having a morning drink. There were four does and one large buck holding his head high and sniffing at the morning air, ever alert to danger. They stood silently watching. The deer moved away, never sensing that they were being observed.

"You know," Alex said, breaking the silence, "A lot of people would just see that and think, 'deer drinking water', but that is one of the most beautiful sights I have ever seen."

"That's life and nature at its finest, Alex. I think we all feel the same way, but I love the way you put it," Brian answered.

Mary put her arm around her daughter. "He says that, but I'll bet he was thinking about how difficult a shot that would be, and how he could get to it once he shot it."

Brian smiled self-consciously and agreed. "But I wouldn't kill one this time of year. The does may still have fawns with them. Plus, we don't need the meat right now."

He had saved strips of the pig's skin just for this purpose, and it was just rancid enough to be really good for catfish bait. In just a couple of hours he and Maurice had caught a stringer full, which they kept alive until they were ready to leave.

Mary and Alex were having a wonderful time collecting and identifying herbs and plants along the bank. Alex made frequent notes in her journal about the types and locations, if they ever needed a fresh supply. Several of their finds were collected, to be dried for later use.

Alex showed them two of the ones she had found. "This is chickweed, good for a lot of stuff, and this one is Saint John's Wort. You wouldn't believe all that it's good for." She ran back to Mary and continued their search.

Brian was only half listening because he had something else on his mind. "Hey, Maurice, remember how we used to set out trotlines across Mulberry Creek?"

"Sho do! We would work dat thang all night in dat li'l boat.

Dose wuz fun times! We had dat ol' kerosene lantern stickin' out de front o' dat boat on a pole, pullin' up dem big ol' catfish— sometimes we got a big ol' turtle. I'se always been a'skeered o' dem. Pap say dey could bite a man's finger off wit' one chomp!"

"Yep. I was just thinking, if we just had a boat, or a raft, we could do that here. But a boat is one thing we don't have. And this current would give us a problem, unless—" Brian went into his thinking mode and didn't even realize he had stopped talking.

"Less whut, Brine? You done got dat look in yo eyes."

"Unless we had a rope or something strung across the river—to hold the boat against the current. It's not that strong here, at least when it hasn't been raining. But before that, we need a boat or a raft."

" Hit `ud be lak de ol' days fer sho," Maurice said.

"Well, it's something to think about. I like the idea of having a boat here, though. It would give us one more escape route if it came down to it."

They checked the several set hooks they had placed along the bank and found two more catfish.

"This ought to be enough for now, since we don't have a good way of keeping them," Brian said. "Let's clean what we have and start thinking about heading back to the cave. We'll have fried catfish tonight … with hushpuppies."

While Mary and Alex gathered their herbs and supplies into their backpacks, Brian and Maurice cleaned the fish, and they headed back to the cave.

On the way back Brian mentioned to Mary, "You know where we were today? I didn't want to spoil the day for everyone by mentioning it, but that was the very spot where those white men killed old Turtle and his son. It was probably close to where Apelka-Haya and the others sank the four men's bodies. But that was almost a hundred and fifty years ago."

Mary looked at him. "I'm glad you didn't say anything earlier. It definitely would have spoiled the day. I keep forgetting that this is the very place you're reading to us about. It just seems so

… so in the past, you know?"

"Yep, I know, but I had the advantage of Keechie actually showing me these places, and telling me the stories of her real-life experiences. It does give you a different perspective. God, I wish that you and Alex could have met her. She would have loved you two."

Alex had to relieve her bladder and went a little way off the trail, asking that they wait for her. A few minutes later, she called, "Hey y'all, come here and look at this!"

"Dad, take a look at this," Alex said, pointing at an old lightning-struck oak tree. "Look at all the bees!"

Maurice was nearest, and he went closer to the tree. "Hit's honeybees, Brine. Alex done foun' us a bee tree, an' I knows how t' get de honey."

"Make a note in your journal, Alex, so we can find it again. We'll come back with some containers and get us some honey. That will be a great addition to our stores," Brian said.

Alex looked around for landmarks and made notes with a diagram in her journal. "How do we get the honey without killing the bees, Maurice?"

"We smokes 'em out. Hit kinda settles 'em down. My daddy usta do it all de time. We had us a bee tree when I wuz a young'un, an' I usta hep him wit' de smokin'."

Alex found another plant, and she wanted to dig up the roots. She knelt down, digging away with her sheath knife, when she suddenly stopped and stood up, looking at her dad with an amazed expression. "Dad! Look at what I found!"

It was a perfect arrowhead made from near-white chert, very much like the one he had found the same day he met Keechie, and still remained in the amulet bag around his neck. Brian told her more about it. The stone was not local, and had probably come from South Georgia, near Butler, where chert was plentiful. "That is a treasure for sure, Alex. Maybe you can make yourself a necklace from it, or add it to your special pouch. It certainly belonged to some of Keechie's ancestors."

"I'm going to keep it forever, Dad. Just think, it belonged to someone who was probably very sad to lose it. Now it kinda connects us. Does that make any sense?"

"It sure does to me, honey. That's the way I felt with every one I ever found."

Alex carefully placed it in the pouch around her neck and pressed it to her chest. "I want to make a necklace from it so I can see it whenever I want to. Will you help me, Mom?"

Mary nodded. "I sure will, baby. I think I have just the stuff we need to make a wonderful necklace. We'll work on it tonight."

They were back at the cave before sunset, and Mary began preparing for the catfish fry. "I've even got a couple of small cabbages ready to be picked to make coleslaw," she said.

They all helped with the preparation. Brian built up the fire under an iron pot of oil, Alex and Maurice went to the garden for the cabbages, Mary was making the batter for hushpuppies and fish. Soon the cave was filled with the aroma of frying catfish. Life was good!

After dinner, while Alex and Mary were working on Alex's necklace, Maurice and Brian began discussing the pros and cons of boats versus rafts.

"A raft would be easier to build, but more difficult to maneuver on the river. And we couldn't hide it as easy as we could a boat."

"Dey oughtta be a lot o' boats just layin' 'roun'. People done leff lots of stuff when dey moved 'way from hyer. I thank dere be mo chance o' findin' one on de other side o' de river, though."

He was right. No one lived between the mountain and their side of the river because of the State Park. No one besides them, anyway. All the houses and farms were on the opposite side.

They began planning a trip to explore the other bank of the river, but Brian knew that a trip like that was not for the entire family. The danger of being discovered was just too great.

The conversation changed to their upcoming Green Corn

Festival, but Brian still couldn't get his mind off boats. He was determined to have one.

Mary and Alex were busy preparing the roots and herbs they collected for drying. Brian had built drying racks for outside use and they spread their shaved roots and leaves onto the screens, ready for taking outside into the sun the next day. Alex labeled them carefully and kept the different ones on different racks. They had an electric dehydrator, but it drained the batteries much too quickly. The sun would do just fine, as long as they brought the racks in each evening in case of rain. It would only take a few days in the hot sun to dry them thoroughly.

Mary was very resourceful in preservation methods, and she was already planning how they would store the herbs using vacuum-sealed bags. She had just the thing – it was a Daisy Seal-a-Meal that she had refused to leave behind. It consumed very little power, and she had a whole large box of the reusable bags.

No one was ready for sleep, so they went outside to sit and enjoy the night sky.

"I wonder about our sanity sometimes," Brian mused. "We've got a perfectly good house in the valley that we could be living in, but here we are, living in a cave instead. What's really strange is that I prefer this." He chuckled.

"I think we're safer here," Mary said. "It seems like every time we go out into the world, something happens."

"But we've only been out that once, and we found Maurice," Alex said, looking at their new friend. "That wasn't such a bad thing."

"You're right," her mother agreed. "Something good did come from that trip. But we almost got him killed because of our presence. But it's always good to find something positive about the hand that life deals you."

"Then it's not just me who wants to stay here?" Brian asked.

"I thought we had already decided that. We love it here. Even if the world suddenly changed back to the way it was before," Mary said with finality.

"And speaking of the world, Maurice, I'm going to go listen to the shortwave radio for a while. Want to join me?" Brian asked his old friend.

While Mary and Alex studied their herb books, the two men went into the storeroom where Brian had his bank of batteries and various radios set up. The shortwave had several different bands – amateur, military and commercial. He switched it on and selected the amateur band first.

"Ham operators always find a way to communicate," Brian said. "Many times in the past they 'saved the day', even when the police or military were working on the case. They do it because they love it."

The limited radio traffic was usually in Spanish or some other foreign language, and even then only one side of the conversation could be heard. There was a bit more in the old Morse code, of which Brian had a limited knowledge. In his Boy Scout troop they had learned the alphabet, but he had forgotten most of it. Then he switched to a frequency typically reserved for police, fire and rescue operations. The reception was very poor and seemed to be transmitting from low power, hand-held units. But whatever was going on was intense, with excited voices and high emotion. Much of it was in police "number code" and they couldn't get a handle on it.

"Write those number codes down while I look for my list," Brian said, tossing Maurice a pencil. "I have those codes printed out from when the Internet was still working."

It took him a few minutes to locate the printout, but he found it. He rejoined Maurice at the radio and continued listening. "Those street names they're mentioning are in Columbus. That's only twenty-five miles south of here, so that's where they are," Brian said. "Sounds like they've got more than they can handle, doesn't it?"

"Sho do. Whut's 'eleven-ninety-nine'? Dey been hollerin' dat one a lot."

"Eleven-ninety-nine … let's see … here it is. 'Officer needs help', it says," Brian answered, referring to the printout.

"An' another one … 'eleven-*fifty*-nine', dey been saying dat one a lot too."

"Eleven-fifty-nine … 'Intensive attention: high hazard, business areas'," Brian said. "Sure wish we knew what was going on. I listen in quite a lot and this is the most I've heard since we got here."

At times there seemed to be several transmitters, all sending at once, making it difficult to understand what was being said; but the overall message from what they were hearing was that Columbus was under some sort of attack. Several times, when a transmission was going on, the sound of automatic gunfire rattled in the background.

Then came several calls of 'signal ten-eighty', repeated from at least two different radios. Then an almost-screamed 'ten-nineteen', repeated over and over – then silence.

"Oh, my God," Brian said, looking up those last two codes. "Ten-eighty is 'bomb explosion', and 'ten-nineteen' is 'return to station' … in other words … retreat."

From the bits and pieces of the radio traffic, they put together the scenario—an armed mob, apparently fairly well organized, had been rioting in the streets, breaking into closed businesses and looting. The police responded, but were simply outnumbered and unable to control the situation.

"You know, before all this happened, we could sometimes see the lights from Columbus reflecting in the sky from the top of the Rock. Want to take a little night hike?" Brian asked.

"Wouldn't mind a'tall," Maurice replied. "Hit's a clear night. We oughtta be able t' see pretty good."

Brian gave Mary and Alex a quick rundown on what was going on. "I don't want to leave you two here alone. Want to go for a little walk with us?"

Alex answered by filling two lanterns and Mary by getting her Colt.

"Ready when you are," Mary announced, patting her rabbit

fur holster.

They walked single-file up the now-familiar path to the base of the Rock. In a few minutes they were standing on top, looking southward toward Columbus. The horizon was glowing reddish-orange.

Columbus was burning.

Then they saw a line of lights in the sky over the city.

"Those are helicopters," Brian said. "Probably military. Fort Benning is right there, bordering Columbus. I was hoping they would get involved."

Then they saw what appeared to be missiles fired from the helicopters, followed by bright flashes from the ground.

"Yep. The military is taking care of business—doing what they do best," he exclaimed with an excitement modified by sadness. "Looks like our decision to stay in the cave was a good one."

They continued watching until the helicopters left, then walked silently back to the cave. No one spoke until Brian said, "If we're going back into the valley anytime in the near future, we had better do it soon, before the bad guys come this way. They may not, but just in case ... I want to get a few things from the barn at my old house."

Alex looked up at her dad with a "don't lie to me" look. "Will they come here?" she asked.

"I don't think so, honey. They'll be looking for things to steal. There's nothing in the woods they want. We'll be safe here," he told her, hoping it was true.

After Alex and Maurice were asleep, Brian and Mary went outside. It was very late, but neither of them could rest, thinking about what they had heard and seen that evening.

"I really do need to get some things from the old house," Brian confessed, "and I don't want you and Alex in danger. Maurice and I can get up early in the morning, make a quick trip, and be back in the early afternoon. Are you okay with that?"

Mary hesitated. "I suppose so. I just hate the waiting, not knowing if everything is all right or not. But I don't want Alex in danger. What is so important that you have to get, anyway?" she asked, putting an arm around her husband.

"Well, there's farming equipment, animal traps, and hand tools of all kinds there. I don't remember what all is in the barn. I just know I don't want to lose it to a bunch of thieves. We may be here a very long time and everything we have may be needed for our future. I just have to go—the sooner, the better.

"If the mobs left Columbus and headed this way on foot, it would take them about two days to get to Hamilton, then another day or two to work their way to the residential places. More than likely they would head straight on up the road to LaGrange, north of us here."

"Remember the radio you took from those men's car? You said we could use it in the truck, to communicate between us," Mary suggested.

"Glad you reminded me of that, baby. It's still in the truck, and it'll only take a few minutes to hook it up temporarily. We can stay in touch. I can even tell you when to have supper ready," he teased.

As they prepared their blankets for the night, Alex began talking in her sleep. "*Yes, I can hear them. I can hear the drums... the drums...* " She woke with a start and called out for her mom.

"I'm right here, darling. Did you have a bad dream?"

Alex shook her head. "It wasn't bad. It was just a dream about this old woman. She was asking me if I could hear the drums. I think it was Keechie. She talked like Maurice. She said that everything was going to be all right. Good night, Mom ... sorry if I woke you up."

"I was still awake, baby. Go back to sleep now. I love you," Mary said.

She looked over at Brian and whispered, "You're not leaving here in the morning without telling her, you know. I know she'll want to go, but you still have to tell her, okay?"

Brian nodded. "I'll tell her in the morning, honey. Maybe you and she can do something special together, but stay close to the cave, okay? And I know that you need to get the herbs and stuff into the sun to dry. Before we leave in the morning, I'll set up the radio for you. Y'all can call us on it. Just don't say anything that would give our location away to anyone listening."

At dawn, Brian woke Maurice and told him the plans for the day. "You don't have to go if you'd rather not," he said. "It won't take long if there's no trouble, and I plan on being very careful."

"I wants to go, Brine. Better to be two o' us anyhow. Do you thank I let you go off by yo'seff?" Maurice said with a grin. He was as anxious to get going as Brian was.

Alex was a different story when she learned that her dad was leaving without her. "I won't be any trouble, Dad. I can take care of myself, you know."

"I know you can, honey, but it's best that only the two of us go. You and Mom stay here and do something together, okay? It's just going to be a quick trip to get some things out of the old barn, then right back here. I would feel better knowing you were safe."

She reluctantly agreed, and soon Maurice and Brian were off. He had set the radio to a clear channel, and all they had to do was use the transmit key on the microphone. He would hook up the radio from the men's car to the truck, and test it as soon as he had it working.

The truck was just as they had left it. They quickly removed the camouflaging limbs and brush from it, and Brian hooked the radio into the 12-volt wiring and attached an antenna.

Then he pressed the transmit button. "Calling Base. Do you copy?"

Alex answered immediately. "Hey, good buddy! Got your ears on?" which was old CB lingo for "Are you receiving me?"

Brian laughed and said to Maurice, "I wonder where she learned that?" He pushed the button again. "Got my ears on and copy you five-by-five, sweet thang! How do you know trucker's talk, anyway?"

"From television, Dad. I saw that old Burt Reynolds movie, *Convoy*, years ago."

"Then we'll check in every hour on the hour," he told Alex.

He slowly backed the truck out to the main road, stopping frequently to listen for traffic. Then he pulled out, heading for the U-turn to the valley below. In ten minutes they were at the old house.

Brian pulled in behind the house so the truck would not be visible from the road, then shut off the engine. Tall weeds and wild blackberry vines had grown up in between the house and the barn; there was no evidence of anyone having passed through them. He had placed a large padlock on the barn door many years before, and it took him several tries to find the right key.

"This has got to be the one," he said as he placed the last possible key into the old rusty lock. It opened with a click and they stepped inside.

It was dusty and dim inside, with the smell of rat droppings almost overpowering. Old cobwebs hung from every available surface. The room was full of an accumulation made over many years. Mostly it was stuff that was too good to throw away, but no longer needed; but to Brian, everything that he saw brought with it a flood of memories.

There was the old fence stretcher that he and his dad used to pull barbed wire tight. One would stretch the wire with the tool while the other nailed it into the post.

His grandfather's old manual plow with its one large wheel, designed for pushing through the soil without the benefit of a mule, leaned against the wall. It was in nearly new condition since Papa discovered early on that it was useless in the Georgia red clay.

A myriad of hoes, hand cultivators, picks and shovels were all standing upright in an old wooden barrel. Some of those would be nice to have at the cave. Then he saw the old army trunk. He had bought it at the army surplus yard when his Boy Scout troop gained permission to buy things there at almost giveaway prices. He remembered it as if it had been yesterday. The trunk itself had 'U.S. Army' stenciled on it in several places. It had cost him twenty-five cents and he had filled it with what he called his 'camping supplies'—mostly all purchased at the surplus yard.

The memories flooded back: ten cents for a military compass, a canteen or a web belt; fifty cents for a huge camouflage parachute, complete with lines; one whole dollar for a K-Bar survival knife (he had bought two of those); twenty-five cents for a mess kit which had a pan, a plate and a cup. All nestled into one small, easy-to carry package. He had bought two of those also. He found he was holding his breath as he opened the old trunk from his childhood.

It was all there—everything he remembered—and more. Right on top were his Boy Scouts' honor badges—knot tying, path finding, map reading, fire starting, plant identification, meal preparation, and good citizenship—all earned and still remembered.

The small local troop he belonged to didn't even have uniforms, and the Scoutmaster was just an old country man who knew and loved the outdoors—and how to survive in it. Keechie had continued his education where the old woodsman had left off.

Brian silently thanked them both. In addition, the trunk contained photographs of a few of his fellow scouts and some of places they had gone on camping trips. All were yellowed black-and-white prints, but still in good condition. *Alex will get a kick out of these.*

Maurice had been looking around the piles while Brian reminisced. "Hey Brine, look at dese. Or maybe I oughtta say, What is dese?"

Brian looked at what Maurice had found. He immediately thought, *Why didn't I think of these things in the first place?* Laughing, he said, "That's our boat, Maurice! That's more of the stuff I bought at the army surplus yard. They're old aircraft wing tanks. They cost me a dollar apiece, then another two dollars to get a man with a truck to haul them home. Then my dad told me that even if we built a pontoon boat out of them, we didn't have a way to get it to a lake where we could use it. I had forgotten all about them."

"People made boats outta dem?" Maurice asked.

"Yep. They float really good, if they don't leak, that is. All you need to do is attach a platform across them and you got a raft … actually a pontoon boat. Perfect for what we need on the river. I think there's even some plywood in here we can make the platform from."

Brian found three four-by-eight sheets of plywood that would do the trick. They would fit in the bed of the truck. He suddenly looked at his watch. "It's been an hour since we left. I'd better go check in with the boss." He went back to the truck and picked up the microphone to call "Base."

Before he could press the transmit button, the speaker crackled and Alex's voice said, "Hey, good buddy, gotcha ears on?"

"I'm here, Injun Walker. I got my ears on. Are y'all all right?"

"Everything's fine, Dad. How about you?"

"We're okay. What are you and Mom doing?"

"We've got all the herbs in the sun, and we were just about to go work in the garden a while. How much longer are you going to be?"

"Another hour or so here, honey, then we'll start back. I love you both. Tell your Mom, okay?"

"Okay, Dad. Love you too. Be careful. Over and out."

He laughed as he wondered what movie she had gotten that from.

They gathered all the items that they thought they might be able to use at the cave, and set them outside the door. The fuel tanks, the trunk, the plow and the hand tools would fill the bed of his truck. There was more that he wanted to take, but it would have to wait for another trip.

He locked the padlock on the door, silently asking the Puma Man to protect the house and barn just as he watched over the cave.

They loaded everything onto the truck, and Brian was just about to start the engine when Maurice whispered, "Wait. I hears sompin'."

An old pickup went past the house with two men riding in the back. They didn't even look toward the house as far as they could tell, and Maurice said he saw cane fishing poles sticking out of the back.

"Probably just some 'good ol' boys going fishing," Brian murmured, hoping he was right.

Sure enough, when they got to the bridge that crossed the creek, the truck was there—parked and empty. Brian drove slowly past and then speeded up, watching in the mirror to see if they were being followed. They had the road to themselves all the way back to the top of the mountain.

When they had the truck safely unloaded and hidden again, Brian made a call back to the cave, but no one answered. He looked at his watch, and realized that it had not been an hour since he had last spoken to Alex. The tanks alone took two trips to get to the base of the Rock, so on the last trip he tried the radio again. It had just now been an hour.

Alex answered immediately. "Hey, Dad. Where are you? How much longer will you be?"

"We're back, baby. We're at the—" He stopped himself from saying where he was. Some locals may guess where "The Rock" was. "We're at the parking place, right where I always park. Why don't you and your mom meet us here?"

"Gotcha. We'll be right there."

"Hey, Sweet Thang, bring a couple of poles and some old blankets, okay? To make a travois. Copy?"

"I understand, Daddy-Boss. Roger and Wilco. Base out."

Still amused at his daughter's TV-inspired radio lingo, which was actually quite good, he turned to Maurice. "Let's wait for them here. They can help us carry some of this stuff." He was feeling very relieved to be back safely, and to know that his family was safe.

The "stuff" took two trips, mainly due to the size of the items. The two wing tanks were not heavy, but their size made them difficult to handle. The plywood sections were heavy, but once on the travois they were not too difficult. Both the tanks and the plywood would have to be taken to the river for assembly, but Brian planned to have everything cut to size before taking them there. He was worried about the tanks leaking, but then remembered that he had a case of aerosol foam insulation that he had no other use for, and it needed to be used anyway. It would fill the tanks like Styrofoam, so that even if the tanks had holes in them, they would still float.

They all enjoyed going through the contents of the trunk. He gave Alex one of the K-Bar sheath knives, just like the one he still carried. The scabbard had its own pouch with a sharpening stone in it, and he showed her the correct method of sharpening the knife. It would be unusual many years later to see her without it strapped to her belt.

After their evening meal, Brian asked if they wanted to hear more of the story of Granny Boo. Maurice was the first to respond with his vote of "Yes!" followed by Mary and Alex in complete agreement.

"Tysoyaha had just proposed to her," Alex reminded her father. "I want to know what happens next."

Mary added, "And he was to become chief when his father died, and we already know that Pu-Can … Granny Boo … always lived here … right? Didn't the men always join the women's Clan?"

"That was their tradition, yes. But the story gets even stranger," Brian said as they gathered around him in front of the fireplace.

CHAPTER 12

Locha-Luste sent word to Pu-Can that he wished to see her before she departed. They were planning to leave at first light the next morning, so she made her way up the hill to his chikee.

Besides, she had a special gift in her pack that she wanted to give him. It was a small amulet that her great uncle Echo-Ochee had carved for her out of a deer antler when she was a young girl. She had noticed that a part of the antler had looked somewhat like a puma and she had shown it to him. He had seen it, too, and over the period of a few days he carved the rest of the figure. He had called it "releasing the spirit" that was already there. The antler had been very special to Pu-Can, but after their shared vision of the Puma Man, she knew that she must give it to Locha-Luste. Echo-Ochee would surely agree.

Locha-Luste was waiting outside his dwelling when she arrived. "Greetings, Spirit Singer. I was just thinking of you," he said. "Would you like some lemongrass tea?"

"Yes, thank you, Grandfather. My mother made that for us, and it is one of my favorites."

He filled a bowl for her and they sat on the log bench beside his fire. Getting right to the point, he said, "Chatto-Nokose told me that Tysoyaha has asked you to be his wife, and that you accepted."

Pu-Can nodded. "That is true. I know it is sudden, but our souls seemed to know each other."

"That is the way of Power, my child. Chatto-Nokose, like me, is getting quite old. His son is to become Mikko upon his death, and you have an obligation to your own Clan. How is this to work? Have the two of you discussed these details?"

"There has not been time, Grandfather. We have not yet decided upon the time of our marriage, either. Surely there is a way to work these things out for both our tribes," she reasoned, knowing that there was cause for concern. "My grandmother told me that a Spirit Singer and Medicine Woman had to sometimes choose between the spirit world and family life, and that it was not an easy choice."

"The spirit world is very demanding, as I am sure you already know, young Singer. However, you must have children in order to pass on the Gift to your descendants. Wind Clan and Puma Clan have always made a powerful combination," he said thoughtfully. "Your meeting Tysoyaha at this time in your lives is not a thing of chance, Pu-Can. It is the way of Power. All things happen for a reason."

"Wild Dancer, my ancestor, was of that combination," Pu-Can said, "and she was renowned for her power."

"Yes, but did she have a family life?" the old shaman asked, already knowing the answer.

"She raised her daughters alone, Grandfather. You have heard the story, I am sure. Her husband was—" she stopped in mid-sentence as the old shaman's meaning became clear to her.

Wild Dancer's husband had been a chief of the Wind Clan, in another tribe. They were together only a few times a year, and then only for short visits. She was Medicine Woman and Spirit

Singer of her own people. It was the custom for the husband to leave his Clan and live with the wife's people – the same set of circumstances in which she and Tysoyaha now found themselves.

"You understand then, Pu-Can. Power has a way of doing these things, but it offers only more proof that it is the Spirit World's plan for the two of you. The Wheel of Life has a way of repeating itself. It is part of the Song. The same one you sing in the Old Tongue that your grandmother taught you. Distance or separation will not affect the love you share with Tysoyaha. It will only make the times you are together all the more special."

"I know, Grandfather. I would feel guilty if Tysoyaha gave up his birthright and his obligation to his Clan to live with my people. He would grow to resent me, and I cannot leave my people. When my grandmother was killed, her duties became mine. Now with her brother, Echo-Ochee, nearing the end of his life, he has already told me that I must take that role also. There is no one else. Our talofa is small, and the white man all too near."

When she mentioned Echo-Ochee it reminded her of the gift she had brought. Taking it out of her belt pouch, she held it in her hand, feeling its familiar shape for the last time, then handed it to Locha-Luste.

"What is this?" he asked, taking the amulet from her hand.

"Echo-Ochee carved it for me when I was a young girl. I think Puma Man wants you to have it now."

He looked at it closely, and then exclaimed, "It is the Puma. I can feel his spirit inside. This is a very special treasure, Pu-Can. Are you sure you want me to have it?"

"I think Echo-Ochee and the Puma Man meant it for you all along, Grandfather. I was the bearer to bring it to you," she answered, feeling that her words were true.

"I will carry it with pride and respect, Spirit Singer. And I also have a gift for you," he said. "Wait here." He went inside his chikee and quickly returned, carrying a small deer hide bag. Opening it, he took out a small, carved ivory owl and handed it to her.

"It belonged to Stands Alone. He gave it to his wife, Butterfly, who was of the Jaguar Clan. It was he who brought the Muskogee people to this country, bringing the corn. Have you heard of Butterfly? In the old Muskogee language her name was Ta-Fo-Lope."

"Yes, Grandmother told me about her. She was one of her grandmothers, I believe. So this owl belonged to a relative of mine?"

"Yes, Pu-Can, and mine also. Stands Alone was my great-grandfather, of the Wind Clan, and Butterfly was of the Jaguar Clan—the Kowakatcu. These two clans have been connected for the life of our people. They had a granddaughter, Wekiwa-Chee, who gave birth to a daughter on the journey here. She was named Paneta-Semoli, the Wild Dancer, and was your grandmother's grandmother. This owl was passed on to her when her grandmother, Butterfly, died."

Pu-Can was speechless. She looked closely at the small owl. It was exquisitely carved from some type of ivory. It had yellowed with age, typical of ivory, but she knew that it had been pure white when it was new. "I thank you, Grandfather. This is a wonderful gift," she said as she placed it gently into the medicine bag around her neck. "I will carry it with honor for the rest of my life."

"The reason I asked you to meet with me tonight, Pu-Can, has much to do with that owl amulet. I carry in my memory the story of our ancestors, Stands Alone, Butterfly and Wild Dancer, and their journey across this land that the whites call America. It is the story of the bringing of corn to this land. Our grandmother told it to my brother Chatto-Nokose and me when we were children. Now since you and Tysoyaha are to be married, we agreed that the two of you should hear the story so that you can pass it on to your children and they to their children. Have you been told any of this journey before, my child?"

"Only some of it, Grandfather. My grandmother knew of the journey, but she told me mostly of Wild Dancer, since she was the one who passed the Gift of the Puma Man to the granddaughters. I would like very much to hear more of the journey and the bringing of the corn."

"Very well, then. Tonight, Chatto-Nokose and I will together try to repeat the story to you and Tysoyaha. It is a long story, but one that should not be forgotten. Now you and Tysoyaha go spend some time together. I will make some preparations for us and try to collect my memories. And, if you will, bring the mask and any other items that you have that belonged to Wild Dancer. The spirits within will help in the remembering."

"Thank you, Grandfather. I can hardly wait to hear of the journey of our ancestors. Would you mind if I brought my special herbs that aid in remembering? I can make us all a tea and an incense smoke that helps one to remember things told, and the teller to remember the stories better."

"I know the ones, Pu-Can. That would be much appreciated. Now go to your young man. We will meet here after sundown," Locha-Luste told her, amazed at the young woman's spirit and knowledge.

Tysoyaha was waiting for her as she started down the hill. "Did my uncle tell you to run away and forget you ever met me?" he asked teasingly. "My father just gave me the same speech, most likely."

"He did not tell me to run away, Child of the Sun, but he did tell me that you ask all the young women to marry you," she teased back.

"Only the pretty ones, Pu-Can, and the ones that have rich fathers."

They walked down to the river and sat on the same boulder as before. It was only a short time before sunset, and they had many things that they needed to discuss.

"Tomorrow I will go with you to your people," Tysoyaha said. "You will not have to walk this time. We will take my canoe downriver."

Pu-Can suddenly remembered that he did not know that she lived in a cave. Many people thought that only animals and witches lived in the ground. What if he was horrified at the thought? What if it changed his mind about her? She bit her lip, knowing she must tell him before they went any further. "Do you know where I live?" she asked softly, not looking at him.

"Two days downriver, between the two mountains. Why do you ask?"

"I mean where I myself live. My house, where my family lives," she said, still not looking at his eyes.

"Some say that you live in a cave in the mountain. I have heard the stories, and I do not think you are a witch, if that is what concerns you. If you are a witch, then I am happily under your spell. It changes nothing," he said, holding her close. He gave her a gentle kiss.

It was their first kiss, and one that she would remember forever.

"Before I was born," she whispered, "when the soldiers came to take the people away, my grandmother took her family and hid them in the cave. It has protected my family all these years. It is really a quite comfortable place to live, and it has everything we need. Puma Man watches over us there," she finished, relieved at his acceptance.

At sundown, they walked back to Pu-Can's fire and gathered the things that Locha-Luste had requested, along with her bag of herbs. On their way to his chikee, she asked Tysoyaha if he had heard the story that they were to hear tonight.

"Many times, Pu-Can, but it is a story that I love to hear. My father told me that we share ancestors from that time, but he assured me that we would not be breaking marriage laws, after so many generations have passed."

The Mikko and Locha-Luste were waiting at the chikee when they arrived. Two women were busy preparing a meal for them, and it was served as soon as they went inside. It consisted of roasted new corn and fresh, uncooked vegetables.

"I thought we should eat lightly for the storytelling," Locha-Luste explained. "I have a pot of water heating for the herbs you brought. They can be steeping as we eat."

Pu-Can took the herbs from her bag, chanting softly as she added them to the water.

"It is important to bless the herbs that help the remembering," Pu-Can said as she placed the last of them into the pot.

They finished eating and talked for a short time. Chatto-Nokose sent the two women away. He spoke to Pu-Can. "I welcome you to our family. The Wind Clan will again join with the Puma Clan. Great Power is at work in our lives, and our two peoples need that Power more than ever. Since the Removal there are all too few of us remaining here in the land of our ancestors. It was this land that they sought so long ago; and it is this story of that journey, and the hardships that they overcame to get here, that we will tell tonight."

Pu-Can stirred the herbal mixture in the pot. "The tea is ready, Grandfathers. We will drink, and then with your permission, I will sing the prayer I was taught that calls the spirits of remembering." She poured them all a bowl of the tea and joined them in the circle around the fire. She threw a handful of herbs into the coals, which filled the room with a sweet-smelling smoke.

When they had finished the tea, she reached into her bag again and took out the leopard mask and gourd rattle that had belonged to Wild Dancer. She put the mask on, began shaking the rattle with a slow tempo, and started a slow dance around them as she sang the Song.

When the Song ended, she lightly touched Locha-Luste and Chatto-Nokose on both of their shoulders with the rattle.

Chatto-Nokose was the first to speak. "This is the story of our people, the Muskogee, who first came to this land from the Great Water where the sun sleeps. They brought with them the very corn that we celebrate and honor at this gathering ..."

CHAPTER 13

Story of the Muskogee as told to PuCan:

The dream had come again to Stands Alone during the night. The spirit being, Owl, entered his sleep and showed him the path his people must take, but Stands Alone had no idea what the vision meant. Owl had indicated a northward journey, directly into the land of his enemies. They were not enemies of his choosing, but enemies nonetheless.

A hunting party was attacked again the day before by a small group of young Alabama warriors. All but one of them was killed with no losses to his experienced warriors. They had twice before encountered small bands of these warlike "Alabamas" and defeated them each time.

The lone captive warrior from yesterday had earned himself a quick and honorable death that was to occur at sunrise tomorrow morning. The captive had displayed courage under torture, and his final but most likely untruthful admission of the location and size of his Nation was more a threat than a sign of weakness. It had been fortunate that Still Water, the widow of one of Stands Alone's fallen warriors, spoke his strange language.

Panther Above, if they had known that they outnumbered us tens of tens to one, we would have ended our journey here in this desert. But Stands Alone also knew that they had been afraid of having to share their hunting grounds with outsiders. *If they had only sent emissaries for a meeting, they would have known we were only passing through their lands. We would have paid them for our safe passage, but their young warriors had seen an opportunity to gain status. They had made their attack foolishly and without plan against my own seasoned warriors, and they had died because of it. Now these Alabamas will be seeking to avenge their young warriors.*

He gazed down from the small mesa that overlooked his people's temporary camp. Fires were being kindled and the women were preparing the morning meals. They had grown accustomed to the hardships of travel over these last few moons, and they were very efficient in the feeding of many people in a short time. His warriors had been well prepared for the attempted attack the day before.

Since their journey had begun, he had maintained scouting parties within a day's run to the north and east of the main body of his people. They had spotted the enemy several hands of time earlier and had prepared an ambush for them. Since leaving their homeland, they had been on full alert and were on duty night and day.

Ten moons ago his people, the Muskogee, had left northwestern Mexico en masse and four hundred strong, seeking a new home where the Sun God rose each day. His first and most powerful vision had come just after the foolhardy Aztec, Montezuma, had attacked the army of the invading Spaniard, Cortez. Montezuma lost not only his own life, but those of most of his warriors. Stands Alone had even sent many of his own finest warriors to join Montezuma's army as a sign of unity toward the Aztec Nation, and they had died with the rest.

Stands Alone's people had listened as he retold his vision in council. The white-skinned invaders had superior weapons, and a method of waging war not understood by the people. They did not speak with truth, but used trickery and cunning in their dealings. The Aztecs were still willing to suffer at the hands of these white invaders, treating them as gods, but Stands Alone's vision told a different story—one of suffering, slave labor and eventual total destruction.

Some began to think of him as the 'Child of the Sun', who had been foretold for tens of tens of generations by the shamans of their ancient homeland from across the Great Water. When he told his people of his encounter with Owl, who told him to seek the land where the sun rose each day, they listened. Then they followed him.

They were carrying a most precious treasure with them. Two summers after their arrival in the land of the Aztecs, one of their hunting parties had encountered a village. They were met peacefully and were given food. They shared some of their fresh venison with the villagers, and in exchange received several baskets of a grain they had never seen.

The Aztec people called it a-chee, or maize, and considered it sacred. To the hunters it was obvious why—it made the most delicious bread they had ever tasted. There was also a kind of gruel made from it that the villagers called "sofkee." Every family they saw kept a pot of it simmering over their fires all day long. When anyone was hungry, they just went to the sofkee pot and filled a bowl. Sometimes they added bits of whatever meat they had for extra flavor.

They remained in the village for two days, gathering all the information they could about this wonderful new grain. They knew they had made an important discovery, but the full impact would not be evident for several years. Little did they know that this grain was the turning point of civilization in this land. It was the foundation of the first communal lifestyle. People began settling in one location, raising this crop and domesticating livestock, no longer having to depend solely on hunting, fishing or gathering wild foods.

The hunters carried enough of the maize for their leaders to taste, and their wives to experiment with in cooking, but the majority of it they planted according to the information the men had gathered. Within two harvests, they became well adapted to this new crop. All the families now had a stone mano and matate, used for grinding the grain into meal. They learned to use the ashes from oak fires to leach the kernels and make hominy. Sofkee was an offshoot of this process.

During the first season of their journey, they had traded some of their maize with the other tribes they encountered. But nearly every time, the other tribes ate all the maize instead of saving some for re-planting.

Unfortunately, one of their affectionate names for their treasure was "The Golden God." This was the message that spread through their chance encounters with others. Within one season, traders carried the message far and wide that the Muskogees were carrying gold, and gold was what the Spanish invaders wanted.

The Spaniards had goods that all the tribes wanted that could be attained nowhere else. Although the Muskogees had never seen a Spaniard, the invaders desired to possess this wonderful gold treasure that they were said to be carrying.

As the first rays of the sun illuminated the barren landscape, Stands Alone offered his prayers of thanksgiving for his warriors' victory and for the continued guidance of his people. He gathered his atlatl, darts and medicine bundle and headed downhill to his people. They must leave this land soon, before the enemy had time to react. *Northward? Why would Owl want us to go northward, into the land of these Alabamas, that he so badly wanted to avoid? Did he not first tell me to go to the rising sun? Owl is of the night and of darkness. The Great Sun rules the day. The Twins of Light and Dark must be playing with my souls,* he thought with a chill of foreboding.

Butterfly was alternating between preparing flatbread cakes and watching her husband as he stood high on the mesa above them. She turned to the other women around the fire and said, "That is how he got the name 'Stands Alone' when he became a man. Even before he could talk, he would go away from the others and stand, just like that, and look at Father Sun. His mother worried about his eyes being damaged by the sun because he would stare at it until he could not see. When he went on his spirit quest, Owl came to him and became his spirit guide. Imagine that! A creature of the night for a man dedicated to Father Sun."

The other women shook their heads in amazement and joined her in watching their leader as he made his way down the mesa. They all knew the story well, but to hear it from his wife of three tens of seasons made it all the more meaningful.

Butterfly's mother, Thorn, had been a Spirit Singer and a great healer among the people. This psychic "Gift" appeared in every other generation among her clan since First Woman, but only in the female lineage. Butterfly had learned all the woman skills from her mother, but the "Gift" was not hers.

She and Stands Alone had only one daughter, Raven, who had spent most of her time with her grandmother, Thorn, learning the rituals and ways of the spirit world. She had demonstrated her Gift many times, and even once during this journey had used her gift of Spirit Singing to call game to the hunters.

Raven's only son, Mushroom, had one older sister, Wekiwa-Chee - Little Spring of Water, who was now pregnant. It was hoped that she would have a girl-child so that the Gift could continue among their Clan. Wekiwa-Chee was approaching the age when women could no longer bear children, and until now only had boys, who were all men now.

As Stands Alone approached the fire, Butterfly scooped a ladle of sofkee into a flatbread cake and handed it to him. He looked at her affectionately and tasted it. The sofkee was hot and he almost spat it out, but grabbed a water gourd and cooled his mouth instead.

"A warning would have been appreciated, woman," he said with mock anger. "How can I speak with my tongue burned from my head?" The women giggled as he stuck his tongue out and asked them, "Is it still there?"

He called to a young boy playing nearby. "Mushroom, go fetch the war leader Tall Bones. Tell him to be quick about it. We have much to decide in the next few hands of time."

His grandson Mushroom was filled with pride as he went to do his grandfather's bidding. He grabbed a flatbread cake and ran off toward the war leader's hide shelter. He was too young to be a warrior, and they had had to restrain him the previous day when the men went to do battle with the enemy. He had been one of the first in the encampment to see the hostage that they'd brought back, and he had watched as the man was tied, beaten and tortured. He felt pity for the man's suffering, but had also understood the reasoning behind it. Some of the other children kicked and prodded the man with sharpened sticks and firebrands, but he had not taken part in it. He had stood silently by and watched. The captive made eye contact with him at one point, and Mushroom admired his courage. He gave the man a solemn nod and walked away.

It was apparent how Tall Bones had earned his name. As he walked toward Stands Alone with Mushroom at his side, he was still adjusting his breechcloth as he ambled along with the loping yet graceful gait that was typical of one so tall. He was extremely lean, his muscles long and rock hard. Every bit of exposed flesh was covered with tattoos, signifying his success in warfare.

"You wished to see me, Mikko?" he asked as he eyed the flatbread cakes Butterfly was piling in stacks.

"Yes, Tall Bones, but first have some of Butterfly's cakes and sofkee. Don't burn your tongue as I did, though. Did our prisoner survive the night?" He indicated by looking toward the staked figure near Tall Bones' tent.

"He still lives, Mikko, and I promised him a quick death this morning. He is a brave one. Even his admission of the size of his Nation was more a warning than a confession."

"Good. I want to set him free. I want him to carry a message to his leaders that we do not intend to make our home here; and that we will pay for our passage through their land. We do not wish to make war with them, but if that is their decision, we will kill many of their warriors whether we are victorious or are defeated. We will ask him to arrange a meeting between his leaders and ours. I think this is why Owl told me last night that we are to go north for a time.

I pray that it is a temporary diversion, and that we will soon resume our eastward journey."

Tall Bones gave a nod of assent, and with a clenched fist, struck his chest in a sign of obedience. "I will see that he is fed well before he is escorted beyond our sentries, Mikko. Alone, they would kill him before he could get past them." Tall Bones saw Mushroom hovering near Butterfly's fire and called him over. "Mushroom, tell Still Water that we will once again need her services. Have her come to my tent. Oh, and tell Bright Star to bring her healing supplies to my tent as well."

Bright Star, the old Medicine Woman, was outside her clan's tent dropping heated stones into a large clay pot when Mushroom and Still Water arrived.

With an air of importance Mushroom announced to her, "Grandmother, Tall Bones needs you right away. He said for you to bring your healing bag with you."

The old woman looked up and nodded. She placed a bark lid over her pot and gathered up her bag. "Is Tall Bones sick?" she asked, with a concerned look on her face.

"No, Elder, I think it is for the prisoner. They are going to free him so he can carry a message back to his people." Mushroom was about to say something more, but realized that he had just told more than he should have, since he had overheard the two men's conversation, but had not been a part of it.

The three of them walked to where Tall Bones was standing in front of the bound captive.

The man was alert and staring defiantly at the war chief, as if he expected to be killed at any moment. When he saw Still Water he spoke to her in his strange language, looked over at Mushroom, then resumed his determined stare into the war chief's eyes.

"He asked if the boy wanted to watch to see how a man dies, War Leader," Still Water translated.

Tall Bones gave the man an evil smile as he drew his shiny metal knife from its rawhide sheath. It had been acquired at a great price—the lives of many of his warriors who were killed in the battle with the Spanish.

The prisoner's eyes widened a bit, but he regained his composure quickly.

"Tell him, Still Water, that not only will the boy watch, but he will be the one to use my knife." Tall Bones handed the gleaming blade to Mushroom.

Mushroom took the knife, which was nearly half his height, with a troubled look on his face—a face that he saw reflected in the shiny metal blade as he held it out in front of him.

"War Chief … I can't …" he stammered, just as Stands Alone arrived with two of his warriors.

Tall Bones gave the Mikko a carefully concealed wink, then told Mushroom, "Go behind him, little warrior, as if you are going to slit his throat. Take your time, and then cut only his ropes."

Mushroom laughed insanely out of relief, which the prisoner misinterpreted and thought, *I was ready to face my death as a warrior, but to have it taken by a mere child is too much. What kind of people are these Muskogee?* For the first time since his capture, fear showed on his face, as he wondered if his souls could ever rest if it was a child who took his life.

Mushroom was so relieved that he would not have to kill the man that he played his part almost too well. Standing behind the captive he could see the expressions on the faces of his Chief and War Leader, and they were having difficulty concealing their laughter. He took the man's hair and pulled his head back until it touched the stake. He passed the knife in front of the captive's face, then, waiting a few heartbeats, Mushroom gave a great shout and with one slash cut the ropes.

The man fell facedown at the feet of the two leaders. As he tried to get to his feet, his arms failed him from being tied behind him all night. He managed to pull himself into a sitting position, then turned his head toward Mushroom and said something to him.

Still Water interpreted, "He said that the young warrior needs more practice with the knife if he was aiming at his throat."

Stands Alone was still laughing as he helped the man up. He

turned to Still Water. "Tell him that all my warriors, even the young ones like Mushroom here, are well-trained with all their weapons. He lives because I wish him to." Then he turned to Bright Star. "Tend to his wounds, and see that he is well fed. I will meet with him later and we will talk." As he turned to walk away he said to Tall Bones, "Guard him well, War Leader. I do not want him escaping before we give him our message for his leaders."

Mushroom stayed with the two women as they tended to the man. He asked Still Water to ask him his name.

After a brief exchange of words, she said, "His name is Lusa-Oka. In his language it means Black Water. He thanks you for not tormenting him along with the other boys yesterday, and for not cutting his throat today."

Mushroom looked at him and smiled sheepishly, then lightly touched the raw flesh on the man's wrists where the rope had been. He took some of the greasy salve from Bright Star's bowl and rubbed it into the wounds. "I am Ekana-Cale," he told Black Water. "I do not yet have my man name."

Black Water looked at him and said with Still Water's help, "In my language your name means Earth Fruit. Like the ones that have no roots." The similarity of meanings between the languages was apparent. A mushroom was certainly an earth fruit that had no roots.

As Stands Alone and Tall Bones approached them, Black Water once again tried to stand. With the help of Mushroom, he got to his feet and faced them.

With Still Water interpreting, he said, "I thank you for sparing my life, Mikko Thlaco, but I think there is more to that than kindness. I will not be your slave, so if that is your plan, you may as well kill me now."

"I have no need for a slave who would kill me in my sleep, Black Water. What I do need is for you to deliver a message and an offer to your leaders. First, tell them that we spared your life because of your courage under torture. The offer I wish to convey is this ... I request a peaceful meeting with your chief and war leader.

We will meet on neutral ground, and we will come with open hands. Will you do this thing for the sake of both our tribes?" Stands Alone waited for the message to be relayed, and watched the man's expression as he listened to Still Water's interpretation.

Black Water, although still unable to fully use his arms, made the universal signal of agreement. He struck his fist to his chest and proclaimed, "I will do as you request, wise Mikko of the Muskogee, but I cannot guarantee how my people will respond. We may have to face each other again in battle. I am but a warrior, but a warrior who follows his leader first, and his heart second."

"Then get some rest, young warrior Black Water, for tomorrow you will be escorted beyond my sentries. We will not want to wait long for your leader's reply." Stands Alone turned and walked away.

Two days passed before they heard the cry, "A runner comes!" echoing through the camp. Stands Alone came out of his tent and met Tall Bones, who was already outside. Blue Jay, the young warrior runner, approached the two and stood with his hands on his knees, trying to catch his breath. Tall Bones handed him a gourd of water and waited for the message, trying not to appear impatient.

"The captive … the one we freed, Mikko … he returned to us this morning. He was carrying the white feather. They have agreed to a meeting with you," Blue Jay gasped. "He said to bring Still Water, although his war chief may speak some of our language. They will meet you in two days at a place near where we met the captive this morning. I know the place, Mikko."

"Then we must leave at sunup tomorrow," Stands Alone said. "Get some rest, Blue Jay. You must lead us there, but at a much slower pace than you traveled today." He took a deep breath and appeared to be lost in thought.

This is a dangerous thing that we are about to do. If it is a trick, my tribe could lose its chief and its war leader; but it is a risk worth taking. There are others who can lead, he told himself, trying hard to believe it. He climbed to the top of the small mesa and stood, watching the sunset. He heard a noise behind him and turned to see Tall Bones scrambling up the last incline.

"May I join you, Mikko?"

"Yes, old friend. I would appreciate the company. Are we doing the right thing?" Stands Alone looked deeply into the eyes of his old friend and war leader.

"I hope so, my chief. We have little other choice, since we are the ones who asked for the meeting. We will not have enough warriors with us if it is a trick," Tall Bones replied somberly.

"We would have too few warriors if we took our entire army with us. Owl told me that we should go north for a time. Perhaps this is what he had in mind."

The sky had darkened before the two men made their way back to camp. They immediately called the council of elders together, and made arrangements for leadership in their absence. To his son, the one who would be chief upon his death, he said, "If I do not return in three days, take our people east. Continue our journey."

He turned to Tall Bones' second-in-command, Oak Leaf, and said, "If we do not return from this meeting, you must take no revenge. Our peoples' survival is more important. Save our warriors to defend the people along the journey. We cannot win a war with these Alabamas now. Later, after you have established a town and rebuilt our resources, you may take revenge."

Butterfly had prepared a special meal for her husband that night.

Mushroom had killed a jackrabbit earlier in the afternoon and had brought it to her. "Grandfather likes long-ears, and this one showed courage. He stopped running and looked at me just before I hit him with my throwing-stick." He looked at her sheepishly and added, "And I thanked his spirit, Grandmother. I did not forget."

"I will tell him it is from you, Mushroom, and I will prepare it very special for him." Butterfly had the meal ready when Stands Alone entered their tent. "Mushroom wanted you to have the long-ears he killed today. He said it showed great courage," she told him as she placed the bowls in front of her husband.

After they had eaten, she prepared their sleeping mats and said, "Jaguar came to me last night. He showed me a great city that you will build on a large river. The ones you are to meet are not to be trusted, but they will make an alliance with you."

"Jaguar still favors you, my Butterfly?"

"The Gift was not for me, my husband, but yes, he still comes to me in dreams."

Stands Alone put his arms around her. "And Owl wanted us to go to the north. Maybe this is what he meant—for us to have this meeting. There is a large river to the east that we must cross. Perhaps that is where the town you were shown will be built."

They made the journey to the sentries' furthest outpost just before nightfall.

Two Crows, the lieutenant in charge of the outpost, met Stands Alone and his party as soon as they arrived. "Greetings, Mikko, War Leader and Still Water. Was your journey without difficulty?"

"Yes, but Tall Bones walks very fast. He kept leaving us behind in his haste to get here," Stands Alone replied as he surveyed the sentry camp. Everything was in order. The discipline of a Muskogee sentry outpost was militarily precise. Scouts were reporting in and out, some taking their turn at sleeping, while others were receiving orders and being dispatched to their stations. Tall Bones had taught them well.

Stands Alone looked intently at Two Crows and said, "At the meeting tomorrow there will be only Tall Bones, Still Water and myself. We will carry no weapons. If this is a trick and we come under attack, you must not retaliate. You must gather your warriors and return immediately to our people. It will require all of our warriors to protect the others and get them moving to the east. The lives of our women and children – and our Nation – are our first responsibility."

Two Crows gave an affirmative nod to his chief and struck his chest in understanding.

Throughout the night, the scouts had watched the planned meeting place intensely, and they had observed no activity there. It was early morning when they approached the agreed-upon location. They stopped on a small hill overlooking the river and scanned the area. Soon a canoe could be seen making its way across the fog-shrouded water. As it neared, they could tell it was Black Water. A lance with a white feather protruded from the bow of the canoe.

"This is it, my friends. Whether we die today or form an alliance, it is a beautiful day to do it," Stands Alone told Tall Bones and Still Water.

They walked openly and proudly toward their former captive. Materializing out of the trees, several men of the Alabamas appeared and began setting up an open-air shelter for the meeting.

Two men, the Alabama chief and his war leader, were getting out of a large canoe manned by four paddlers.

Black Water said to Stands Alone, "There is no need for concern. Our leader and our war chief wish to meet you and hear your offer." Still Water translated his words to the two men with her.

"Tell him we come in peace as well, Still Water," Stands Alone replied, never breaking eye contact with Black Water, who took the feathered lance and planted it in front of the newly constructed shelter.

The chief of the Alabamas had apparently dressed in all his finery. He was a short, stocky man who carried himself with an air of arrogance. Never making eye contact with Stands Alone, he spoke directly to Still Water. "Tell your chief that I am Chatto Isto, ruler of this land. Ask him why I should allow this trespass to continue."

When Still Water repeated the words to Stands Alone, he replied, "Your name means Big Stone in our tongue. Is that close to your meaning?"

The other man looked surprised, and said, "Yes, that is my

name meaning. What is your name and clan?"

Still Water answered for him and told him, "Our Mikko is Stands Alone. He is of the Wind Clan. All of our leaders are chosen from that clan."

That seemed to have an effect on Big Stone, who said, "My father was of the Wind Clan, but we no longer follow that old tradition. Let us sit and discuss this situation."

The two chiefs with their war leaders entered the shelter and sat on furs around the small central fire.

Tall Bones removed a pipe from his pack and loaded it with the dried herbal mixture that he always carried. He took two small twigs and picked up a glowing ember from the fire and lit the pipe. He passed it first to Stands Alone who took a deep draw and blew the smoke to the four directions. He then passed it to Big Stone as he said, "Let us first smoke the pipe of peace, Chatto Isto."

The smaller man took the pipe and drew deeply, repeating the blowing of the smoke to the four directions, then passed it to his war leader. "This is Nokose Ili, my war chief. Does his name have a meaning in your language?"

Still Water, who was standing behind her chief, smiled and translated his words.

Stands Alone laughed. "In our language it means Bear Paw, or the footprint of a bear."

The Alabama war chief blew the smoke from his lungs and turned his back to them. On it was a birthmark that looked like the track of a bear's paw.

"It seems our languages are not that different after all, Big Stone. Could it be that our hearts are as similar?"

"Too similar if we both intend on using the same hunting grounds," Big Stone replied. Only then did he make brief eye contact with Stands Alone.

"We are only travelers through your land, Big Stone. We have no desire to settle here. Our journey takes us much further. Our destination is yet unknown, even to me."

"Black Water told me the same thing, Stands Alone. He

learned many things during his short visit as your guest," Big Stone said. Trying to appear casual, he added, "He also told me something about a new food that you possess. Tell me more of this."

"It is called a-chee by the original inhabitants of the land we left. It is a grain that can be made into bread or gruel. It can be prepared in many ways. It is a gift of the Sun God."

"Then that is what I demand as payment for crossing my land. That and someone who can teach our people how to plant and harvest this food," he said with finality. He looked pleased with himself as he took the pipe and re-lit it with satisfaction.

"A wise decision, Big Stone. A-chee, or maize as we call it, has changed every Nation that has honored it and used it properly. People who do this no longer have the need to follow the game to have enough food. I will ask for a volunteer from my people to remain with you for one season of planting and one of harvesting."

Still Water, who was standing behind her chief, offered quietly, "I will remain, Mikko, if it is agreeable with you. I have neither a husband nor children to leave behind. I speak their language and I know the ways of maize."

Stands Alone turned and looked at her in admiration. "Are you sure you want to do this? You are young enough to take another husband, and I have seen several of our unmarried warriors look in your direction."

"I will do it for our people, my chief. I have no fear of these people," she said with what she hoped sounded like sincerity.

"Then tell Big Stone what we are saying, my brave Still Water. Tell him also that I will have many baskets of maize sent to him within two days. There is time left in this season for one crop to be harvested. It is a bit late, but it should be enough to get a good seed crop for the next season."

After he heard the proposition, Big Stone stood abruptly and gave a grunted assent, and with very little formality, left the shelter and walked toward his waiting canoe.

Black Water remained behind and said to Stands Alone, "I will see that Still Water is treated well, Mikko, as payment for you sparing my life. My chief does not allow men prisoners to live and the women are kept as slaves. You are an unusual man, and I offer you my respect."

"You are a brave and honorable man, Black Water. I thank you for watching over Still Water. She will be no man's slave," Stands Alone replied to him. "I expect for her to return to our people safely."

"How much further is it to the big river from our camp?" Stands Alone asked Tall Bones when they arrived back at the sentries' outpost.

"For the entire camp, about two days' hard march, Mikko. That is, if you mean to the east as we were traveling."

"I think we should find a safe crossing and get our people across this river as soon as possible," Stands Alone said. "I do not trust this Big Stone. His eyes never met mine as we were talking. His words were like smoke in the wind."

"I agree. His war chief was the same. I do not trust them. I am glad you feel the same," Tall Bones said with resignation. "As soon as we get back I will get my scouts together from the east and plan our departure. I will have Two Crows remain here with the sentries for one day, then follow us by one day."

They reached the river called Yazoo on the third day following Stands Alone's return. Finding a ford to the north had taken an extra day of march, but it was a fortunate delay. On the east bank was a perfect place for a town to be established. There was fertile ground for raising crops, especially for the corn.

They followed their age-old custom of river crossing. First to cross, led by Stands Alone, was the Wind Clan, from which all tribal leaders were selected. Then came the Bear and Jaguar Clans. The army was the last to cross, led by the war chief, Tall Bones.

When all the people had made the crossing, Stands Alone told them that this was to be their home for a few seasons, until they could replenish their stores of maize.

"This is good land. The river will provide fish, and it will offer the means to trade with others. We will establish a great town here. In time, there will be those among us who wish to continue the journey to the home of the Sun God. The Muskogee will become the greatest Nation in this new land."

At that moment, Mushroom came running up to Stands Alone and Butterfly. "My sister Wekiwa-Chee, her baby is coming! She almost had it in the river."

"This is a good omen for the people," Stands Alone said to Butterfly.

"Yes, and if this is the girl-child that Raven dreamed of, she will carry on the Gift for our people. Jaguar told her that she will be the most powerful Singer born since my mother Night Flower came to this land. That was Raven's Power Dream of the night before we began this journey. It is truly an omen."

Night Flower had been a young maiden when the first of the Muskogee had crossed the big water to come to this land. She had foreseen the coming of the white-skinned ones.

"The white faces will destroy the ones who were first in this land," she had proclaimed. It was only after her death, when the Spanish invaded and scattered the Aztec people, that her words were remembered.

Butterfly was the first to get to her granddaughter. She took charge immediately, issuing orders for a temporary shelter and for water to be boiled. She gathered her packs and selected the herbs and amulets she would need. "Mushroom, go find your mother and tell her that her grandchild is being born, maybe before she can get here. Hurry!"

"Yes, Grandmother. She is on the bank of the river!" Mushroom called out over his shoulder as he ran. He did not want to miss the birth of his niece, or leave his sister.

The girl-child was the first to be born in what was to be the Muskogees' new town. Construction began immediately, and soon the people had settled into a peaceful life. They raised their crops and their children and within only a few years had grown to be a large town. Within those few years, they had established trade up and down the river, and they thrived.

One spring day, three summers after they had built their town, a canoe appeared on the river. One of Tall Bones' warriors saw it first and recognized the markings as those of the Alabamas. He sent word to the war chief and Tall Bones met it at the landing. It was Still Water and the Alabama warrior Lusa-Oka—Black Water.

"Greetings, Still Water. We welcome your return," Tall Bones said.

"Greetings, war chief. It is good to return to my people." Still Water climbed out of the canoe. "I come with my husband, Lusa-Oka, and, as you can see, our child." she indicated her belly, which was heavy with child.

"Ah, so our former guest wishes to again experience the hospitality of the Muskogee. Welcome to our town, Black Water," he said as he offered his hand in friendship.

"I greet you, war chief, and also my old friend, Earth Fruit," Black Water replied as he saw Mushroom running to meet them.

Mushroom went first to Still Water and gave her a hug, grinning at Black Water the whole time. When he turned to Black Water, he pointed at Tall Bones' knife. Laughing, he made a throat-slashing gesture with his hand.

"Do not remind me, Mushroom. You were much smaller then. Now you are tall enough to reach my throat with that knife." Black Water chuckled.

"Did you teach the Alabamas of the maize, Daughter?" Tall Bones asked, still laughing at Mushroom's humor.

"Yes, war chief, but they make more war than maize, I am sorry to say," Still Water answered.

Black Water looked at Tall Bones intently. "I have much to say to you, war chief, but later, with your chief present, if that is acceptable. For now, I will just say that I can no longer follow Big Stone. Evil spirits took away his souls. I place myself at your service."

"I knew you were a man of honor, Black Water. We will talk of this later, with Stands Alone. Now, we must get you and Still Water settled. You have learned our language very well."

"Still Water is a good teacher, war chief. It was from her that I learned that the way of my people is not the way that I wish for our child."

What Black Water had to tell them later was disturbing. Big Stone had gone completely mad. He was making war even against other Alabama tribes. He had begun a religion based on human sacrifice, and there were even stories of him and his priests eating the flesh of their victims.

Still Water added, "He is planning an attack on this town, Stands Alone. I do not know when, but he will attack. It has become his way."

Stands Alone took immediate action. Leaving only enough warriors at their town, Tall Bones led his army across the river and then turned north. His surprise attack on Big Stone's camp was a complete and successful victory. The women of his own tribe killed Big Stone as he tried to escape the camp dressed as a woman. All the women and children were spared, and taken into the Muskogee Nation; the warriors who escaped with their lives fled to the west and south. Their reign of terror was over.

Soon there were so many Muskogee people in the town that some of them, feeling that same old urge that their grandparents had felt, left to establish their own town, still seeking the Place of the Rising Sun.

They crossed another river to the east, called the Chatta-Hochee, the River of the Marked Stones. Among the ones who settled there were Wekiwa-Chee, her husband and her young daughter, who had been born on the day they crossed the Yazoo. Her name was Paneta-Semoli, the Wild Dancer.

Stands Alone, although now quite old, continued his dream quest, and built another town, then another, always to the east, until the Muskogee were the largest Nation in the entire southeast.

In the town on the Chatta-Hochee, the girl-child, Paneta-Semoli, the great-granddaughter of Stands Alone and Butterfly, became a woman. She was known throughout the whole land as the greatest of all the Spirit Singers.

"And that is the story of our people, and how they came to this land, Pu-Can," Locha-Luste said, his eyes showing the lateness of the hour.

Chatto-Nokose, who had also offered some highlights of his own in the telling of the story, appeared to be as tired as his brother. "You young people leave us old ones now to our dreams and our blankets. That story always makes me want the old ways to return to the time before the white men and his guns and fences and broken promises."

Pu-Can and Tysoyaha embraced the two elders, thanked them for the remembering, and left the chikee, heading for the river. The moon lit their path as they made their way down the hill to the now-familiar boulder.

They sat silently, watching its reflection in the water and thought of the great people from their past, whose struggles and determination had made their existence possible. They also felt the weight of responsibility that fell to them to continue the traditions and culture that had begun so many years ago.

CHAPTER 14

"Wow!" Alex exclaimed. "First we're listening to you read about what Keechie told you about Granny Boo and her life, and now Granny Boo is getting told about *her* ancestors. I need to keep notes to keep all these people and time periods straight. Did Child of the Sun ever come here to live with her?"

"As far as I know, he never did actually stay with her for more than a few weeks at a time, but the next installment explains that a bit more. You'll have to wait to find out," Brian teased. "That last part about Stands Alone and his people up to Wild Dancer I learned from Keechie over a period of several years."

"She must have had a great memory," Alex mused. "All those details about their journey, and the conversations—"

"Not all of that came from Keechie," Brian explained. "Some of it came from my studies of the early migrations. Like the part about Cortez. They didn't know his name, but it is known that he was the one who invaded the territory."

"What about Pu-Can and Tysoyaha at the Green Corn Festival? That didn't come from history books."

"I really picked Keechie's brain on that part. I was working on my thesis at the time, and studying the migration stories of the Creeks, and all I had to work from were the legends and myths of the Muskogee. Usually when asked about their origins, the ones remaining on the reservations would simply point to the west and say, 'we came from over there'. Keechie filled in the gaps."

"I wonder how the people in Indian Territory are handling the situation now," Mary spoke up. "I'll bet they're better off than most, since they have had to do for themselves mostly anyway."

Brian nodded. "I would hope so, but they've been adapting to the white man's ways for so long, only a few of them remember and hold to the old ways. I worry about them a lot, since I know some of them, especially Long Walker's family. They were the ones related to Keechie."

It was late when Brian finished reading from his journal, and they soon settled into their blankets for the night. Brian went to sleep thinking about the friends he had made in Indian Territory. He wondered if any of the ones living there now would even have heard of "Yoholo", or Loud Speaker, the name given to him by the tribal elders when he and Keechie had visited them all those years ago.

Mary was the first to awaken the next morning. She loved to sit on the rocks outside the entrance and watch the sunrise while she had her first cup of coffee. This morning she wanted time to think about the recurring dream she had been having.

It was something about the Puma Man and plants, and her lifelong ability of "knowing" a plant's properties and uses, even if she had never seen or used that particular plant before. The Puma Man seemed to be trying to tell her how this "Gift" came to be. It had something to do with the spirit world and shamanism, with images of old Indian medicine men and women. Her own Cherokee grandmother appeared many times, and that was the strangest part of all. She was always holding a rolled parchment scroll and was trying to unroll it. She could see strange hieroglyphic characters on it, but it rolled back up before she could see it clearly. She attributed those images to her becoming so involved with the stories that Brian was reading almost nightly now.

But there was something more—something deeper that touched her soul. "Maybe Granny was a witch," she said to the sky. *I have always felt this connection with plants,* she thought, *but then I have never had to rely on it for survival. It was always for the culinary herbs and spices. I never related it to the spirit world, or shamanism. I never knew of the Puma Man until Brian told me about him. Can I trust a vision over scientific books?*

There was one way to find out, but she wasn't sure it would work. Usually her "Gift" occurred when she encountered the plant or herb, when somehow she knew its properties and uses. But what if the need came first and she needed to know which plant fulfilled that need?

So she planned to test that very thing. She would find a medical condition among the four of them, and then meditate on it. If a certain plant was "shown" to her, then she could look it up in the herb guide to see if it agreed. All she needed now was to come up with a real need among them, and she thought she knew just the patient.

Maurice had been complaining of mouth ulcers and sore gums. As soon as he was awake, she would ask him to help in her experiment. If it worked, he would benefit from it. If it failed, no harm would have been done.

Everyone else was beginning to stir inside the cave, so Mary went in and began preparing breakfast. While they were eating, Mary asked Maurice about his mouth.

"Hit sho be sore, Mary. Hit ain't my teeth, though. Dey's alright. I juss got dese places on de inside o' my cheeks, an' my gums hurt."

"I may be able to help, but I don't know for sure. Would you be willing to try a cure, even if it sounds strange?" Mary asked, sounding uncertain.

"Sho, I try anythang. Hit cain't get no wuss, I don' thank. Unless you gonna pull my teeth out er sompin' awful lak dat," he added, laughing.

"I wouldn't do that. I just want to see if there's an herbal remedy that will help, that's all," she said, wondering what the next step should be.

When they finished breakfast, Alex began clearing the plates and cups and washing them.

Mary looked at Maurice's mouth and tried to concentrate on the condition alone, and not think about anything else. In her mind's eye, she saw blackberries. Not only the fruit, but the entire plant, right down to its roots. "This just isn't working," she said. "All I can think of is blackberry bushes. We saw a lot of those the other day. Let me try again."

"Blackberries?" Alex asked. "I read something about them in the book. Wait, I'll get it." She went to her pack and retrieved *The Field Guide to Herbs*, looking for the reference to blackberries. "Here it is, Mom. Listen to this." She read aloud: "*Blackberry is edible and medicinal. Used extensively by the Native American tribes, it had many surprising uses. The leaf is more commonly used as a medicinal herb, but the root also has medicinal value. Externally, they are used to treat sore throats, mouth ulcers and gum inflammations. A decoction of the leaves is useful as a gargle in treating thrush and also makes a good general mouthwash.* Wow, Mom, how did you know that?"

Mary was stunned and didn't have an answer, except for, "I have no idea, but I think the Puma Man or my grandma may have something to do with it. All I know about blackberries is they're good to eat, and they have these really nasty thorns. I think we should gather some of the roots though, don't you think?"

"The leaves and roots both, according to the book, but I still want to know how you knew that," Alex said. "And there are blackberry vines right here within twenty feet of the cave. I'll go dig some up right now."

"I heps ya, Alex," Maurice offered. "Dose briars be mean. I'll get my gloves an' a shovel an' be right behind you."

Mary picked up the herb book to see if it gave any instructions on preparing the roots and leaves. It was good for many things, but the only recipe was a tea, to be taken internally. Since she wanted a mouthwash, she figured that it could be made much stronger, since she wasn't planning on Maurice swallowing any of it. She put on a pot of water so it would be boiling when Alex and Maurice returned.

Alex washed the roots carefully and chopped them, handing them to Mary. "Tell me when you have enough," Alex said. "We can save some for tomorrow, and there's plenty more where these came from."

Mary added them to the water until she felt that she had enough. She put some of the leaves in as well. "We'll let that steep for a while, then when it's cooled enough, you can just rinse your mouth with it," she told Maurice. "Hold it in your mouth as long as you can, then spit it out, unless you have diarrhea, of course. The book says it's good for that too." She smiled while making a mental note to retain that little bit of knowledge.

Maurice took a cup of the concoction and went outside. He took a large mouthful and swished it around. He let it stay as long as he could, then spat it out. "Hit ain't too bad. Hit kinda bitter, but if hit helps, I kin do dat all day long."

They all tasted the brew. "It seems to have a lot of tannic acid in it, you know, like tea," Brian mused. "It dries out your mouth like that, anyway. What gave you the idea?" he asked his wife.

"Just a hunch, Brian. Just a hunch."

"Your grandmother was Cherokee, right? A Medicine Woman at that."

"She never actually said she was a Medicine Woman for the Cherokee, and she married my grandfather and went to live with him when she was very young. He was a fur trader, according to the family stories. He had to pay a high price for her though, and that was because of her knowledge of medicinal plants. She told me once that she thought she had been adopted into the tribe since she didn't look like a Cherokee. All the other children were taller than she was. She was a tiny woman, much like you described Keechie."

"When was your grandmother born? Did she know the year or anything?" Brian asked, suddenly remembering a story Keechie had told him once. *This would be just too coincidental for normal circumstances, but when the Puma Man is involved, anything is within the realm of possibility.*

"She didn't know when she was born exactly, but she thought she was close to fifteen when she married Grandpa, and that was around 1928 or so. That would make her year of birth close to around 1914."

He quickly did the math in his head. If Keechie had been born in 1898 like they had figured, she would have been close to fourteen or fifteen when the event she had told him about had occurred. That would have been near 1913 or 1914.

Mary frowned in concern. "What is it? You've got that strange look in your eyes again. Why are you asking about Granny's birth date? I was just thinking about her this morning, and this dream I keep having about her."

Brian shook his head. "It's probably nothing, just a strange thought I had about your grandmother, and a story Keechie told me once. It's one I never wrote down or even told you about. In fact, I think I'm the only one Keechie ever told. She said she never even told her mother or Granny Boo."

"Well, you have to tell it now, Dad!" Alex exclaimed from behind him. She and Maurice had been listening the whole time, caught up in the conversation between him and Mary.

"Okay, I don't think Keechie would mind, but it probably has nothing to do with us. It was just a weird thought I had. Gather around and I'll tell you what I know before we get going on our visit to the bee tree so Maurice can show us how to get the honey. But first, I have to get something from the storeroom." He returned in a few minutes with a rolled-up parchment, tied with a piece of ribbon.

Mary almost dropped her cup of coffee, staring open-mouthed at the scroll. It looked exactly like the one her grandmother had been trying to show her in the dream. "Brian, before you unroll that paper, I can tell you what is on it. It looks like hieroglyphics, doesn't it? I'm almost afraid to know."

Brian stared at Mary with a puzzled expression, and then looked at the rolled-up parchment. "Have I shown this to you already? I don't remember if I did."

"No, I have never seen that before, except in my dream. But it's the same – right down to the color of ribbon."

"I'll open it after I tell y'all this story, but what you just said almost confirms what I've been suspecting, and why I asked about your grandmother's birth date. It is just so 'far out'… is that the right term, Alex? But it would sure explain a lot about your Gifts," Brian said, nodding first at his wife, then at his daughter. "It appears that the Puma Man has been busy arranging all the details."

"I think we're about to hear the drums again," Alex spoke solemnly. "Tell the story already."

"Okay, here it is. One day, Keechie and I were in the storeroom, and she was telling me the stories behind some of the relics we were looking at." He held up the parchment roll and continued, "I picked this up and asked her about it. This is the story she told me…"

"Dat be a Cherokee thang, Brine. Hit ain't sompin' I'se proud of. I keeps it t' `mind me of a bad time."

"May I open it?" I asked her.

"Sho you kin. Hit jus' some Cherokee Injun writin'."

I carefully unrolled it and she was right. It was covered with handwritten characters. The ink was smeared in places, but it was entirely legible – if I could have read it. I asked her if I could make a copy of it because it looked like the Cherokee alphabet writing that Sequoyah had invented over a hundred years ago.

"'Y kin keep de real thang. Hit done serve hit's purpose." Then she became silent and stared toward the wall of relics, but not appearing to be looking at them.

"What was its purpose, Keechie? If you don't mind my asking."

She looked at me intently, then said in a low voice, "'Member I tol' you dat de Gift could be used fer bad thangs, well as good 'uns?"

"I remember. Granny Boo taught you to use your Gift for only doing good for people."

"Well, dis one time I used it to witch a man. Hit wuz de man dat wrote dat paper in yo hands. You needs t' have somepin dat belonged t' da one you be a'witchin'. I shoulda burned hit, but I din't."

"He must have been a bad man for you to want to put a bad spell on him."

"Brine, I nevva tolt you dis befo', but when I wuz juss a li'l gurl, juss havin' my firs' moontime, I wuz up at de women's cabin, all by myseff, an' dis Cherokee man—guess he wuz out a'huntin' er sompin'—foun' me up dere. He hel' me down an' took me lak a man take his wife. Den he took me off wit' him. I'se gone a whole year, fo' I ran away from him, an' made it back hyer."

"He raped you and kidnapped you, Keechie?" I asked, horrified.

"He sho did. Put a baby in me too, he did. One day he caught me tryin' t' run away wit' my baby. He beat me 'til I pass out. When I woke up, he done kilt de baby an' burred it. He showed me de grave. He say dat what gonta happen t' me iffen I tries t' run away agin. Dat be why I witched 'im. He killed dat po li'l girl baby juss t' get back at me. He wuz a bad man. I wanted t' kill 'im, but he wuz too big."

"You had a baby?" I asked in disbelief. "You never told me that."

"I tries t' not t' thank on hit," she said sadly. "Dat wuz de onliest time I evva knowed a man in dat way."

"How did you get away from him after that?"

"A coupla days later, while I'se cookin' his food. I put a li'l sompin' extra in his tea so he go t' sleep real soun' lak. While he wuz a' sleepin', I took dat paper o' his an' leff, hopin' dat he die. Den I made it back hyer. I nevva even tol' Mam er Granny Boo dat I done had a baby. Granny Boo always wanted me t' have a baby girl, so's I pass on de Gift. If I tol' her I done had dat girl, an' dat she wuz kilt, it wouda broke `er heart. Den she probly start a war wit' de whole Cherokee tribe."

"And that's the story. I remember it like it just happened," Brian said as he carefully unrolled the parchment and showed it to them. "I never did get it translated." Before he even opened the scroll, Mary already knew what she would see. Her grandmother had already shown her the same scroll.

When she was able to speak again, she asked, "How are we ever going to get that writing translated? I've got a feeling that the truth in all this is in that document." In her heart she knew that what they all now suspected was the truth: she and Alex were Keechie's direct descendants.

"I still don't understand what that has to do with us," Alex murmured. "If he killed the baby."

"What if he didn't kill Keechie's baby?" Brian proposed. "What would have been the point? What if he lied to Keechie to scare her into obeying him, and the baby wound up being raised as a Cherokee? Remember, Keechie said that she only saw the grave, not the baby. The time period is almost perfectly aligned with your mom's grandma. And she was a Cherokee, and she told your mom that she wasn't like them. She always thought that she was adopted."

Alex gasped. "If that's true, then that would make Keechie my great-grandmother!"

"Great-great-grandmother, and my great-grandmother," Mary said with as much astonishment in her voice as Alex. "And it wouldn't surprise me a bit, knowing how the Puma Man works; and remember, Keechie had already predicted that I would have a girl-child with the Gift."

"Puma Man done tol' her dat!" Brian carefully re-rolled the parchment and tied it with the ribbon. "We'll find a way to get it translated, honey. Somehow, we will find a way. There are Cherokees still in North Georgia who never left for the reservations. Eventually we'll find someone who can read this script. I promise you. Now, is everyone ready for a trip to the bee tree?"

"I wants t' get somma dat honey, Brine. I gots evvathang I needs all ready," Maurice said. He had wanted to go back to the bee tree for the honey ever since Alex had discovered the tree, and he had already spent several hours making himself a smoker out of a used gallon can. It needed to hold smoldering pine straw and have a way of pushing the smoke out. He finally came up with the solution by soldering a piece of copper tubing to the can into which he could blow. Another piece of tubing at the top of the can directed the resulting smoke out of the can. It was primitive, but seemed to work well enough to get the job done.

By mid-afternoon they were all on their way back to the bee tree. Maurice wore several layers of clothing and Mary helped him tie the wrists and ankles to keep the bees from getting inside. She had an old hat and upon that, she placed mosquito netting, tucking it in at the neck. By the time they got to the tree, he was sweating profusely.

"Nex' time I'se gonna wait 'til I gets t' da bee tree 'fo I gets all dressed up!" he panted.

He had brought some live coals from the fireplace, and placed one large one into the bottom of the can. He added pine straw on top of the coal, and then capped the can. After a minute, smoke was seeping out of the top spout. He blew into the bottom tube and tested his invention. It worked! Smoke billowed from the top tube. He waved everyone away and approached the tree. Mary passed him a plastic pail and a long knife for gathering the honeycomb.

He placed the upper tube into the hole in the tree and began blowing into the other one. In a few minutes the bees had settled down, and he reached inside. He came out with a large section of comb that was literally dripping with honey.

A few bees landed on his arms and shirt, and a few more were circling his head, but there was no major swarming or vicious attacks. He blew more smoke into the opening and continued to withdraw honeycomb after honeycomb until the pail was nearly full.

Maurice shook off the few bees from his clothing and moved away from the tree.

Brian helped him remove the netting from around his head, shaking off a few more bees in the process. "Are you all right, man?" he asked.

"I sho is. Only got stung once't, I thank. Bit me on da wrist, but I used t' dat. Honeybee stangs ain't nuttin lak wasps er hornets. Reckon dat's 'nuff honey? I don' wanna take more'n we need. De bees need it, an' dey'll leave iffen we take it all."

Mary took the pail. "We have enough honey to last us for months," she said. "And we can use the wax from the comb for a lot of things. You did good, my friend." She covered the pail with a cloth and suggested that they hurry back to the cave. The honey needed to be placed into jars quickly to preserve it.

They didn't have a honey extractor, but she planned on leaving a piece of the comb in each jar anyway. Since it was still several hours before sundown, they had time to make a quick detour to the cornfield. There they found a few remaining snow peas and a large quantity of running beans that were ready for picking. They all joined in and gathered all they found.

The corn, which Brian checked closely, was within a few days of being fully ripe. Just in time for the full moon and their own Green Corn Festival.

Mary already had water boiling in the fireplace for sterilizing the Mason jars. She and Alex placed the jars into the water for a few minutes, and then they filled them with the honey. When they were finished, they had filled sixteen of the jars with wild honey.

"We have sixteen pints or two gallons of honey, thanks to Maurice, and there's still enough to have some tonight. I'm going to make biscuits," Mary announced happily.

They were a joyful bunch that night - fresh ham and green beans topped off with biscuits and honey just seems to have that effect on people.

After dinner, Brian went to the storeroom to listen in on the shortwave for news of Columbus and the rioting. There was no radio traffic from any of the bands, so he switched it off, not knowing whether to feel relieved or worried.

On his way back to the main room, he grabbed the journal he had been reading. Earlier at the cornfield, when he had mentioned their planned Green Corn Festival, Alex had asked for more of the story tonight. She was becoming more interested in the story of Granny Boo than she had with Keechie when he had read that one to her. That was over a year ago—just weeks before the terrorist attacks and their sudden, unplanned escape to the cave. Now with the distinct possibility that Keechie and Granny Boo were related to her, she wanted to learn everything she could about them.

They gathered in front of the ancient fireplace and Brian began reading …

CHAPTER 15

Pu-Can's people had already gathered their belongings and assembled at the river. Those walking were the first to leave, and they were glad to be returning to their homes. Several marriage alliances were made, but only two of the young men would not be returning with them. They were going to live in their new wives' italwas, which fortunately were only a few miles upriver.

There were even more young men coming to live with them. Five of the girls had accepted proposals, and would be bringing their men home with them. They were also from nearby clans, so the alliances would benefit both italwas greatly. Three of the men had canoes, so they would not be walking with the others and could lighten the loads of some of those walking.

Pu-Can and Tysoyaha had their own canoe, and the gifts that she had received from Tysoyaha's father and uncle nearly filled it. The portage around the shoals would be a minor problem, with all the extra items to carry, but Tysoyaha thought they could drag the canoe with some of it still inside.

There were many of the people gathered at the river to bid them farewell, and many promises were made of visits and meeting again at the next Green Corn celebration. Tysoyaha's father and uncle were there, dressed in all their finery for the farewell.

It had been one of the best Green Corn Festivals that either of them could remember, and it seemed to be due, at least in part, to this remarkable young woman that Tysoyaha was marrying.

"She is truly a child of Kowakatcu, Brother," Chatto-Nokose said with a tone of reverence. "I have never felt so much Power in a person before. This union will bless our people. I believe that the Wild Dancer has returned."

Locha-Luste nodded, "I agree. The only time I have actually seen the Puma Man in his man form was when Pu-Can was present. If I had been alone I would probably have run away. It was the most Power I have ever felt."

The walking party had already left when the canoes got underway. They had agreed to meet at the base of the shoals and make camp for the night, with a few of the men who were walking waiting at the head of the shoals to help with the portage. It had been Pu-Can's idea, and she had asked Apelka-Haya for volunteers.

Pu-Can and Tysoyaha were the last to leave. Even with the load of gifts and supplies they were carrying, their canoe was the least loaded and would be the swiftest of the lot.

Pu-Can carried a very special clay pot between her feet that she checked periodically. It contained live coals from the New Fire. It would be used to re-light all the fires of her people. One other woman carried an identical pot in case anything happened to the other. When they arrived, all the fires would be extinguished, and then re-kindled with the coals Pu-Can carried. All the clans of the Muskogee Nation that were represented at the Festival would then share the same New Fire that she had started with Wild Dancer's fire drill. It was just one more way to maintain a connection between the various tribes. She opened the pot to let it breathe, and then added a few wood chips. To lose the Sacred Fire would be a very bad omen.

The other canoes were already pulled onto the sand above the shoals when they arrived. It was very close to sundown, so they quickly unloaded the heavier packs from their canoe. The young men who were going to help with the portage were there waiting for them. The rest of the walking party had gone on ahead to begin setting up the campsite at the base of the shoals.

It was dusk when they arrived at the campsite and beached their canoe, ready to be loaded the following morning. They could hear singing and loud whoops from the campsite. The Festival had rejuvenated the spirit of the people, and they were happy to be on their way home.

I too am happy, Pu-Can thought. *My mother and uncle will be joyful when I introduce them to Tysoyaha, especially when I tell them he is the son of a chief, and a member of the Wind Clan.*

Just as they entered the campsite, lightning flashed, illuminating the startled faces of the people. It was followed closely by a loud crash of thunder that echoed and rumbled for many heartbeats. The sky was nearly clear, with only a few clouds overhead in the darkening sky. The storm moved closer and the lightning and resulting thunder were occurring almost simultaneously. Yet there was no rain. The people were becoming afraid because the lightning appeared so close.

One of the old men who had been in one of the canoes went to the main campfire and called the people together. "Have no fear; it's only Thunder Helper laughing. Gather around and I will tell you of the Thunder Helper."

Pu-Can had heard this story many times, and she knew that it would be a good thing. Everyone loved a good story well told, and this old man was very good at it. They all gathered around the fire as he prepared to speak. He waited until there was complete silence, except for the booming of the thunder, and then he began...

In the days of First People, there was a boy whose parents died when he was very young. The other children wouldn't play with him so he took long walks in the forest. One day he was walking along a creek when he heard a great Thunder. When he looked up, he saw a Tie-snake and Thunder fighting.

The Tie-snake said to the boy, "Kill Thunder, and I will teach you about all the things that are under the earth."

The boy put an arrow into his bow and was about to shoot when Thunder spoke to him.

"Do not listen to the Tie-snake. I, Thunder, can help you to be brave, strong and wise. Shoot Tie-snake."

The boy shot Tie-Snake, who fell dead into the creek.

Thunder kept his promise and made him strong and wise, but said he must never tell anyone who gave him these gifts.

Soon the boy became the best hunter in the village. Because of his new wisdom the people listened when he spoke. One very cold time the people became hungry, for there was no meat or corn. Many days passed and the boy came to them and said, "Last night an owl talked to me. He told me to come to his tree for there was a bear sleeping in a hole in the ground nearby."

The young men laughed at him for saying that the owl spoke to him, but the old men listened, for they knew the boy was wise.

Only one young man did not laugh. "I will go hunt the bear with you," he said.

The young man and boy went to the tree with the owl in it. Just as the owl had said, they found the bear sleeping in a hole. They killed the bear and took it back to the village. The people were happy to have so much meat to eat.

Now whenever the boy said something after that, all the people believed him.

War broke out with another tribe and the men went into battle. They were outnumbered and many of their warriors were killed. The women were afraid because they knew the enemy would now come, steal their food and burn the village.

The boy told the women, "Do not be afraid. I will go and kill the enemy. They will not burn our village." Then he went into the woods and found the remaining men of his village. He said to them,

"Stay where you are. I will go to the enemy and kill them. Never again will they try to burn our village."

The men watched the boy as he went to meet the enemy alone. They heard the Thunder and saw the Lightning far away. The Thunder and Lightning came down upon the enemy and killed them all. The men waited a long time for the boy, but he never returned. He was never seen again.

Now, when the people hear Thunder and see the Lightning, they know that it is the boy calling in the Thunder, and when the Lightning flashes in the sky, they are sure they can see the face of the boy. "The Thunder Helper laughs," the old men say, and then they go to sleep unafraid.

(*Author's Note: Thunder Helper is an authentic Creek legend that was edited from historical documents and several Internet sources, and is believed to be in the public domain. The author was listed either as "unknown" or "anonymous".*)

By the time the old man had finished the story, the strange storm had passed. There was not one drop of rainfall, which only made the story all the more appropriate for the occasion.

Pu-Can went to him and thanked him. "Where did you hear that story, Grandfather? We have never seen any bears this far south. The bearskin robe I have was traded for many years ago. The traders were from far to the north."

The old man answered, "I heard it from my grandfather, Spirit Singer. He heard it from his grandfather, I suppose. I have never seen a bear myself," he said with a toothless grin. "But it is a good story."

Pu-Can laughed and asked him to join her and Tysoyaha at their fire for some dinner. He thanked her, but declined. "My old woman has already fed me, Granddaughter, but I thank you for the offer. You and your new young man have no need for an old man at your fire."

Pu-Can got two of her bowls out of her pack and filled them with sofkee for Tysoyaha and herself. One of the women had roasted some of the new corn from the Festival and gave her two of the ears. Pu-Can and Tysoyaha sat at their fire and ate. It was the first meal they had shared alone since they had met. Soon they would share a blanket, but not until they had made their vows in front of her tribe, hopefully with her uncle Echo-Ochee performing the binding ceremony.

She went to sleep thinking about Echo-Ochee. She wanted to tell him the story of their ancestors that Locha-Luste and Chatto-Nokose had told them. He had not heard that story or he would have told it to her himself. *After all, Wild Dancer was his grandmother. He should know the story,* she thought as she drifted off to sleep.

It was morning and the canoes were loaded and ready to continue the trip down river. Dawn had brought a light rain that had ended as the sun rose higher in the sky. Pu-Can had saved her embers before the rain extinguished the fire, and she was about to start another to warm some sofkee for Tysoyaha and herself when one of the other women offered to share what she had remaining.

"I was about to throw it out rather than carry it," she told Pu-Can, "and I hate to waste food."

Pu-Can accepted her offer and thanked her. It would have been difficult to start a fire with wet wood, and they were in a hurry to begin the final leg of the journey. By late afternoon they should be back at their home fires. There would be a feast for them, and everyone would want to hear their stories of the Green Corn festival.

Pu-Can smiled as she thought of her mother meeting Tysoyaha for the first time. Even the news of her being chosen to be the Firestarter would be overshadowed by her bringing the son of a chief home with her.

She watched the people who were walking as they left the campsite. The love she felt for her people was almost overwhelming. There were so few of them left, but they retained their joy of life and celebrated even the smallest things. When the last of them disappeared into the forest, she looked around the campsite. Once again, there was no sign of anyone ever having been there. Even the fires that were extinguished had been covered with sand.

She walked down to the canoes where the rest were waiting. With Tysoyaha already at the stern, she pushed their canoe out into the water and hopped in without even rocking the craft. She took her paddle and with long, graceful strokes, helped speed their passage down the river and to her home.

No one was waiting at the landing, but that was expected. The ones who were walking had not yet arrived, and besides, no one at their village knew when to expect them. One of the young men volunteered to run ahead and let the people know they were returning.

Pu-Can was showing Tysoyaha where their talofa used to be and where old Turtle and his son were killed when the first of the walking ones appeared. They had made much better time on the return trip, and were in good spirits. Soon they were all gathered at their old town site. It was late afternoon, and if they continued to the cave now it would be dark before they arrived.

Some of the people lived nearer to the river and could have gone to their cabins, but everyone wanted to congregate with the ones who had remained. There was to be a celebration and a sharing of the New Fire. They all agreed to continue on to the cave, where everyone was accustomed to gathering for big events.

The path was familiar and the excitement was high. The runner had already left to alert the others that they were at the river. As they started the last part of their journey, Pu-Can began a familiar chant that everyone knew. They all sang along as they made their way back to the home that they loved. It was as much a part of them as their own bodies, and it was where the bones of their ancestors' were buried.

The ones who had not attended the Green Corn Festival were already on the way to meet them when they heard the singing. They met them halfway on the trail, and soon the entire population was together. Everyone began talking at once. The new husbands-to-be were welcomed, especially Tysoyaha, who was to be the husband of their very own Spirit Singer.

They extinguished all the fires when they arrived at the cave. Pu-Can still carried the embers from the New Fire, and quickly began rekindling with them. They started several other fires around the meeting area as they exchanged news of home and of the festival.

Echo-Ochee wanted to meet them on the trail, but was too weak. He was waiting at home for them, dressed in his ceremonial attire when he stepped out of the cave. He raised his arms and everyone became silent.

"We are pleased to have our people return safely to us, bringing the New Fire. Let the drums be heard! Let the dancing honor this reunion, and let it please the souls of our ancestors."

At first, he had thought to have their own New Fire ceremony and a separate Green Corn Festival for the ones who did not make the journey, but the old corn was plentiful, so he had waited.

Pu-Can introduced him to Tysoyaha and asked if he would perform the Joining Ceremony for all the new couples tonight.

"Of course, my Pu-Can. I would be honored to welcome the nephew of my old friend Locha-Luste into our family, and the other young men into our Clan. Gather all the couples and the mothers of the girls. We will have a Joining and a Green Corn Festival to remember."

They formed a circle around the central fire with the mother of each girl clasping the hands of the couple together. A single blanket was wrapped around them both as Echo-Ochee performed the age-old ceremony. The entire assembly formed a circle around them and began a slow Stomp Dance. The drums began slowly, increasing in tempo with every revolution of the dancers. The mothers of the newly-joined couples then pulled the blankets from the couples, revealing them as man and wife for the first time.

The new corn was brought out and was soon roasting over the coals while the dancing continued. The festivities lasted well into the early morning hours, and when it had broken up into several small groups, each sitting around their own fire, they recounted the stories of the big Festival.

Pu-Can and Tysoyaha took Echo-Ochee, her mother and Apelka-Haya into the cave. They told them the story that they had heard from Tysoyaha's father and uncle of the first Muskogees. Pu-Can then told of the night she and Locha-Luste combined the Power Bundles, and the vision they had shared.

Echo-Ochee laughed as he heard of his old friend's encounter with the Puma Man. "It seems that we both had our encounters with Kowakatcu because of you, Pu-Can. The first time I ever saw him was when he gave me your name on the day you were born. You carry his Power with you wherever you go, my little Spirit Singer."

"We saw the same vision, Grandfather. It was so real ... as if we were actually there in our bodies."

"You were there, Pu-Can. The Wheel of Life cares not of past, present, or future. It is all the same. It is only us who are caught in the present who see the passing of time as we do," the old shaman said. "You are fortunate to have seen this for yourself. Many seek what you already know in your heart."

As the evening progressed, Echo-Ochee sat silently, watching the fire in the hearth and then dozing off to sleep. Pu-Can wrapped a blanket around his shoulders, and then she and Tysoyaha went back outside. Almost all of the people had gone to their own fires. Only a few remained, reluctant for the evening of storytelling to end.

The old man at the fire nearest them was about to tell the story of "How the Indians Got the Medicine". It was one that Pu-Can knew well, having heard it many times from both Hechee-Lana and Echo-Ochee. The old man was doing a good job, and she saw that Tysoyaha was listening intently. The man said, "Echo-Ochee tells it much better than I, but this is how the Indians got the medicine ... "

The first Indian who ever killed a deer and ate its flesh became sick. The Deer Spirit was angry and said to the Indian, "I gave you the first sickness for killing me, but if you will bring me your wisest man I will teach him the cure."

The tribal elders tested all the Indians and when they found the wisest one among them, they took him to the place where the Deer Spirit spoke.

"Only the one man will be given the secret of the medicine," the Deer Spirit said.

After the elders left, the Deer Spirit told the wise man "You must go into the forest alone and fast for many days. You must not speak to anyone. When you have done this, I will come to you."

After many days in the forest the Deer Spirit spoke to him again.

"You have been chosen to be the Keeper of the Medicine for all of your people. You will be their first Healer. Each animal gives a disease to man, but each one also has the cure for that disease. You must find those cures. Take these secrets that you find and put them in a medicine bundle. There will be many who will try to steal the medicine from you, so it must be guarded well.

"When there is a new sickness among your people, I will give you a sign at the New Fire. This sign will help you cure the new disease. Each year bring your medicine bundle to the Green Corn Dance and share the cures with your people.

"When you grow old, you must teach a young man how to make the cures. Test him to be certain that he will make a good medicine man. Many false healers will want to get the secrets from you. Now I give you part of my breath. Go and blow on the sick. Give them the medicine of the herbs and roots that I tell you. This will make them well.,"

The first Medicine Man returned to the deer he had killed and cut off the tip of his antler. This was the first magic object in the sacred medicine bundle of the Muskogee.

(Author's Note: How the Indian Got the Medicine is an authentic Creek legend that was edited from historical documents and several Internet sources, and is believed to be in the public domain. The author was listed either as "unknown" or "anonymous".)

The old man stood and bowed to the group of applauding people around the fire. "It is growing too late for this old man. I must go to my blankets," he said tiredly before departing for the night.

"I told you my mother was Yuchi," Tysoyaha said when the story ended. "Even though their language was completely different, that story was nearly the same as the one she told me. There must have been some sharing of knowledge a long time back in our histories."

Pu-Can nodded agreement. "I think so, too, Sun Child. Perhaps both our people came from the same place in the west, just at different times. That may be why my people said that the Yuchi were already here when they arrived."

Tysoyaha added, "The Cherokee were already in the east too, but they are very different from either of our people. Not only is their language different from either of ours, but also their customs and their looks. Some say they came from the north."

"And now the white men want us all gone. They have almost succeeded, too. My grandmother—" Pu-Can's voice broke as she became emotional. "She ... she said that if only the white man would try to understand our ways ... instead of trying to kill us or drive us away ... and if only the Indians would try to understand that they really fear us more than they hate us ... we could have shared the land. But instead, they killed her." She stood up, turning away from him so that he would not see her tears.

Tysoyaha stood and wrapped his arms around her. "I know, my Pu-Can. I know. They killed many of my family too, and took many to the reservations, just as they did with all Indians."

"Tomorrow I will show you the valley from the mountain," Pu-Can said, drying her eyes. "There is a Place of Power there, at a big rock where we bury our people. From the top of the rock you can see the whole valley. You will then see why we chose to remain here, even with the threat of the white man. But it is very late and we should get some sleep, before the sun peeks over the mountain."

She took him inside the cave and made a place for him near the fire. She went to her own blankets near Echo-Ochee, who was snoring softly, and was almost instantly asleep.

When she woke, her mother and Tysoyaha were talking while her mother prepared sofkee and fry bread. It smelled wonderful, but she lay there pretending to be asleep, listening to the two as they got to know each other. They were discussing her mother's cooking, but Tysoyaha seemed to be especially interested in the herbs and spices that she was adding to the sofkee.

Both she and Pu-Can had learned how to cook from Hechee-Lana. She could take the simplest foods and make them appealing to even the pickiest eater. By the smell, she knew that her mother had added bee balm and wild onions to the sofkee.

Tysoyaha brought Pu-Can a bowl of the sofkee. "How long have you been lying there, waiting to be served?" he asked teasingly.

"Just long enough to hear you try to win my mother to you, Sun Child," she teased back. "Did she not tell you how lazy I am?"

He smiled at her. "No, she actually said that you were usually the first one to wake. She knew you were tired from the journey, so she let you sleep."

Echo-Ochee stirred, and then sat up. "It is good to wake smelling food that I did not cook myself," he yawned, stretching his arms. "I have not slept so soundly in many years."

Achena-Nakla brought him a bowl of the sofkee, which he began eating as if he were starving.

"This is just like what my mother and sister made. I am glad someone remembered the bee balm." He took a piece of the fry bread and wiped his bowl clean with it. "And this bread ... surely it is made from the new corn?"

Achena-Nakla and Pu-Can both laughed at the old man's perceptiveness. "It does not take a shaman of great power to tell old corn from the new, Uncle. But you do know your food," Achena-Nakla said, still laughing.

"It is not just the ingredients that make the food good, Niece. There is much to be said for the one who prepares it," he replied as he wiped his mouth on his sleeve.

"Grandfather, Tysoyaha and I will be going to the Rock today. Will you walk with us?" Pu-Can asked him.

"Thank you, Pu-Can. I will go as far as my cabin with you. That mountain trail is too steep for these old legs these days," he said. "Are you leaving right away?"

"As soon as I prepare some food to take with us. Would you rather wait a while?"

"No, I am ready when you are. I want to talk more with this nephew of my old friend, Locha-Luste. He and I have known each other since we were children, but it has been many moons since we have talked. Much has happened since we last saw each other."

"I would be honored to tell you all I know about my uncle, Grandfather Echo-Ochee. He has spoken of you many times," Tysoyaha said as he helped the old shaman to his feet.

Achena-Nakla handed Echo-Ochee a bundle. "Here is some sofkee and fry bread, Uncle. You can heat it when you get hungry today. It was good to have you stay here with us, even if it was only for one night. You are welcome to stay longer if you would like."

"Thank you, but I have some things I must do today. I must be about my duties while I still feel the strength to do them."

CHAPTER 16

Brian closed the notebook. "Just think, those conversations with Echo-Ochee took place right here where we're sitting. He was the last Hilis-Haya of the Osochi Creeks that lived in this area."

"And Hilis-Haya means 'Medicine Man', doesn't it?" Alex asked.

"Yep, but the Muskogee Creeks didn't use the term 'Medicine Man'. Actually it means 'Keeper of the People' or 'Medicine Maker'. He was next to the Chief in ruling power, but sometimes he had even more power than the Chief, depending on what the Clan was facing."

As they prepared for sleep, Mary reminded Maurice about the blackberry root rinse for his mouth. "How is it feeling?" she asked.

"Dat's de reason I fergits 'bout it," Maurice confessed. "Hit's so much better dat hit don' remind me to use it. I had dat problem my whole life, an' hit better'n hit's evva been. Dat be good medicine."

Brian went into the storeroom just before turning in for the night. He wanted to check the shortwave radio to see if there were any recent developments. The last they had heard, Columbus was under attack and burning. It had sounded more like a rioting mob than a planned military-style operation, but he wanted to know how widespread the rioting was. Chances were that even if it progressed northward, it would be at the next largest town of LaGrange, bypassing their cave altogether. Rioting mobs usually weren't interested in forests and remote areas. That was his hope, anyway.

The only radio traffic that he found was in Spanish, and from the tone of voice it was not anything exciting or indicative of a problem that would affect them at the cave. He turned the receiver off and went to his blankets.

Brian and Maurice began the day working on their plans for the pontoon boat. They needed to carry the fuel tanks and plywood to the river, but Brian wanted to have everything cut and sized to fit first. All his tools were at the cave and there was no need in having to carry them there too.

The tanks were twelve feet long, and the plywood was in four-by-eight foot sheets. Using only three of the panels, they could have an eight-by-twelve-foot pontoon boat. The biggest problem they would have was the method of attaching them to the tanks.

They finally decided on making the deck itself as a separate unit, with two-by-four runners sandwiching the tanks. Threaded metal rods would pass through the two-by-fours with a tank in between them. Everything was cut to size, and then they began hauling it all down to the river.

By noon they had it assembled and sitting at the water's edge. They cut a couple of long, two-inch-thick oak saplings to use as push-poles, but they both knew that the current would be a challenge.

Mary and Alex came to check on them just as they were

about to push it into the water for a test. Brian had attached a long rope to one end and tied the other end to a tree, just in case they couldn't handle it against the current.

"Wouldn't it be great if you had a rope all the way across the river?" Mary asked. "You could pull the pontoon back and forth along it."

Brian gave Maurice a wink. He had already thought about the rope across the river, but exclaimed "That's it! Thanks, Mary, I hadn't thought of such a simple solution. But we can't leave the rope. It would be an advertisement that we were here. But with it we could work a trotline all night long without having to paddle against the current. So now it's time for that test, Maurice. We may wind up a little downstream from where we want to be, but I think we can drag a rope across, don't you?"

Alex wanted to go along, but Brian wanted to test the pontoon boat without risking her safety.

"Let us see how well it works first, honey. If it works like I hope it will, then we can all go for a ride, okay?"

She reluctantly agreed, but made him promise that she would get a trip today. "I can help, you know. I'm not a baby anymore."

Brian tied one end of the nylon rope to a tree, and then the two men pushed the boat into the water. By holding the rope tightly and poling across the river, they maintained a relatively straight course. They found that by pointing the pontoons with the current worked much better, so they poled the craft sideways across to the other side and pulled the boat onto the sand and attached the rope tightly to a tree.

Brian took another short line and made a loop over the main rope, attaching the other end to the boat. If they let go of the main line while crossing, it would hold the boat against the current. All they had to do was pull the boat along the main line, letting the looped line slide along.

They made the crossing much easier the second time, and the pontoons seemed to be working well.

"I believe we could carry a Volkswagon across the river

with this thing," Brian wagered. "It isn't drawing but an inch or two with the two of us on it, and it's much more stable than I thought it would be."

Maurice chuckled. "Hit's ridin' juss fine, Brine. A feller could live on a boat lak dis."

They picked Mary and Alex up and went to about midstream, letting the rope hold them against the current. The water was fairly deep so Alex, Mary and Brian went swimming. Maurice confessed that he had never learned to swim, so he remained on the boat.

When they tired of swimming, Mary and Alex wanted to investigate the other side of the river. Alex had brought along *The Field Guide to Herbs*, and that was excuse enough. They pulled themselves along the rope to the opposite shore, and then pulled the boat onto the sand. They saw several human-made trails, most of them leading toward the homes in the valley—the nearest of which was almost a mile away. They spent most of the afternoon investigating the trails near the riverbank, but when they returned to the boat, Brian saw two men standing there, looking it over. They appeared to be fishermen since they had all their tackle with them.

Brian had the other three remain out of sight while he approached them.

"Hi, guys! Having any luck today?" he asked, noticing immediately that one of them was wearing a large revolver on his belt.

"Just got here, friend. Is this your boat?" one of the men asked, seemingly friendly enough, but Brian noticed his interest in the crossbow that was slung over his shoulder.

"Yep. Just got it put together today. Are y'all from the Valley?" Brian asked.

"Yep. Sorry," the man said, offering his hand. "I'm Bobby Causey, and this here's my brother, Hugh. We've lived here almost ten years now. Before the riots, our mom ran a beauty shop near the crossroads. Since then we've been living hand-to-mouth, hunting, fishing, raising a few vegetables—you know—like everybody else.

Where do you live?"

Brian thought quickly before answering and pointed upstream. "Up that way about a mile. I used to live here when I was a kid. Brought my family here from Atlanta to escape the craziness. We kinda camp around here and there. I just found these old tanks, and my friend and I made this boat out of them. Planning on running a trotline – do some night catfishing."

"You sure did a good job on it. And this is a good spot for it too," Hugh said, admiring the boat. "Hey, man ... I know you can't trust anybody these days ... and you don't know us, but we're good guys, okay? We've had our share of trouble from the bad ones. Two men broke into our house a couple of months ago. They killed our dad. Would've killed us too, I reckon, but Bobby and I were out hunting. When we got home we found our dad dead in the yard and Mom tied up inside. She got beat up pretty bad, and I think they left her for dead. All they wanted was our food and the keys to our truck."

"Two guys? What kind of vehicle were they in?" Brian asked, trying to sound nonchalant.

"Little black car, Mom said. She thinks it had a Louisiana license plate, but she wasn't sure about that ... but those two guys ..." Bobby continued describing the men that had killed their father.

Brian had goose bumps when he finished. It sounded just like the men who had kidnapped Maurice. The ones who drove a car with Louisiana plates. The ones he had killed. *This is not the time to tell that bit of news,* he thought.

"Sorry to hear about your father, guys. We've had some trouble ourselves. We heard on our shortwave radio that Columbus was under attack a few days ago. We could see the fires from the top of the mountain."

"We heard something about that over the grapevine when we were in Hamilton yesterday. The guy at the store said that some of the rioters had come through there, but went on through, heading for LaGrange, I suppose," Hugh said.

Bobby pointed at Brian's crossbow and asked, "Is that your

only protection?"

"It serves its purpose, I reckon, and it's a lot quieter than the alternative," Brian said, indicating the big revolver on Bobby's belt.

Bobby laughed and patted the sidearm. "I never carried a sidearm until they killed our dad and hurt Mom," he said. "I didn't even know if I could kill a man or not until then. Heck, the bullets in this thing are so old they might not even fire. It was Daddy's from when he was a deputy sheriff in Hamilton. He only shot it off every Fourth of July and New Year's Eve. It was his way of celebrating— kind of a tradition in our family that ..." Bobby's voice trailed off as he remembered better times.

Brian felt that these two young men were not troublemakers, and decided to bring his family and Maurice out of hiding. "Excuse me just a minute, guys ... there's someone else I want you to meet," he told them, and went back to where the others were waiting.

"Come meet these guys, y'all. Just don't mention where we live, or anything that's happened recently," he told his family, with the last part directed at Maurice. "Their father was killed a couple of months ago, and I think it was those same two guys we had trouble with that did it. Maybe we'll tell them later, okay?"

When Maurice and Brian's family walked out of the woods, the men were very polite, and acted like it was every day that they met a family out in the woods, in the middle of nowhere.

Brian introduced them to the two brothers, who were obviously impressed with the survival skills of these new acquaintances, especially when Mary fed everyone with some of the best venison jerky they had ever eaten.

They had a pleasant visit, apparently because they all needed and craved outside contact with people—something that was taken for granted before the terrorist attacks, but much too dangerous when you could trust no one's intentions.

Just before sunset, Brian asked them if they would like to join them that evening running a trotline. "We can share any fish we catch. I didn't come prepared for doing it tonight, but we can make do with what I did bring along."

"Heck, yes!" Bobby exclaimed. "We've got bait, and enough hooks and stuff. We just don't have a line long enough to cross the river."

"I've got that covered," Brian told him. "And I have two lanterns. This just might be fun."

It turned out not only to be fun, but very rewarding as well. The four men worked their way back and forth across the river all night, with Mary and Alex going with them at times. Their biggest problem was handling so many catfish. They didn't have enough containers to store the fish, so they had to keep them alive until the morning. They had full stringers pegged into the bank on both sides of the river. At first light they were all tired and sleepy, but they estimated that they had almost a hundred pounds of catfish to share with Bobby and Hugh.

They parted early in the morning, and Brian waited until they were out of sight across the river before he and his family started back to their cave. He had told them that they lived upriver and didn't want the two brothers to see them walking downriver—not yet. It was just too early in the friendship to show too much trust.

He told them that they could use the pontoon boat any time they wanted, and where it would be hidden, but that was kind of a given. There was no way he could move it anywhere other than drag it to the edge of the forest and cover it with branches. They had removed the rope from across the river on their last trip over, so that would not be a problem.

Hugh and Bobby had told them where their home was, and invited them to visit any time. Their mother would appreciate the company, they had said.

When they arrived at the cave they were so sleepy and tired from staying up all night, they took barely enough time to get the catfish cleaned. When Brian and Maurice finished they estimated that they had nearly twenty-five pounds of dressed fish. Mary and Alex had a huge pot of oil hot and ready for a deep fry. They feasted on fried fish and hushpuppies, and then salted the rest of the fish down with the last of the bulk curing salt.

Although it was only just past sundown, they all went to their blankets, even giving up the nightly reading of the Granny Boo story.

"Before we go to sleep, I want to see if y'all are agreeable with making another trip into town tomorrow," Brian said. "We need more curing salt, and probably a few other things. We can also ride past Bobby and Hugh's house. I think I know the people who used to live there, if I'm thinking about the right house. We just have to look for the two mountain laurels they said were in the yard. There aren't many houses on that section of C Street. That road runs into the mountain road just below the old rock underpass. You've been there, remember?"

"Sure do. King's Gap, right?" Alex was proud of herself for remembering. "King was an old Indian man who ran a stagecoach stop there in the old days," she added for Maurice's benefit.

"When we get back tomorrow," Brian continued, "We'll go harvest the corn. We have a Green Corn Festival to celebrate. The full moon is in three days."

They were up at dawn, and quickly prepared for the trip into town. Maurice was anxious to talk to some of his friends and find out what he could about recent events. Mary had food enough to last them several days, Brian noted jokingly, but was glad to know it was there, just in case.

Alex wanted to stop at the burial ground and "show her respect" as she put it. Brian smiled as she correctly pointed out the various places where Keechie, Bull Killer and the others were buried. She really had a good memory when it was something in which she was interested.

Suddenly she stopped in her tracks. "Dad, look at this!"

Brian went to her to see what she was looking at so intently on the ground.

"Isn't this where Echo-Ochee was the day Granny Boo was

born? You know, when the Puma Man gave him her name?"

"Sure is, honey. Why do you ask?"

"Look at this!" She held up a vine for him to see. It was a passionflower vine with several fully-opened flowers. The vine the Creeks called Pu-Can. It was not unusual for it to be growing there, but it was just so appropriate for the story that he had been reading to them.

"It may be a relative of the same vine old Echo-Ochee fell on that day. I think it's a sign that the spirits appreciate your honoring them today," Brian said as he gave her a hug.

They cleared the brush away from the truck, and Brian backed it slowly out onto the highway. There were no other cars in sight as they began the trip into town.

"I just thought of something," Mary said. "We never cross the river when we go this way. There's only the creek that you used to follow to Keechie's cave below your old house. What happens to the river?"

"Just downstream from where we were yesterday, it turns almost due east," Brian explained. "It crosses the highway south of Hamilton, then it runs into the Chattahoochee just north of Columbus. Then there are several dams further downstream. Why do you ask?"

"I was just thinking. If we got on the pontoon boat and just let the current take us, how far and where would it take us?"

"We would go almost to Columbus, baby; but then the dams would stop us. If it weren't for them, we could go all the way to the Gulf of Mexico." He laughed at the thought, but had already thought it through when he first had the idea of building a boat. There were roads where the river crossed that they could use to meet and pick up passengers, if it ever came to that.

It was just another of what he called his "escape plans", to be available if in an emergency they had to use the boat to get away. It would be a good time for him to show Mary and Maurice the bridge crossing below Hamilton where they would meet if anyone ever had to use the boat to get away.

He first drove to Hamilton and parked in front of his dad's old store. Everyone piled out and went in, except for Maurice, who saw two of his friends sitting outside on the steps.

Mr. Epstein greeted them as they entered. "Hello, folks. What can I help you with today?"

"Just wanted to look around, Mr. Epstein, and get some curing salt if you have it."

"Sure do. Salt hasn't been in too much demand these days. Nobody has anything to preserve. Meat is so scarce that it gets eaten before it has a chance to go bad. How much you need?" Mr. Epstein asked, remembering that Brian paid in cash.

"How much is it?" Brian asked.

"Twenty dollars for a fifty pound bag. Probably one of the best deals I have left."

"I'll take two bags if you have them, and do you have any kerosene?"

"Sorry, no kerosene, or gas, for that matter. I could sell a tanker truck full if I had it," Mr. Epstein said, shaking his head. "I had a little kerosene last week, but those rioters came through from Columbus last week and stole it."

"Was there any trouble here? I heard a little about it on the radio."

"Not anything you would call really bad – that is, no one was killed. They just came through and stole anything that wasn't nailed down. Shot out a few windows—that kind of stuff. It was late at night and there weren't any people around. Country folks usually go home at night, you know."

"Glad to hear that no one was hurt," Brian said. "Say, could you use some fresh catfish on occasion? Sometimes I have more than I can use, and I could bring you some every once in a while."

"I'll take all the fresh meat you can bring me. Any kind! There's good trade value in fresh meat. In fact, I would love to have some fresh catfish for myself." Mr. Epstein chuckled. "I would have to get some ice from this one guy I know to keep it, but I wouldn't have to keep it long, once word got out that I had fresh fish."

Mary and Alex found a few canned items that they wanted and a gallon of peanut oil, but nothing much else. Just as the last time they had come in, they found that they actually had more staples than the store.

One of the things that Alex did find, though, was a jar of peanut butter. She carried it to the counter as she thought of when she used to sit on her bed, watching TV and eating peanut butter right out of the jar with a spoon.

"I think that's about it this time. How much do I owe you?" Brian asked.

"Well, let's see … forty dollars for the salt, ten for the peanut oil, and eight dollars for the canned goods … that comes to fifty-eight dollars."

Brian gave him three twenties and put the two ones in change in his wallet. "Thank you, Mr. Epstein. We'll see you soon, I hope. Maybe I'll have some catfish for you next time."

"I hope so. Brian, is it?"

"Brian it is, and this is my wife, Mary, and my daughter, Alexis," he answered, shaking the man's hand. "We'll be back." He picked up one of the bags of salt and threw it over his shoulder.

They met Maurice at the door. He was laughing at something one of the men outside had just said, but wanted to wait until they got back in the truck to tell them what it was. He picked up the other sack of salt and carried it to the bed of the truck.

What's so funny, Maurice?" Alex asked him as they pulled away from the curb.

"Hehe … dey saw dose men put me into dey car, an' dey thought I wuz a'joinin' up wit dem. You know, like I'se gonna be a gangsta er sompin'. Den I don' come back fer a while an' dey thought I done got myseff kilt. Den I comes a'ridin' up wit' white folks, an' I ain't de one a'drivin'! Hehe. Dey wants t' know my secret. I tol' dem hit wuz my good looks. Hehe."

Mary and Brian both laughed with Maurice, but Alex wasn't old enough to remember the racial prejudices of her parent's generation, so Brian had to explain it to her.

Brian drove south, toward Columbus, to show them where the river crossed the road. "If any of us ever have to take the boat downstream, this is the first place where the river is accessible from the road." He pulled over and stopped just past the bridge and they all got out. He pointed down at the embankment. "See that sandy area there? There's a little road that goes right down to it. You can pull the boat in there, and whoever is looking for you will know to come here first to find you, or me, if that's the case. This is just one of those 'just in case' preparations, okay?"

As they were about to turn around and head back into town, the first vehicle they had seen on the road all day went past, heading toward Columbus. It was an old pickup with two men inside, and they were pulling a rickety trailer with a boat on it. The bed of the truck had several fishing poles sticking out.

"No trouble there," Brian said with relief.

Just past town Brian turned east, heading toward Pine Mountain Valley. It was only five miles away, and the road where Bobby and Hugh lived was just past the crossroads that led to Brian's old home.

When they passed the house, they saw the two mountain laurels in the yard. No one was in sight, but it looked occupied, since it had curtains in the windows and the yard was well kept. He drove on past.

He pointed to a little weed-covered trail off to the left. "That's the 'Stagecoach Trail'. It's all that's left of the old stagecoach road that led up to King's Gap. We used it to park with our girlfriends when I was young. It now just goes to the underground reservoir for the Pine Mountain Valley water supply - takes electricity to run the pumps, though."

Further up the road was the hairpin turn that led up to the top of the mountain. "We called this 'Devil's Hairpin' when I was living here. One of my classmates was killed right here, trying to make the curve going much too fast. It happened just before graduation. Her little brother was in the car with her, but he survived."

They made the sharp turn to the left and just ahead was King's Gap, the rock underpass that Roosevelt's W.P.A. workers constructed in the 1930s. Just as they went through, Brian blew the horn. "Dad did that every time he came this way. It has a nice echo, doesn't it?"

He made another sharp left turn onto the Scenic Highway, passing the rock "Tavern" that was built by the same workers.

"Many of the stones they used to build these places, like the underpass and this building, came from an old Indian ceremonial ground near here. I wish they had left them where they were. Keechie's ancestors built a huge stone-walled circle, and she remembered going there when she was a young girl."

"Have you ever been to the spot, Dad?" Alex asked.

"Yep. There's nothing left there, though. I never even found an arrowhead there. The W.P.A. was pretty thorough."

A half-mile further was the old trail that led to the Rock, and Brian turned in slowly, making sure there was no traffic to see him pull in. After unloading the truck and carefully concealing it again, they hauled the salt and the few items down to the base of the Rock. Brian made a travois out of a blanket and two dead tree limbs to drag the salt to the cave.

After a short rest and a quick meal, they left again for the cornfield. Not only was the corn ready, but there were still a few snow peas that needed gathering. The running beans had gone wild, climbing up the cornstalks. They picked almost a full bushel basket of beans before even beginning to pick the corn.

The Osochi corn that Keechie had preserved all these years was beautiful. Alex and Mary gathered the ripened tassels and shook the remaining pollen into a cloth bag, just as Keechie had shown Brian how to do. Not only was it used to insure the pollination of the new crop, but it was considered sacred, to be used as offerings to the spirit world.

It took them two trips, even using the now-familiar travois, to carry all the corn back to the cave.

Mary had taken it upon herself to collect the biggest, most

perfect ears and keep them separate from the rest. They would be the seeds for next year's crop. *Puma Man, this is the corn of your chosen Clan. We are a part of that Clan, by whatever means. Through our labor, we honor the people who brought it to this place, and we consider it sacred by continuing to preserve it.*

Mary was amused with herself for beginning to think more like a pagan than her minister father would have ever wanted to hear about. *After all,* she thought with a smile, *I just might be the great-granddaughter of one of the most powerful Spirit Singers you have ever trained, Puma Man.*

Brian had prepared a special place for the corn in the storeroom that included netting that he hoped would keep the rodents out; but strangely enough, they had experienced no problems with them in the cave. Keechie had even commented on the absence of rats and insects, saying that it was due to the "pertekshun o' de Puma Man." He could offer no better explanation.

With the new corn safely stored away, they dined again on catfish. Brian wasn't sure about the salt preservation method, and wanted to eat as much of it as they could, just to keep from wasting it.

Mary rinsed off as much of the salt as she could, but this time, instead of frying the fish, she broiled it with margarine and fresh herbs. It was even better than fried. She took out a few of the smaller ones from the salt and hung them over the fireplace, just to try smoking them as a preserving method. *Never had smoked catfish,* she thought, *but you never know until you try.*

It was the drums that woke Alex in the middle of the night. They seemed to be echoing as she lay there listening to the sounds of the night. She remembered Keechie's words: *'As long as dere's someone who kin hyer de drums, de people will nevva die'.*

"I hear the drums, Keechie. We can all hear the drums. They woke me up," she muttered under her breath. She had to relieve her bladder, so she made her way very silently to the outside latrine. The stars were brilliant and the moon was so nearly full that it illuminated the path almost as well as day. She loved to come outside alone like this, when the night creatures were active. An owl hooted nearby, sounding like it was asking her a question.

"Who? It's me, that's who, the double-great granddaughter of Keechie," she said to the night. She sat on the boulder above the entrance and thought about the Green Corn Festival that they were planning. She wanted badly for it to be a real Festival, done for the right reasons rather than a meaningless holiday—only for their entertainment. She knew there was a spiritual and cultural meaning to the event that she understood in her heart, although she did not have the words to describe it.

I hope my dad plays the drum and rattle just like he did with Keechie when they did the Singing. I hope the old language comes through him as it did then. That is what I want this ceremony to be like.

Then she added a special request to the Puma Man to make it so. As she looked up at the sky to make her plea to Kowakatcu, a shooting star streaked across the sky, leaving a visual trail from west to east. She took it as a sign from the Puma Man that he had heard her plea.

Alex sat there a long time, just listening and feeling the night. It seemed alive with the spirits of the people who had lived and died right there. Surely they must have felt the very thing she was feeling at that moment. She felt that this was an enchanted place—a place that she knew would never be far from her heart. She and her parents were meant to be here, as was Maurice. It was all recorded within The Wheel of Life, which kept turning and turning—

"Here she is!" was the next thing she heard. "Alex, are you all right, honey?" her dad asked, hugging her tightly to him.

"Gee, uhhh, I'm fine, Dad," she answered, trying to regain her senses. She had fallen asleep on the boulder during the night. The sun was almost up, but it was already daylight. "I came out to use the latrine, and it was such a pretty night ... I just sat here for a minute. I saw a falling star ... and then—"

"It's okay, baby. I've done the same thing myself, but I fell off the rock when I did it," Brian joked, relieved that she was okay.

"I started to get up las' night an' lissen t' y'all a'playin', but den you stopped. Den I went back t' sleep," Maurice mumbled, rubbing the sleep from his eyes.

"Playing? What did you hear, Maurice?" Mary asked.

"De drums. Dey wuz pretty loud. Woke me up. Den dey stopped. I thought y'all wuz a'practicin' fer da Green Corn Dance er sompin."

Alex looked at her mom and dad, nodding in agreement.

"It was the drums, Dad. You know—like Keechie said. It was the drums that woke me too, Maurice. They're from the spirit world. Welcome to the club. We all hear them now."

Maurice's eyes widened as he realized what she was talking about. "Den I ain't crazy, er nothin' lak dat, is I?"

"You're not crazy," Mary assured him. "I think it's a good thing, in fact. It means the Puma Man has accepted you, and now you are under his protection. I've heard the drums too, and feel comforted by them. It took me a while to accept it, though."

"I remember Brian readin' dat to us ... as long as dey's someone dat can hyer de drums, de people will nevva die. Is dat right?" Maurice asked.

Brian nodded. "That's what Keechie was told, and it seems to have happened with all her ancestors. It was a recurring thing that seemed important to the Kowakatcu Clan. The Puma Man has indeed taken you in. It was probably him that caused us to find you. He wants you to be here," he told his childhood friend.

"Dad, have you thought about who's going to start the New Fire at the Green Corn Festival? Alex asked.

Brian had indeed thought about it, but had never mentioned it. Keechie had told him about "his girl-child carrying on the Gift, but Alex had never tried to start a fire with a fire drill.

"Do you think you could start a fire with a bow and drill?" he asked her.

Alex nodded. "I think I can, but I've never tried. Can I be the

Fire Starter?"

"I think it would please Keechie and the Puma Man if you did, baby. I'll get out the one that Keechie and I made to practice on, For the ceremony though, you will use the old one that Granny Boo used," Brian said, pleased that Alex had thought about it on her own.

He went into the storeroom and found the ancient fire drill and bow that had belonged to Wild Dancer. It had aged beautifully. The wood was dark with age and the patina of the years of care and handling it had seen. He quickly did the math and realized that even if it had been new when Wild Dancer had used it, it would be at least two hundred and fifty years old now. He rubbed his hands over the wood, feeling the imbedded memories and the Power within. There was a small bag tied to it and he opened it to look inside. It contained the chaff and fine wood shavings needed to start a fire. Golden pollen was mixed throughout.

Brian located the one that Keechie had helped him make and handed it to Alex. "Let's go outside and I'll show you how to use it, but we'll need fresh tinder. What Keechie saved is special. We'll use it tomorrow when you do the real thing."

That told Alex that her dad felt the same as she did – that this was a serious event, and not just a symbolic gesture. She held the fire drill with a feeling of reverence. She could feel the Power within it, and silently asked the permission of Keechie's spirits for her to hold it.

Brian shaved some fine curls of dry cedar bark and gathered a handful of dandelion seed heads. He showed her how to hold the bow and draw the drill back and forth into the hollow of the fireboard.

In just a couple of minutes, she had a wisp of smoke rising. He added some of the dandelion fluff as she continued to drill. He showed her how to blow gently into the ember. A lick of flame appeared. They added tinder, then the wood shavings, and soon had a small fire.

"And that's how it's done, Fire Starter!" Brian gave his daughter a very special hug. He extinguished the fire, and they went back inside for a quick breakfast of grits and ham, which reminded Mary of eggs. She wanted some real eggs, not the powdered ones they had in their stores, but fresh eggs, laid by a live chicken.

"Is there any way we could get some chickens here?" she asked her husband. "I miss having fresh eggs to cook with. For that matter, I miss having chicken to eat – fried, with dumplings, chicken with rice, barbecued … whatever. I want some chickens!"

"I guess we could ask Bobby and Hugh next time we see them. Maybe they either have some, or know where to get them. We might be able to trade some corn for them. We have plenty of that," Brian said.

He and Maurice had planned to search the nearby woods for large logs to use for building the New Fire. They used small-diameter wood for the fireplace, and that was usually deadfall.

What Brian wanted was four large logs from a fallen tree. They needed to be dry and well cured. He found his bow saw, gathered up his crossbow, which was always hanging just inside the entrance, and was about to leave when Mary and Alex joined them.

"We may as well all go. Alex and I can look for herbs while the two of you play Paul Bunyan," Mary suggested. She had *The Field Guide to Herbs* in her hand, and Alex had a knapsack with food and water inside.

Maurice carried two old blankets to use as a travois for the logs, which would be heavy. They first went toward the burial ground and the Rock, turning northward into the deeper woods where most of the trees were hardwood.

The rocky soil and the steep slope of the side of the mountain caused many trees to fall during heavy winds, especially after several days of ground-soaking rain. Any that had fallen during the winter would be sufficiently cured by now, and the proximity to the cave would lessen the labor of transporting them back. They found the perfect one within minutes of entering the stand of timber. It was a huge hickory, and had probably fallen no earlier than the previous winter since dirt was still clinging to the roots. It was at least eighteen inches in diameter at its base, and had fallen across another old dead tree. That would make cutting it that much easier.

Brian went to work with the bow saw. It took almost a half-hour to make the first cut, removing the tree from the root ball, which slammed back into the hole with a loud "whump" when he made the final cut.

Maurice made the second cut about three feet up the trunk. "At leas' hit gits smaller evva time," he said, wiping the sweat from his eyes. "Dat sho be some tough wood!"

The smell of hickory filled the morning air. Alex gathered the sawdust carefully and placed it into one of the small plastic bags she carried for herbs. "Won't hurt to have this when we want to add a little hickory smoke to the fire."

Soon they had their four logs for the New Fire. Mary asked for help in digging some roots from a plant she had found. She was very excited about her discovery, and she and Alex were having a whispered conversation about it.

"What's such a secret?" Brian asked as he looked at the plant she had found. It was a beautiful plant, with a huge single plume of white flowers, higher than his head.

"It's black cohosh. The roots are good for many things, menopause being one of them," Mary explained, reading from the herb book. "Never mind. It says that the roots should be harvested in the fall after the fruit has developed. I can wait. It can also be poisonous if you take too much. Dis be powful medicine," she added in her best Keechie imitation. "Mark the location in your journal, Alex. We'll come back in the fall and get some of the roots. Says here that the Indians used it to treat snakebite and the shaman would use it to produce visions. We don't need any help with that."

They were fortunate that the trip back was mostly downhill. The logs were heavy, and Maurice and Brian took turns dragging them on the travois. They stopped about halfway back for a snack of jerky and a drink of water.

"I want to get the rest of that tree to the cave before winter," Brian said. "The way we use the fireplace for smoking meat— hickory is the best, especially for pork. It's too bad that mesquite doesn't grow in Georgia. I like it for beef and venison."

They spent the afternoon preparing for their Green Corn Festival. They would use the clearing in front of the cave since it was only the four of them. It was also where Pu-Can's people had celebrated their own Festival when she and the others returned from the larger tribal Festival upriver.

Mary and Alex were making ankle rattles out of small cans and pebbles for the Stomp Dance, and they were putting together their costumes. Mary found enough colored cloth to make several yards of ribbon for the Ribbon Dance. They both had beaded and quilled deerskin shirts and dresses, but Alex wanted to wear one that she had found in the storeroom. It had belonged to Keechie, and it fit her perfectly.

Brian and Maurice went into the storeroom together and were very secretive about their plans for the Festival. Alex was dying to know what they were up to, but finally agreed to wait.

That night, before going to sleep, Brian read again from the first journal he had ever read to Alex. He read the passage of the Green Corn Festival that he and Keechie had attended in the Creek Territory. It was the one in which Keechie had been selected to be the Fire Starter. It was the perfect thing to read that night, for tomorrow night his "girl-child"—the one who would carry the Gift into the future—would be the Fire Starter.

All four of them spent the next afternoon clearing and cleaning the area for their Festival. They also cleaned the cave and made a pile of all the old stuff that was broken or no longer needed to burn later in the evening.

This marked the New Year for the Muskogee Nation, and it was a time of renewal. Old grievances were forgiven, old clothes and possessions were thrown into a fire, and gifts were exchanged. Just before sunset, Brian took his compass and marked the four directions in the center of the clearing. He and Maurice oriented the four logs to these points, with their ends placed together in the center, leaving enough room in the center for the New Fire to be started. They all went inside and changed into their costumes.

Brian still had the deer hide shirt that Keechie had made for him for his graduation, and it still fit, although rather tightly around the midriff. He came out first, beating a slow tempo on his old drum, using a gourd rattle as a drumstick. He made four circles around the clearing, chanting softly as he and Keechie had done those many years before. Then he stopped and walked to the center of the clearing and took new pollen from a bag around his waist. He threw it to the four directions, then to the sky. Finally he sprinkled it over the four logs, asking the Master of Breath to bless this Festival and offering thanks for a bountiful year. Then he began playing the drum again.

Mary and Alex entered the clearing next, wearing the colorful ribbons and stomping out the rhythm with their feet. The ankle rattles sizzled in time with the drumbeat. The Ribbon Dance had begun. They were both somewhat self-conscious at first, but soon, with the increasing tempo of the drum, they became totally absorbed in the Dance. After they completed the fourth circuit of the clearing, they paused.

Brian began a fast tempo on the drum that they accompanied with their rattles. From out of the cave emerged an apparition that was almost frightening, even to Brian. It was Maurice, dancing, spinning and waving his arms in time with the drum. He was wearing the ancient leopard mask and robe and screeching like a banshee.

If there were any evil spirits within a half-mile of here, they're long gone now, Brian thought.

Maurice walked to the four logs and said loudly, "Dis be a spechul night when we begin all thangs new. Leave all yo bad thoughts an' hurtful feelin's outside dis hyer circle." He took tobacco from his belt pouch and threw a pinch to the four directions, saving a bit to throw onto the New Fire after Alex got it started.

Brian walked to the center of the clearing and announced, "We ask the blessing of Kowakatcu, the Puma Man, to accept our offerings tonight as we begin this New Year. We also thank our god, the Master of Breath, for our bountiful harvest and for this sacred place that we maintain in his honor. We ask for their protection and peace as we begin this New Fire, which represents a new beginning for us here, and for all the world." He paused and looked directly at Alex. "Kachina, Spirit Singer of the Osochi, passed the Gift of Spirit Singing to this young woman who stands before me. Kowa-Tikose, Girl of the Puma, do you accept the sacred duty of Fire Starter, and your new name?"

Alex walked up to her dad. "I accept them both, Yoholo, and I thank you for the honor."

He passed her the ancient fire drill and bow, which she took from his hands as gingerly as if they were holy relics. She knelt down beside the logs and said a silent prayer, then began drawing the bow back and forth, spinning the drill in the hollow of the fireboard.

Brian began a soft, slow beat on the drum as he watched her, just as he had watched Keechie over forty years ago.

A wisp of smoke finally appeared, and Alex, Kowa-Tikose, added tinder and blew gently as she continued to use the bow. Another wisp of smoke, then, as she blew, a tiny spark of an ember glowed. She added a bit more tinder as a small flame appeared. She carefully added wood shavings, continuing to blow gently. To her great relief, the New Fire was born.

She and Brian transferred the small fire to the center of the logs, and continued to add larger and larger twigs until the ends of the logs had begun to burn. The sweet smell of hickory smoke filled the clearing as they began the Stomp Dance. Mary and Alex made a slow circuit of the clearing, and then Maurice and Brian joined in. They both now had a drum and a gourd rattle that they played loudly, increasing the tempo as they danced faster and faster around the circle.

When they were all exhausted, Mary took the last remaining embers from the hearth inside the cave and started another fire outside the perimeter of their circle with them. She then extinguished the fire in the ancient hearth completely. All their old clothes and items they no longer needed were thrown into the second fire.

Brian called for the New Corn to be brought to him. Mary had roasted a dozen ears of the new harvest, and she handed him one of them. He pulled the shucks away and bit into the steaming ear.

"It is good!" he proclaimed, and everyone cheered and grabbed an ear. Mary brought out bowls of vegetables, fresh from their garden. The feast was superb, and their first Green Corn Festival was as successful and meaningful as any that had ever been held.

After they had eaten, Alex lit a torch from the New Fire and took it inside the cave to rekindle the fire in the hearth. It would not be allowed to die until the next year's Green Corn Festival.

As they sat around the New Fire that night, Brian told stories from his memories of Keechie. Maurice wanted to hear the story about Brian's exploration of the cave, when he had discovered the bones of Keechie's father and brother. The night was perfect for storytelling, and by the time they finally went to their blankets, their minds were full of images of the ones who had lived there long before them.

CHAPTER 17

Brian was up early the next morning. He wanted to remove any evidence that they had left the night before. He spread the ashes from the two fires and covered them with sand. He swept their footprints from the circle and raked leaves and pinestraw over it. Satisfied with his work, he went back inside where Mary and Alex were preparing breakfast.

"Where's Maurice?" he asked, noticing that his friend was not in the room.

"I'se back hyer, Brine, in de sto room," Maurice answered from behind the door curtain. "Puttin' away de stuff we used las' night, an' straightnin' up a li'l bit."

Brian joined him in the storeroom, and was amazed at the work Maurice had done. Everything was stacked and ordered neatly. He had even swept the floor and dusted off the old relics of Keechie's ancestors. It looked like a museum, ready for public viewing.

"This looks great, Maurice. I've never seen it look this good, not even when Keechie lived here."

Thinking about their Green Corn Festival the night before, they all wanted to pay their respects to the ones who were here before them. They had all felt the presence of the spirits of the ancestors the night before during the Festival, and they had seemed pleased.

They spent the rest of the day at the burial ground and the Rock, just talking about the different ones that they knew from hearing Keechie's stories.

Sitting in front of the fireplace that evening, Brian continued reading the story of Pu-Can and Tysoyaha ...

Pu-Can and Tysoyaha stayed with Echo-Ochee at his cabin for most of the morning. His fire had died and Pu-Can started him a new one, and then made him a pot of herbal tea. They shared the venison jerky she had brought along for the day. He asked Tysoyaha to tell him of his uncle, Locha-Luste. They had known each other since they were children and had walked the shaman's path together.

Tysoyaha tried to recount as much as he could remember of his uncle's life since Echo-Ochee had seen him last. He told him of the time when they all thought the old man was dead after eating mushrooms. He had been trying to help a man recover his lost souls by going on a Spirit Walk to find them. For two days, he had lain in his tent as if he were dead. His sister and Medicine Woman, Owa-Hatke, was about to prepare his body for burial when she detected signs of life. She nursed him back to health as a mother would a small child. She found the few remaining mushrooms he had not eaten and scolded him. He had used the wrong ones and nearly killed himself.

Echo-Ochee laughed and admitted that he had made similar mistakes, but had only gotten very sick. "Sometimes you must learn things the hard way. If you don't die, you are a much wiser man."

Pu-Can and Tysoyaha began preparing to leave for the burial ground and the Rock, and again they invited the old shaman to accompany them.

"No, no, you two go on and enjoy the day. I have a few things I must do today," he answered. "Thank you, Child of the Sun, for the stories of my old friend, and for watching over my Pu-Can. The people need their Spirit Singer. I bless you both and hope to see many children. You two make a fine union that the spirit world arranged even before you were born. I know this here," he said, placing his hand over his heart.

Pu-Can showed Tysoyaha where the bones of all her ancestors lay. Some of them were his ancestors as well, although most were of a different line descending from Stands Alone and Butterfly.

At sunset they stood on the top of the Rock, holding hands as they watched the sky change colors. Tysoyaha took her in his arms and embraced her. They sank slowly to the ground beneath an old tree and made love for the first time, lying on a bed of leaves.

If Pu-Can had not known the path so well they would have had difficulty getting back down the mountain, but she had traveled this way many times in the dark. When they passed her uncle's cabin she noticed it was dark, and no smoke was coming from his chimney. Knocking on his door and calling him got no response, so she opened the door and slipped inside.

"Grandfather!" she cried out. Tysoyaha was right behind her and watched as she shook the old man, who was sitting slumped over in front of his cold hearth. He was dressed in all his finest robes and was holding his special drum. He was dead.

She held him tightly for a moment. "He knew he was dying. This was the thing he had to do today. He prepared himself in his ceremonial robes and sat here, waiting for the spirits of his ancestors to come for him." She held her uncle for a long while, trying to think of what she must do. Someone had to remain with his body for four days before he was buried. It was their way.

"Tysoyaha, will you remain here with my uncle until I can bring the others? He wanted to be here, in his cabin. Otherwise, we would take him back to the cave."

"I will stay here, Pu-Can, or I will go tell the others."

"I have walked this path since I was a little girl, my husband. It will not take me long. I will return soon with others."

He was pleased when she called him "my husband", because it reflected how he felt about her, but this was not the time to discuss such matters. When Pu-Can left, he laid the old man onto his back and covered him with his blankets.

"I wanted to spend more time with you, Grandfather," he said to the corpse, "but it seems that you had other plans."

Pu-Can hurried to the cave where her mother and brother waited. She told them how they had found Echo-Ochee dead in his cabin, dressed in his ceremonial robes. "Tysoyaha remains with him until we can let the others know. Should we bring him here, to the cave, or should we sit with him at his cabin, Mother?"

"He would want to remain at his cabin, I think. I will get my things and go there. I must first tell the others though," Achena-Nakla said with finality. She had lost her mother and uncle in such a short time, and was deeply saddened.

Apelka-Haya took the old conch shell and blew it, calling for an assembly of the people. Within a few hands of time, the others were gathered outside the cave.

Pu-Can told the people of Echo-Ochee's death, and they quickly began preparing for the four-day vigil. Sadly, they had much experience at these things, and everyone knew exactly what must be done in preparation for the burial of their beloved friend and Keeper of the People.

Tysoyaha sat beside the old shaman until Achena-Nakla arrived. He offered to stay with her until others came, but she told him to go to Pu-Can.

"She carries a large burden for one so young. She needs you, young warrior. I thank you for sitting with my uncle. He wanted to know you better, and I am pleased that you brought him news of his old friend, Locha-Luste. I think that was what he was waiting on – that and to see Pu-Can one last time. He loved her as if she were his daughter."

"My uncle told me many stories of the great Echo-Ochee, Mother. I am pleased that I had the chance to meet him. Locha-Luste will be saddened to learn of his death," Tysoyaha said as he prepared to leave.

The path back to the cave was dark, but his instincts led him until he saw a torch moving up the trail toward him.

It was Pu-Can, coming to meet him. "Did my mother arrive safely, my husband?" she asked.

"Yes. I offered to stay with her, but she told me to return to you."

"My mother wants us to be together as much as possible. She understands that our marriage is to be from a distance. She knows the obligations of the Spirit Path all too well. Her mother, the feared Hechee-Lana, taught her well."

"Did your grandmother really have the eyes of a cat? That was the story I heard."

"Her eyes were yellow, like a cat, yes, but the stories of her being a witch and eating babies and such were untrue. She was very kind and caring toward others. She sometimes played the part of an evil witch, but everyone who knew her knew it was a game she played."

Pu-Can and Tysoyaha remained at the cave when the others left for Echo-Ochee's cabin. It was decided who would stay each day with his body during the four days of vigil. The burial would be attended by all. Pu-Can would be there for the last night before the burial, since she was now the priestess and Spirit Singer. She would lead the ceremony at the burial. There was no one else trained in the rituals that were necessary to send the departing souls safely into the spirit world.

The burial was carried out in the traditional manner. Echo-Ochee was buried in the low-lying swampy area near the river. In about two years they would dig up his bones, sew them into a deerskin bundle, and then inter them in a place of honor at the Rock.

As Pu-Can conducted the ceremony, she remembered that it was Echo-Ochee who had taught her the ritual and the words she was now using. As she sang the Song for the Dead, she could almost hear his voice joining with hers. The spirits of their ancestors had been present, for she could feel them all around her, and as she finished the Song, a large hawk swooped low over the assembly and flew up, circling high into the clouds above them.

Tysoyaha stayed with her for the next two moons. He had to return to his people for a short time to help them prepare for the winter, and he had his birthright to consider. Upon his father's death, he would assume the responsibility of the Mikko. Both he and Pu-Can had obligations to their respective tribes that did not allow either of them to live with the other. They had known that their marriage would be this way, limited to only a few visits each year, and they had accepted these restrictions.

But their plans were not to be.

One half-moon passed when Tysoyaha left to return to his italwa, a runner appeared and asked for Pu-Can. He was taken to her and he asked, "Where is Tysoyaha? He was to return to us on the new moon."

"He left here at his agreed-upon time," Pu-Can replied, fear creeping into her souls. "I watched him as he paddled up the river until he was out of sight."

Her brother Apelka-Haya and several other young men went to their canoes and began searching the river for signs of her husband. They found his bullet-ridden canoe upstream around the second bend of the river. It had lodged upside-down between rocks, but there was no sign of Tysoyaha. On the east bank of the river, a little further upstream, they found several spent cartridge shells. The boot tracks in the sand told them that there had been at least three men standing there, firing their rifles. The spent bullet casings fit snugly into the holes in Tysoyaha's canoe.

"It was the new white man rifles, Pu-Can," Apelka told her. "The ones that shoot many times without reloading."

They searched the river for two more days, looking for him, but he was never found.

Pu-Can hugged her belly where the unborn child of her husband grew. She had not had her moontime since they had lain together at the Rock.

Tysoyaha's tribe was the largest in the area, and there were many people at the special ceremony. They had no body to bury, but his spirit was honored as a fallen chief. Pu-Can attended the ceremony, staying with Tysoyaha's family until the next full moon.

Several of the young warriors wanted to take revenge, but the tribal elders decided that any retribution taken would only incite the old hatred toward the Indians. They would not stand a chance against the white man's guns.

After Pu-Can left to return to her own people, several young warriors from Tysoyaha's tribe slipped away in the middle of the night. They burned two of the white men's houses nearest the river where Tysoyaha's canoe was found. When the families ran out of their burning houses, they were killed, down to the last man, woman and child.

The state militia, already waiting for any excuse at all, took immediate action. They murdered every Indian they could find. Tysoyaha's italwa was burned to the ground. There were no survivors.

The slaughter continued all up and down the river. Even Pu-Can's people, who lived in single dwellings scattered about the forest on the western side of the river, were hunted down and killed, their cabins burned to the ground.

Within a month, only Pu-Can and her immediate family remained, safely concealed in the secret cave.

She named her daughter Wekiwa, the same as that of Wild Dancer's mother, and raised her alone, with only the help of her mother. Achena-Nakla died when the child was only three summers old. Apelka-Haya, however, lived to see his niece grow into a young woman.

When Wekiwa was fifteen summers old, she was staying at old Echo-Ochee's cabin for her first moontime. She discovered a young black man on the roadside near the Rock. He was near death, but with the help of Pu-Can, he regained his health.

His name was George Washington, and when he and Wekiwa married, they had two children—a girl she named Kachina, whom George nicknamed 'Keechie', and later a boy named Stikini, which meant Screech Owl, but George called him 'L'il Gawg', after himself.

Keechie, unable to say 'Pu-Can' when she was very young, called her 'Grandmother Boo-Can'. Later they shortened it to simply Granny Boo.

CHAPTER 18

"Well, that wasn't a very happy note to end on," Alex murmured. "I sort of knew Tysoyaha wasn't going to be in the picture long, but my gosh ... he and his whole tribe were killed?"

"Yep, honey. The farmers and settlers in Georgia wanted the Indians out of there. That just gave them the excuse to commit murder with the government's approval. The only thing that saved Pu-Can and her family was this cave," Brian said, looking around the familiar room.

"And that last part. In just a couple of sentences you covered the birth of Pu-Can's daughter, and then her daughter finding George Washington, the man who became the father of her children, Keechie and Screech Owl ... what was his Indian name? I feel like some of the story is missing."

"Stikini was Keechie's younger brother," Brian explained. "He was the one that I found way back in this cave, honey. I guess I just kinda rushed that part because I had already written most of it in the first journals—the ones that I read to you about Keechie. Remember?"

"I know, but there must be more … you know, like what was Pu-Can's life like after she lost her husband and then her whole tribe? She had just become the Spirit Singer and the Medicine Woman for a tribe that was wiped out."

Brian thought for a moment. "Keechie didn't tell me a lot about that part of her grandmother's life. You see, Pu-Can didn't care much for George Washington. She put up with him for her daughter's sake, but he was trying to change them. He knew how the white man thought about Indians." He looked at Maurice apologetically, and then added, "At that time, Indians were treated even worse than blacks. A black man could at least interact with whites. They spoke the same language at least, and they had accepted the white man's religion. They were still considered somewhat less than human, but still better than a savage, heathen Indian."

Maurice grinned at Brian. "I done heerd dat some Injuns owned some o' us back den, too. Splain dat, mista white man!"

Brian shrugged. "I can't, except that if some escaped slaves made it to an Indian village, they were usually accepted into the tribe. Indians didn't have the racial prejudices that the white men had. By the time of the Removal, there were not many Indian families left that were not of mixed race. Yet, some of the tribes did own slaves, but it was during the time when the Indians were making the white traders rich. Deer hides and animal furs were traded for much less than their actual worth. It was still the white man's greed that ruled. When the demand for land exceeded the demand for trade items, they got rid of the Indians."

"But back to Pu-Can, Dad. Okay, she didn't like him because he was afraid for them, because they were Indian. What was wrong with that?" Alex persisted.

"Granny Boo, Pu-Can, had the Gift," Brian continued. "Her daughter did not. The shaman's path is difficult when you have a family, a husband, children, and so forth. After Pu-Can's husband died, she spent more and more of her time in the spirit realm. She became even more powerful than Wild Dancer, who was said to have been the most powerful Spirit Singer to ever live.

"Our Granny Boo surpassed her, according to Keechie, but she had no tribe to share the knowledge with, or use for their advantage. All she had was her daughter who, according to the Rules of Power, did not have the Gift, but her granddaughter, Keechie, did. George Washington was trying to change that. He was the son of slaves, although he himself had been born free. He had learned to live in the white man's world. Keechie spoke the Muscogulge language. He wanted her to survive. He even worked and saved his money for her to get an education in the white man's world. Pu-Can wanted her to be Spirit Singer, so that was the conflict."

"I think I understand," Alex said at last. "But it's so sad. They had to live in hiding all their lives, just because they were Native American."

Brian nodded "And here we are, white people and a black man living just as they did, in hiding, and for what reason? And there isn't an Indian among us," he said, hoping he had made his point.

"Because of greed? Because we have food? Is that what you mean?" Alex asked.

He nodded again. "That pretty well sums it up. Don't feel sad for Keechie and Granny Boo having to live here. They wanted no part of the white man's world. They were content living here, just as we are … or at least I am," Brian said. "I would like to think we live here because we want to, not because we have to. Does that make any sense?"

"It does to me. And for your information, I'm content here too," Mary replied, putting her arm around her husband's shoulders. "We came here because we had to. We stay here because we want to. Does *that* make any sense?"

"Mom, Dad, I love it here, and I don't really miss socializing all that much," Alex spoke up. "What I really want to do is make my vision quest."

"A vision quest? You mean go out alone in the woods like the Indians did?" Mary asked.

"I know it was mainly for the boys, but I feel like I'm supposed to. I keep having this dream about the Puma Man. He shows me myself, sitting at a small fire at night, beating a drum and singing. It feels so right, somehow."

Brian looked at Mary intently. He knew that this was important to Alex. He also knew that as a father his natural reaction would be to forbid it. The potential danger was enough to make him forbid it without a second thought, but as a coming-of-age experience, it would be a memorable one.

Quite unexpectedly, Mary said, "If your dad thinks it's okay, I think you should do it, Alex. You're not afraid to stay alone up on the mountain at night?"

"I would be afraid enough to not do anything foolish. I think I just need to prove to myself that I can do it."

"The moon is still close enough to being full that it won't be totally dark," Brian pointed out. "But to do it right, you should fast beforehand. Tomorrow I'll help you with the purification ritual and teach you as many of the words as I can remember for the Singing. Do you remember the Indian name that I gave you? You should think of yourself with that name."

"I remember, Dad. Kowa-Tikose, the Puma Girl, right?"

After Alex was asleep, Brian and Mary sat outside and talked.

"You sure surprised me by giving your approval so quickly," Brian whispered.

Mary smiled. "Well, I knew it was important to her, and I knew you were feeling very proud of her, Yoholo. What I want to know now is, how are you going to protect our daughter and still allow her to feel alone? I know you already have a plan. I could see it in your eyes."

"I'll know exactly where she is, and I won't be more than a

hundred yards away. I'm not so much worried about watching her as I am making sure that no one else is. She'll be just fine, and she'll never know that I'm there, covering her back."

While Maurice and Mary worked in the small garden near the cave the following morning, Brian and Alex rehearsed as much of the Song that he could remember.

"When Keechie was singing and I was just playing the drum, it would come to me and I would join in. Power does that. It's not so much the words but your intent while singing, anyway. At least that's what I think."

"I'll take the new fire drill that you made me to start my fire with, and some corn pollen for blessing the ceremony. I'm really excited about doing this, Dad. Thank you for letting me."

"Your mom and I are very proud of you, Kowa-Tikose. Keechie and her ancestors will be watching over you. Make your camp at the top of the Rock. And while I'm thinking about it, here's the spare key to the truck. If there's a storm, or any trouble, you can get inside it. Use the Citizens Band radio if you need help. We'll leave the one in the cave turned on."

Alex placed the key in the pouch she always wore around her neck. "Thanks, Dad. I don't think I'll need it, but it feels good to have it."

"I sho hope dose turnip greens come up, Mary. My mama always put in a fall crop o' dem," Maurice was saying as they approached Alex and Brian from the garden.

"Me too, and the spring onions should have just enough time to make, too. Those can be dried and used in soups and stews. Hey, you two, are you ready for some lunch? Maurice and I picked the last of the veggies."

Alex shook her head. "I'll pass, Mom. I'm fasting for my vision quest tomorrow. Dad said I could have water or tea, though."

"I'm sure ready for lunch, honey. What are we having?" Brian asked as he handed Alex the drum he'd been playing.

"I made a pot of sofkee earlier," Mary replied. "I just need to make the fry bread to go along with it. We'll have a fresh garden salad too, with vinegar and oil dressing."

"Dat sound good to me too," Maurice answered. "Dose `maters wuz a'fallin' off de vine."

Alex insisted on keeping her fast, and stayed outside while the others ate.

"She really wants to do this right," Brian said. "I'm going out to watch the sunset with her. Great meal, Mary. I'll take us both a cup of tea."

Brian found Alex on the rocks above the cave. She had the small drum and rattle with her and was playing them softly.

"Hi, Dad. I think I've got the general idea. Listen to this."

She closed her eyes and resumed playing. In her young voice she began singing and chanting the old Song that Brian had learned from Keechie.

A wave of nostalgia flooded through his mind, carrying him back to the time he and Keechie had sung on that first day at the town in Creek Territory. As he listened, he began accompanying his daughter.

Just as the sun set behind the mountain, Brian felt that feeling again – the air became electrified and pulsed with Power. Both he and Alex stood simultaneously, singing the words to the Song in the Old Language. The sound of drums seemed to be coming from everywhere at once. Then right above them, covering the entire sky, appeared the image of the Puma Man. He stretched out his arms toward them as if to embrace them. Then as the sky darkened and the Song ended, the image dissolved.

"Brine! Alex! Where y'all at?" Maurice was shouting.

"We're up here!" Brian shouted back. "Is everything alright?"

"Dose drums! Dey wuz a'shakin' de whole mountin', seem lak. Din' y'all hyer dem?"

"We heard them. Alex was playing the drum and I guess she got a bit loud," Brian explained, winking at Alex.

"Dat weren't no li'l drum I be a'talkin' 'bout, Brine. Dis wuz a'boomin' lak thunder, whut I heerd."

Mary looked at Alex, and with a mother's knowing look, said to her, "We heard the drums, honey, and as Keechie said, 'the people will never die'. Now the two of you come on down from there before it gets any darker. You have a long day tomorrow."

After her mom and dad were asleep, Alex went quietly into the storeroom. She located the fire drill and bow her dad had made for her. As she was leaving the room, she noticed something on the floor directly beneath Granny Boo's Power Bundle that hung from a peg on the wall. When she picked it up, she knew immediately what it was, although she had never seen it before. She recognized it from the story that her dad had read to them. It was the ivory owl that Locha-Luste had given Pu-Can at the Green Corn Festival. It had originally belonged to Stands Alone, who gave it to his wife, Butterfly. It had then been passed down to her granddaughter, Paneta-Semoli—the Wild Dancer.

Alex reached for Granny Boo's Bundle to return the owl, but as she did, her own medicine pouch grew warm against her chest. *Am I to keep it, then?* Just as she had the thought, an owl hooted from outside the cave. Placing her hand on Granny Boo's Bundle, she said, "Thank you, Granny Boo. I will keep it always, and remember you every time I look at it." She placed it reverently into her pouch.

Alex had her backpack ready before sunup. She had been thinking and preparing for her vision quest long before she had ever mentioned it to her parents. She'd been surprised at their immediate approval when she finally had the courage to say anything about it, but she also knew that her dad understood, and that her mom was beginning to. She went through her backpack once more. Satisfied that she had everything she needed, she closed it and slung it over her shoulders.

"I want to get started early," she told her dad. "Last night when we were singing … that was special, wasn't it? We both saw the Puma Man. That was not my imagination, was it?"

"No, Alex. I saw him too, and it wasn't the first time. You weren't frightened, were you?"

"Not at all. Actually it made me feel safer—like he approves, and is watching out for us."

"That's exactly what I felt too, baby. Are you sure you want to get started this early? It's not even daylight yet, and it'll be a long day on the mountain, all alone."

Alex nodded. "I thought about that. I'm going to take the field guide and look for plants and stuff before I make my campsite. And too, I want to visit the burial ground and talk to Keechie and everyone there. Let them know that I remember them. And Dad, last night when I was in the storeroom getting my fire drill, I found this." She took the ivory owl out of her pouch and showed it to him.

"Where did you find this, Alex? It must be the owl that belonged to Pu-Can, don't you think?"

"It was on the floor, beneath her Power Bundle. I think she wanted me to have it."

"I thought I had seen everything in Granny Boo's Bundle, but Keechie never mentioned the owl other than in the stories she told me. Do you remember the story I read to you? When it was given to Pu-Can?"

"Yes I do. It was Stands Alone's, and then it passed on to his granddaughter, Wild Dancer, then to Granny Boo. It must be very old."

Brian nodded. "Very old indeed, Kowa-Tikose. The Puma Man must have wanted you to have it for your vision quest. Nothing ever happens by chance when he's around."

Mary, Maurice and Brian walked to the beginning of the trail with Alex.

"I am so very proud of you, Alexis. Be very careful and pay attention to your instincts, okay?" Mary told her daughter. "I love you so very much."

"I love you too, Mom, and I'll be careful. I'll even look both ways before I cross the trail."

Brian laughed. She was only trying to lessen the tension of the moment, and hearing his style of humor coming from her was funny.

Maurice didn't say anything. He just went to her and gave her a long hug. *Dis be one brave li'l girl Lawd. Watch ova her, an' brang her back home safe,* he prayed silently.

Alex looked back at the three of them just before the turn in the trail would place them out of sight. She smiled, waved, then quickly turned and continued up the mountain toward the burial site and the Rock. *This is way beyond spending the night at a friend's house,* she thought, while her heart pounded in anticipation of the adventure that lay before her.

As she approached the burial ground she stopped and removed her shoes. She took a small amount of corn pollen from her pouch and blew it gently to the four directions, sending her intentions of honoring the dead to the spirit world. She sat down in front of Keechie's grave and tried to form an image of her dad's old friend, and very possibly her own ancestor.

"You meant so much to my father, Keechie. Because of your friendship we are safe in your cave. Because of what you taught my dad, he was able to teach me. I wish I had known you as he did."

The wind picked up suddenly and whistled through the trees, lifting her hair. It sounded to her like voices singing. Memories that were not hers seemed to fill her mind. There was Wild Dancer and Pu-Can and the ancestors of Keechie - all Spirit Singers - singing in harmony and welcoming Alex as the new Singer. The feeling of their acceptance was humbling to her, and she silently repeated the words of the Song with them.

She looked high up to the top of the Rock, trying to visualize old Bull Killer as he stood there that day in his ceremonial robes, holding his great spear and shouting his defiance to the world of the white man. Raising her hand in greeting to him she called out, "I honor you, my grandfather."

Alex gathered up her pack and proceeded to the top, where she planned to make her camp for the night.

Brian took a longer, more indirect path to the top of the mountain where he could see the road that ran close to the Rock. He picked a spot where he could also see Alex's fire after it became dark. He didn't want her to know that he was anywhere near her, and he wanted her to have this experience, but the danger of her being discovered by unscrupulous humans was just too great for any father to risk.

He would be far enough away for Alex to have her privacy, yet close enough that he could respond quickly if she were in danger. She would never know that he was there.

He sat and waited for sundown ... and her fire. He would not have one of his own. It was going to be a long night with the mosquitoes.

Alex explored the area around the Rock, looking for plants that she didn't know. She made a few journal entries and looked through the field guide. Her stomach had stopped demanding food, but she took a few sips of water from her canteen. She went to where the truck was concealed and checked her pouch for the key. Assuring herself that it was there, she began gathering deadwood for her fire. Finding a small clearing on the rock itself, she arranged a circle of stones to contain her fire and made a bed of pine straw for her blankets. Then she sat and waited for sunset.

What does one do on a vision quest? Last night when Dad and I saw the Puma Man, and we sang the Song together—words that neither of us knew—isn't that the same? What if I just spend a lonely night up here and nothing happens?

She reached for the medicine bag around her neck and pressed it tightly to her chest, finding comfort in the act. The valley below her was already dark with the mountain shadowing the last few rays of the sun. Behind her, to the west, there was still daylight enough to see the entire horizon, which was starting to display the purples and magentas of a beautiful sunset.

She took the fire drill out of her pack, along with the bag of tinder, and began the process of making fire. Chanting the words to the Song that she could remember, she drew the bow back and forth on the drill. A wisp of smoke appeared. Adding tinder and continuing to draw the bow, she blew gently into the bed of tinder until a flame sprang to life. Soon she had a small fire going, and she sprinkled a pinch of corn pollen into it. She removed her pot from her pack and poured a small amount of water into it. When it began steaming, she added some of the special mint and lemongrass tea that she and her mom had prepared. She heard an approaching car on the highway and quickly grabbed a blanket and held it in front of her fire, blocking its light so that it wasn't visible from the road. The car went on by, the sound of its engine dying away in the darkness. She was far enough away from the road that it probably wouldn't have been seen anyway, but she didn't want to take any chances.

Brian had heard the car too, and listened closely until he could no longer hear it. He had smelled the smoke from her fire before he actually saw it, and was watching the flame when he heard the car. He saw the fire disappear at the same time, and then re-appear when the car had passed. *Smart girl,* he thought proudly. He heard the hoot of a nearby owl and the ever-present tree frogs' shrill calls. A rush of wings and the dying squeak of a mouse told him that the owl was successful in its hunt.

Then came the mosquitoes. He applied repellant to his face and arms, hoping that Alex wouldn't smell the familiar odor because the wind was blowing toward her from his direction. He settled in for a long, sleepless night.

Shielding the fire from the passing car had given Alex an idea. She hung a blanket from two overhanging tree limbs between her fire and the road. Now, if she went to sleep and missed hearing an approaching vehicle, the fire would not be seen from the highway.

She heard the owl and remembered the one she had in her pouch and the story of Stands Alone—when Owl had come to him in a vision. It had caused him to take his people eastward, and eventually settle in this very same valley that stretched out below her. She felt the gathering of Power and as she did, she took out the drum and rattle. Clearing her mind of distractions and sending her positive intentions to the spirit world, she began softly beating the drum with the gourd rattle.

Brian heard the drum and the sizzle of the rattle, smiling as he thought, *Yes, I can hear the drums, Keechie.* In his mind he saw Keechie as she stood on that hill in the center of the small Oklahoma town, beating the drum they had bought at the local gift shop. That was the first time he had actually seen the Puma Man materialize in the clouds above them.

The sudden, very loud shriek of a large cat cut through the night, freezing his blood. All other animal sounds ceased—even the tree frogs. He had heard that sound only a few times in his entire life. When he was a boy living in the valley, he had heard the cry of bobcats. They could sound like a woman's scream or a baby crying—but this was no bobcat. This was a much larger cat, probably what they locally called a mountain lion, also known as a cougar. *Or a puma,* he thought.

Judging by the sound, it was close enough for him to be concerned for their safety, but he knew that they only hunted at dawn and dusk—not at night.

Alex had paused briefly in her playing, but now resumed. Brian knew that it must have frightened her as much as it had him, but the night sounds soon began again as if nothing had happened.

Alex had indeed been startled. She had never heard that sound before, except on nature programs on television, but she recognized it and accepted it as a sign that her request had been heard. She resumed her drumming and began to chant the words that she remembered.

A sudden gust of wind blew sparks from her fire and swirled in an upward column, growing wider as it rose above her. As she watched the rising spiral of sparks, clouds drifted across the moon and the sky darkened, until it seemed that she was inside a small cocoon of firelight. Everything outside the cocoon was blackness and void. It seemed to her that even her voice was contained within that small space, and that time itself had stopped.

Lightning flashed across the sky, and thunder boomed, echoing between the two mountains that enclosed the valley. Chilled air swept down from above as Alex raised her arms above her head, still beating the drum above her head. The words that came from her were unknown, but she thrilled in their meaning and felt their Power.

She looked up and saw the image forming above her, filling the cloud-darkened sky. The Puma Man had come. She stopped drumming and looked into his eyes, which seemed to bore into her soul. Then he opened his mouth wide, and before she could react, he lunged toward her, engulfing her in his huge, gaping mouth. In the next instant, she was on his back, soaring high above the mountain, above the clouds, looking down on the world below.

This is a dream, or the vision I was seeking. Either way, this cannot be real, she told herself as she clutched the silky fur on the Puma Man's neck. *Keechie had done this too. She saw the lights of cities that she had never seen from high above. I am not afraid. I am not afraid.*

"And why would Kowa-Tikose be afraid?" the Puma Man asked in a voice as real as any she had ever heard. "Did you not call me this night? Did you not hear me when I answered? Are you not the Spirit Singer?"

"Yes … no … I don't know," Alex stammered. "Keechie–Kachina told my dad that I was to receive the Gift as her granddaughter, but I'm not sure that I am of her bloodline."

"Power recognizes neither race nor bloodline, Spirit Singer. You are of the bloodline, but it is the intention in your heart and your acceptance of the path that caused you to be chosen. Now look! Look down upon your world as it is now."

Alex looked down and saw cities in flames, and, as they

swooped lower, she could see mobs of people running wildly in the streets, with no apparent purpose except that of destruction and devastation. He carried her higher and higher, toward the west, where the sun was just setting below the horizon.

"This is where your present path takes you, Spirit Singer. It is but one of the many destinations you could choose, and it is not the easiest one. The choice is yours to make, just as your ancestor, the Spirit Singer Kachina had to choose."

She looked down on a desolate town square where two people stood alone on a hill. One of them was a small Indian woman playing a drum and singing, and the other was a young, blond-haired white man that looked like someone she had seen before in her family's old photo album. It was her father. He was singing along with the woman in the Old Language.

"That's the place where my dad took Keechie. She found some of her people there. My dad worked there with the children before I was born. They brought them the corn!" Alex cried out as she remembered the story.

"And even now, in their poverty and seemingly hopeless conditions, notice that their city is not burning. It is because they can hear the drums, Kowa-Tikose. Because of you, they can still hear the drums … *still hear the drums, Kowa-Tikose. They can still hear the drums…*"

Alex awoke with rain spattering on her face. She was sitting at her fire with the voice of the Puma Man still echoing in her head. She could still feel his fur in her clenched fists as she tried to bring herself back to reality. Or was what she had just experienced reality, and this the dream?

The rain, which was now falling in torrents, made the decision for her. She quickly unrolled her poncho from her backpack and covered herself and her fire as best she could. Somehow it didn't seem nearly as important as the message she had just been given. Her resolve was to remember what had just happened. Somehow, she had to cause it to be. Her dad would understand.

When the thunder sounded, Brian thought, *At least rain will* cool things off some. *Maybe the mosquitoes will take a break too.* He could still hear Alex beating the drum, so he knew she was all right. He hoped that if the storm got too intense she would get into the truck. There were many lightning-struck trees on the mountain and storms there were frequently violent.

Then the drum stopped. He waited for the next flash of lightning and saw that she was sitting at her fire with a blanket around her shoulders. He got his poncho ready for the approaching rain.

Alex moved some of her wood closer to the fire to dry, and added a few sticks to the flame. The smoke collecting under the poncho was almost choking her, but she didn't want to lose her fire. Her heart was still racing from the flying journey with Puma Man. It was so much like Keechie's journey that her dad had read to her. The only differences were the conditions of the cities, and the journey back in time to when Keechie and her dad were singing in the town square. She had seen so much detail that she knew she could describe what they were wearing. And for the first time, she had literally heard Keechie's voice. Then she realized that the Puma Man had referred to Keechie as her ancestor. *Dad was right about the connection after all.*

She poured water into her pot and prepared herself another cup of tea. Sleep would be impossible now, not only because of the rain, but from the excitement of having ridden on the back of the Puma Man. She knew that one day she would go to the Creek Indian Territory. The Puma Man had told her as much. Surely, there were living relatives of Keechie, Long Walker, and the others still living there. And if she was needed, and could benefit the community by being there, then that is what she would do.

Brian waited until Alex scattered the ashes of her fire and cleaned the area before he started back down the mountain. He took a slightly different path so he would not leave any sign of his passing. He had taught her well, and she had become very adept at tracking. The sun was just rising as he entered the cave. Mary and

Maurice were already up.

"I don't think I slept at all last night, worried about the two of you," Mary told her husband.

"Alex should be right behind me," Brian told her. "She was gathering her things when I left. "Let's go meet her halfway."

The three of them only had to go about a hundred yards before Alex emerged from the trees.

"Hey, y'all! I wasn't expecting a welcoming committee!"

They gathered around her and listened as she told them of her experience the night before.

"It was just after the thunder and lightning started. I was drumming and trying to remember the words that Dad taught me. Then they just seemed to come out of my mouth. And there was a big cat scream just before that, and—"

"Whoa, honey. Slow down. Let's get inside and fix something to eat. Then you can tell us all about it. I'm sure you must be starving," Mary said.

"Dad, remember the story you read me about Keechie— when she rode on Puma Man's back and saw the cities?"

"I remember, honey. She had never seen a city before, yet she described a large city as seen from high in the air. I was convinced that her experience was real."

"He took me for a ride last night. I saw a city in flames and people running wild in the streets. Then we went very high and went toward the setting sun. I saw you and Keechie on that hill in Creek Territory, singing. You were dressed like an Indian, Dad. You were shaking a rattle and Keechie was beating a small drum."

Brian remembered. He had been wearing the deer hide shirt that Keechie had made him. They had made a special trip back to the motel that day just to change into those clothes. He had been playing a rattle. Keechie had picked out a small drum at a local gift shop just so they could use it at the town square. That was the day that Keechie had found Long Walker, one of her relatives. They shared a grandmother.

"Did he say why he showed you that scene?" Brian asked.

"You described it perfectly."

"He said that it was my path—or one of them. I could choose it if I wanted. I think he showed you and Keechie to me so I would know where the place was. The people there were having a terrible time, but their city was not burning like the one he showed me first, and they still had hope because they could still hear the drums."

Brian remembered Keechie's words from long ago – before he had ever left the valley, and many years before he had married Mary. Keechie's prophecy replayed in his mind ...

You's gone ta have a girl chil' wit' da Gift, same as me an' Granny Boo. Puma done tol' me dat too. She gonna make a diff'ernce in dis worl'.

"Maybe one day we can make that trip again, Alex. It's a long way, and the world is still too dangerous for a cross-country journey—not to mention trying to find gasoline, but we'll take you there one day. I promise you that. Surely there are still relatives of Keechie living there. Maybe they will have heard the story of Kachina, the Spirit Singer, and Yoholo, the Loud Speaker."

Alex grinned. "Oh, and another thing ... he said that Keechie was my ancestor. You were right about Mom's grandmother."

Brian nodded. "We'll get that scroll translated one day, but if the Puma Man said it was so, then that's good enough for me."

Mary and Brian both saw a change in Alex after that night on the mountain. She asked to read Brian's old textbooks on anthropology, and concentrated on the ancient myths and religions of the indigenous cultures of the world. She had acquired her mother's instinct in medicinal herbs, but now that ability had blossomed into what could only be called supernatural. She had become a Medicine Woman that any culture in the world could appreciate.

She was Spirit Singer.

Reviews on Phil Whitley's First Novel - KEECHIE

New Book Reviews – ... KEECHIE was selected as the 2006 New Book Review's *Spotlight Best Book of the Year* ...

"Phil Whitley's *Keechie* is a tale of kindred spirits between young Brian and Keechie, an elderly half-breed lady. Brian and Keechie would realize why her spirit guide has brought them together, and how each one of them helped the other to realize their dreams that seemed unattainable in any way. Thoroughly enjoyed this historical fiction, well written and told, a tale that should make any reader smile and share the magic between the two main characters of this book. A Must Read! Story telling at its best! *Keechie* is a great story, and author Phil Whitley has done a superb job of marrying fact with fiction. The final twist is unexpected and powerful!"

Tim Donaldson, Editor

"Phil Whitley's brilliantly written novel, Keechie, blends ancient lore and mysticism with basic survival skills. The author's major character, a simple yet enchanting Native American woman, warms the heart, but also reminds us of our potential vulnerability. He provides a stern warning to a society whose over-dependence on technology endangers an entire population. Analyzing the consequences of natural disasters in recent history validates his concern that so many people know nothing of surviving in emergency conditions."

David S. Rosenberg, author

"Phil Whitley is a master storyteller and one that I am sure will be writing more books in the future. Keechie is one of those books that is destined to be a classic and you owe it to yourself to obtain a copy."

Tom Ward, author
"The Enemy Within"

"*Keechie* is a book that transcends the gap between local lore, superstition, present realities and old memories. This book is a great read for both adults and young people.

Jim Elders, author
"Flatwoods and Lighterknots"

"***Keechie*** is a novel full of spiritual wisdom. It charts the relationship between a white American, living in the state of Georgia, and a North American Indian hermit called Keechie. Although there are some interesting parallels with the work of Carlos Casteneda, Keechie is not at all like the cantankerous Mexican shamen Don Juan. She is gentle and vulnerable, protected by a powerful spirit guide called Puma Man.

Phil Whitley writes with great affection about the rituals and wisdom of the indigenous peoples of North America.

This is a well-researched and delightful book which deserves to be widely read and pondered upon.

Andy Lloyd, author
The Dark Star

Made in the USA
Charleston, SC
03 March 2010